T0165550

GUNS OF THE HEART

When a Gun is Not Enough

KERMIT L. KRUEGER

iUniverse, Inc.
Bloomington

Guns of the Heart
When a Gun is Not Enough

iUniverse books may be ordered through booksellers or by contacting:

iUniverse
1663 Liberty Drive
Bloomington, IN 47403
www.iuniverse.com
1-800-Authors (1-800-288-4677)

ISBN: 978-1-4697-8483-0 (sc)
ISBN: 978-1-4697-8484-7 (e)

Printed in the United States of America

iUniverse rev. date: 3/2/2012

Introduction

The West has always been a land of adventure and opportunity for those who sought a new life. It was a land of wild, untamed beauty that encouraged the adventurous spirit in a man. It offered the chance to build a dream if a man had the courage to take up the challenge. It was born out of a spirit of greed and conquest and grew into a place where a man could prove he had what it took to match the challenge of building a new empire. As the East became settled and homes, farms and industry overtook the land, it left a certain element of the population restless for change. With the restrictions that came with the expansion of the Eastern cities there was a constraint that oppressed their freedom-loving spirits. When gold and silver was discovered in the far West, hope was ignited. Many chose to follow their dreams and create for themselves a new world.

New opportunities drew a mixed group of people with wide-ranging ideas of what constituted happiness. It began with the conquistadors, who were motivated by the dreams of gold. Then came the mountain men in quest of furs and freedom. As they followed that dream they inadvertently became the trail-blazers for those who would follow. Over the period of a few decades they made a way for those who would settle the land. Then with the discovery of gold in California, the land was filled with prospectors, miner's, gamblers, shady ladies and some of the elements of society that sought a place where they could escape a troubled past. For a period of time the land was ruled by violence and without law to protect the people; a man had to make his own law. From this chaos emerged the law of the gun. From those who had the courage to stay, a new culture was born. The West was no longer a direction, but a way of life. These hardy souls ruled the land and while civilization was catching up, they created an empire of freedom and opportunity like the world had never seen.

It was into this land that Bruno Turnbull rode. He carried with him a dream that could not be achieved in the East and a determination that was not to be denied. 'Come Hell or high water' he had resolved to build his own world and there was no quit in him. When he found Kitty, he found a woman of beauty whose courage matched his own. In the course of their lives, there came an unexpected turn of events that would challenge them to follow a higher path. It led them to a future they could not have imagined was possible.

CHAPTER 1

The rider paused at the top of the grade to survey the land before him. It had been a long ride and his destination was very close. It had been weeks since he had left Bodie, but Bruno Turnbull was not a man to be easily turned from his purpose. For the past weeks he had lived on hatred and the man he sought would soon be his.

A soft wind moved the boughs of the trees as he started down the grade. The rock-strewn trail was difficult and the horse stumbled, but quickly regained his footing. Reaching down, the man patted the animal on the neck. "Easy Hawk, it won't be much further and you will get your rest. God knows you've earned it."

Bravely the horse gathered himself and moved forward. Bruno had been fortunate to find such a game animal; in the two years he had owned Hawk the horse had proven his courage many times. He had won the horse in a poker game that had nearly cost him his life when the Hawk's former owner had accused Bruno of cheating. Life in Bodie had been tough from the day he had come to that town; in the two years he had lived there he had worked himself up from a hand in the mines to a mule skinner and finally to the job of bouncer in the Lucky Boy Saloon.

Born in New York, Bruno had been raised by an alcoholic father and an abused mother. Life had been 'Hell on earth' from his earliest memories and there were times that he had wished he had never been born. When a man is addicted to the bottle it becomes a family member and it takes over the time that belongs to the children. As a result, the chance to know what a loving father was like had been stolen from him. Money was often in short supply, so to make up the difference his mother had taken a job scrubbing the floors in an office building that was close to their home. As a result Bruno found himself alone and neglected much of the time and he wished there was some way he could rescue her from the trap they were in. When he was 12 Bruno pleaded with her to leave with him so they could find a new life that would be free of overwork and neglect. It broke his heart to see the pain in her eyes when she struggled to explain that she had a duty to stay by her husband's side. In spite of his best efforts to change her mind, she resolved to stick it out. Finally, in desperation, he gave up. Against his mother's wishes, he quit school and began looking for a job. The opportunities for a young man in the city were very limited; he managed to come by a few small jobs, but the pay had been disappointing. Soon he discovered that breaking into houses and stealing valuables paid much better and he developed a system to know when there was no one at home and the risk of being caught was small.

By the time he turned 15, the strains of a life of overwork and abuse caught up with his mother and after a short illness she died. With her death, all loyalties to his father were severed and the decision was made to strike out on his own. One thing he had learned from his mother was to save money and from his various enterprises he had managed to put away a little savings of his own. His prospects in the city were not improving and the thought of living out his life there was not an option he cared to entertain. He knew it was time to leave. The sooner he could shake the memory of this place from his heart, the better he would like it and a dream had been growing inside of him. Somewhere in the world there was a place where he could be free to follow his dream and build a life for himself. For some time he had been reading stories in the magazines and listening to the tales of how people lived in the West and his heart was drawn to that magical land of excitement and adventure. Great fortunes were being made in the mining camps and cattle industry and the stories he heard told of much free land that was still there for the taking. Living in the city was slowly draining the life from him and he had used up all the patience he could muster. The crowds of people and the shabby tenements that his family had lived in were not the life for him. Now was the time to make his move and if he didn't act now he would become a prisoner of this cramped and regulated life. His mind was made up, it was now or never.

In 1863 he packed his meager belongings and headed west. For several years he had been hearing of the great silver bonanza on the Comstock and how men were getting rich. Following the dream, he soon found himself in Virginia City. For the first weeks in the silver camp he wandered the hills, digging holes and anticipating a great new strike. With no real knowledge of how to prospect or even how to recognize what would be a rich find, his efforts had been in vain. After much effort and frustration he had to admit that his knowledge of prospecting was not going to make him rich. Besides, all the good claims had been taken and if he was going to eat it was time to find a job. He found one in the Shamrock mine and entered a world that was totally foreign to him. The mine was dark and dusty and he was given no quarter because of his youth. Without options, he quickly made the adjustment and a new toughness began to grow in his spirit that was necessary if he was going to survive. The work was backbreaking, but a couple of years of swinging a double jack had built him into a lean, powerful machine.

During that time he had continued to save a little money each week and his stash of gold coins had grown. He knew the future of a miner was not very bright and his dream of a ranch of his own began to grow. Even with free land, it would take a good bit of money to start his own outfit and borrowing the money was out of the question. He would be beholden to no man. No matter how much time it took, he was going to make it on his own. The days of free land would not last forever and he knew his window in time would soon close. He became even more frugal and the pile of golden coins continued to grow. Even though the clock was against him, he was making steady progress and failure was not an option. By 1874, the mines of the Comstock were so deep that the removal of the water had become a real problem. The rich ores had also begun to run out and one by one the mines began to close. With the slowdown the jobs were also disappearing and it was time to look for greener pastures. For years he had been hearing of the rich gold strikes in California, so he saddled Hawk and headed west. For several years he drifted from mining camp to mining camp until he found himself in the booming gold camp of Bodie. With no better place to go, he decided to try his luck there.

The mines at Bodie were much different than the ones he had worked in the other camps. They had been in operation for many years and the shafts were already very deep. Here the rock was much more stable and the square sets that had been used for support in the Comstock were not needed. The working sections of the mine were also very deep and the heat that was produced was unbearable. Bruno found the adjustment hard to make, but the dream of the ranch kept the steel in his resolve and he learned to live with it. It had been hot in the Comstock too, but the winters were not as harsh, making it easier to handle the extreme temperatures. Bodie was further north and the winter winds that blew across the barren flats were much colder. Many miners died from the pneumonia because of the drastic changes in temperature when they left the mines. Bruno had never had a problem with the heat before, but this time it had almost cost him his life. The adjustments from the 90 degrees of the work area to temperatures that often reached 20 below at the surface, took a heavy toll and finally even Bruno had fallen victim to the deadly winter temperatures. For several days he had lain at death's door and if it had not been for the help of Rosa May, 'the local Florence Nightingale', he would have surely died. His constitution was strong, however, and he had made a rapid recovery. It had been a close call that had taught him an important lesson. He would never work in the mines again.

His next job was as a mule skinner. The work was easier, but the pay was not going to bring him the money he needed.

He began to look around to see how he could improve his lot. On the night a fight broke out in the Lucky Boy Saloon, his luck improved. A fight had started over some senseless argument and when a man spilled his beer on him, he hit him on the head with the empty mug, laying him out on the floor. Several men had joined the brawl and he waded in with both fists swinging. By the time the fight was over, he was the only man standing. He was immediately offered a job as bouncer. At six foot-two and 200 pounds of solid muscle, he was well qualified for the job and he accepted the offer.

The work was easier than anything he had ever done and he discovered that he enjoyed the power that came with maintaining order in a place of tough, short-tempered men. He was quick with his fists and gave no quarter in a fight. After breaking a few heads, he establishing a reputation for being a man to listen to. He began carrying a gun and learned to wait for that moment of truth when it was time to put lives on the line. He soon earned the reputation as the fastest gun in town, which gained him the respect of the lawless element. The pay had increased with his reputation and he continued to add to his savings. In a couple of years his stash had grown. He knew it would not be long before he could get out of this country and head for the open range of Kansas where he could finally set up his ranch and begin living the dream.

And then it happened. Because he did not trust banks he had been stashing his money in a satchel he kept under a loose board in the floor in his bedroom. One night when he came home he discovered that the floor had been ripped open and the money was gone. Panic set in, but was quickly replaced by anger. Who had known about the stash and who would have the guts to steal from him? He had no personal friends and he had never allowed anyone into his place. Calming himself, he knew he had to keep this under his hat until he could do a little investigating. He would find the money and somebody was going to pay a big price for their foolishness.

It had not been hard to find out who the thief had been. After a little checking around, he had learned that Ben Allison had been spending freshly minted Carson City half-eagles. Much of Bruno's stash had been gold coins from the Carson City Mint. Not many of those coins were circulating in Bodie and he knew he had his man. Word travels fast in a gold camp and when Bruno went looking for him, he found Ben had left town.

Ben had not had many friends in town and had never been known to have any money, but he had been buying drinks at the Wild Horse Saloon. When Bruno asked around he learned that he had a brother named Dan who was working the mines in Central City and he had lit out for Colorado. Colorado would be his next stop.

Hawk walked on into the stillness, tired from the many miles. Drawing from his master's anticipation, he sensed the end of the journey was near and moved bravely forward. Softly Bruno spoke to the horse with words of encouragement. He knew he enjoyed the sound of his voice and over the brief time they had been together they had developed a bond of understanding that comes from mutual trust and dependence.

Before them, the narrow canyon leveled off and the trail wound its way along the ragged slope. Stumps and deadfall timber now filled the once-beautiful canyon and in the bottom ran a poisoned creek that had been destroyed with the runoff of the mines. Scattered throughout the canyon were yellow mine dumps that ran down from the portals of mines. Many had been long abandoned and stood as phantoms of better times. In the distance, a large glory hole appeared marking the edge of the town of Nevadaville. Soon the long ride would be over and the day of reckoning had come.

Although the town had been in existence for many years, the flavor was very much like many of the booming mining camps of the West. The main street was filled with ragged miners who had just finished their shifts. Some of the men had gathered together for the purpose of talking and singing. One group had gathered in front of the Mountain Boy Saloon and were harmonizing melodies that they had brought with them from Cornwall, where their families had worked the mines for generations. These "Cousin Jacks" were highly valued miners, who were known for their hard-working ways. The Cornish songs they sang seemed out of place as they lifted the haunting melodies that had been sung in the mines of England.

Moving through the crowded street, Bruno made his way down the hill from Mountain City to Central. In the gulch many clapboard homes and businesses had been thrown together and it was difficult to tell where one town left off and the next began.

The scene that lay before him was all too familiar; it reminded him of some of the camps of California. Over the years Bruno had followed the stories about the mines in Colorado. Like Bodie, this mining town had begun in the late 50's and had set off the mining boom in the state. Early in its history, the placer deposits had been cleaned out and the big money interests from the East had set up the deep mines that now supported the industry.

Tying his horse at the hitching rail, he loosened the girth and stepped up onto the board walk. It felt good to be out of the saddle and he paused for a moment to take in the scene before him. Unlike Bodie, many of the buildings here were constructed of brick and stone. Some of the lintels above the Victorian windows bore the date of 1874. Like many of the mountain towns of the 70's, Central City had experienced a disastrous fire in that year and had been built back with the more-fireproof materials.

All of the new sights of the city were very interesting to the man, but he had more important business on his mind. The man he sought was a simple man; he should not be very hard to find. The chances that he would be successful in prospecting were very remote and it was likely that he would put off the inevitable fate of working in the mines until there were no other options. The most logical place to find him would be in one of the many saloons that lined the streets.

One place was as good as another, so he walked to the Silver Slipper and stepped inside. Standing at the bar was a man whose clothing was much different than the miners that made up most of the crowd. He was a lean, well-muscled man with a deeply tanned face. Lines showed evidence of a life that had been lived in the open. From his dust-covered hat to the striped pants, his appearance was that of a man who did not work in the mines. Unlike most of the men in the bar he wore a tied-down Colt revolver that showed evidence of much loving care.

Stepping up beside him, Bruno laid his Winchester on the bar and ordered a beer. The trail had been dry and the drink quickly disappeared. The second one met the same fate and he ordered another.

"You must have come down a mighty dusty trail, Partner," said the man. "Can I buy that one for you?"

9

Bruno turned and did a quick appraisal. "Suit yourself. I never turn down a drink."

Nodding toward the bartender, he smiled. "Toby, another beer here for my friend." He put out his hand. "My name is Coffin, Clay Coffin. What brings you to the fair city of Central?"

Bruno stared at his glass. "You might say I'm here on a louse hunt. This looked like a good place to start."

Clay smiled, "We sure have plenty of those in town. What makes you think he is here?"

"Just a notion. As soon as I figure this place out, I will find him."

"Maybe I can help. I'm new in town but I know plenty about this place. A man by the name of Gregory found gold here about 20 years ago. That started the boom and the place has been growing ever since, but you probably know all that. You don't look like a miner, though. You look more like a man that knows how to use that gun you're wearin'. You wouldn't be a bounty hunter, would you?"

Bruno Frowned at the man. "I've paid my dues in the mine, like most everybody else and I've moved on. Right now, I have other things on my mind."

"Tell me who you are looking for and maybe I can help."

"He's the brother of a local miner by the name of Dan Allison. You know him?"

"I know Dan. Are you sure this man is his brother? Dan seems like a decent-enough man."

"This man is of a different stamp. I followed him here from California and I'm guessing he hasn't been in town long."

"What did he do?"

"It's a personal matter."

Clay spat in the general direction of a spittoon, missed and looked back at his friend. "I wasn't fixin' to interfere with whatever kind of business you have with him. I just thought I could help."

Bruno studied his new friend in the back bar mirror. "I don't need any help in dealing with him. He made a big mistake when he stole from me and I can take care of it. If you can help me find him, I'd be obliged."

"Don't know where Dan lives, but I'll bet Toby knows. He knows everybody in town."

Turning, he motioned to the bartender and he joined them. "Another drink, Boys?"

"We need a little information and I'll bet you're the guy who has it."

"What do you want to know?"

"Ever heard of a man called Dan Allison? I hear tell he has a mine here somewhere."

Toby smiled. "Sure. Everybody knows Dan. He owns the Troubadour Mine, up behind Mountain City. He's a good man. What do you want with him?"

"I heard he has a brother that has come to visit. Do you know where we could find them?"

The man scratched his head. "Now let me see. Dan's not much of a drinking man, although he does come to town once in a while for a beer. He's a hard worker, been in town since the early days. Comes here sometimes, but you'd be more likely to find him at the mine."

"Where do you think he would be if he wasn't at the mine?"

"You might try the Shoo Fly. He goes there once in a while. You sure you don't want another drink?"

Bruno picked up his Winchester. "No thanks." Turning toward Clay his eyes narrowed. "Thanks for your help, Partner."

Clay downed the last of his beer and set the mug on the bar. "I got nothing else to do right now. Mind if I tag along?"

"Suit yourself."

Together the men headed for the door; it was a short walk to the Shoo Fly. When they arrived, they found the saloon was on the second floor. Mounting the stairs, the men stepped into the room and stopped to look things over. Unlike most saloons Bruno had seen, this one was divided into several rooms. The layout was designed to accommodate the theater next door and on one side there were several private rooms used for costume changes. In the back were more rooms for gambling. The theater featured vaudeville type shows and had a chorus line whose most obvious talents were to display as much flesh as they could safely get away with. The main room was the saloon. On one side was a small band consisting of a nervous piano player and a man laboriously trying to make music with a battered banjo. Most of their efforts were drowned out by the crowd of boisterous miners, teamsters and other assorted types trying to escape from the drudgery of their work.

While Clay faded into the shadows by the door, Bruno stepped up to the bar and ordered a whiskey. Carefully his eyes surveyed the room, taking in every detail. Standing at the end of the bar was the man he sought, engaged in a conversation with a scar-faced man. He didn't notice when Bruno slipped up beside him and set his glass on the bar.

"Hello, Ben. Long time no see."

At the sound of the voice, Ben's face went stone sober. At

a loss for words, he stammered, "Bruno. What are you doing here?"

"I might ask the same of you. Where is it, Ben?"

"What are you talking about?"

"Don't play stupid with me; you know what I am talkin about."

The scar-faced man began to move away from the bar slowly, while his hand dropped toward his gun. Ben backed away toward the end of the bar.

Pointing toward the scar-faced man, Bruno's eyes remained locked on Ben. "You just stay put and keep your hands away from that gun. Where is it Ben? Where's the money?"

"I don't know what you are talking about."

Lashing out, Bruno slapped the man across the face. "I haven't got time for your games. Tell me where the money is and I might let you live."

Fire came into Ben's eye,s but before he could move Bruno slapped him again. "Talk to me, because I'm about out of patience!"

Ben picked up his bottle and poured a drink. Picking it up, he downed the drink and turned toward his antagonist. "I think someone has given you a bum steer. Here, have a drink on me and we will talk about it."

"I don't drink with scum like you. You got about two seconds to tell me where the money is or I'm going to take you apart."

Downing the drink, he poured another. Slowly he turned. "Have it your way."

Suddenly he swung the bottle and Bruno ducked, but the bottle grazed his temple. Regaining his balance, his eyes narrowed. "That wasn't very smart. Now I'm going to give you what you got coming."

Ben was a big man and he outweighed Bruno by 30 pounds; his towering height would have discouraged most men. Like many men in the mining camps, he had been in his share of fights and his confidence showed. Instead of being intimidated, Bruno stepped in quickly, grabbed a handful of shirt and shoved him up against the bar. He followed with a right to the belly, doubling the man over. Then he shook him to the heels with a right uppercut. From the corner of his eye, he caught the movement of the Scar-faced man and he jerked Ben upright and pushed him into his friend, throwing both men off balance. They fell to the floor, but the scar-faced man came up in a mad rush. Bruno saw him and caught him on the side of the head with a right that sent him crashing into the bar.

By now the crowd was cheering for the big stranger. Squaring off, both men began slugging each other with bone-jarring punches. It was clear that Bruno was winning the advantage in a slugging match, so Ben went into a clench. Unable to free himself, Bruno delivered a punch to the solar plexus that knocked the wind out of him. Another blow to the jaw sent him crashing into the scar-faced man and back onto the floor. Gasping for breath, he regained his feet and came in swinging. Standing his ground, Bruno caught him on the side of the head, breaking his jaw and sending him back to the floor. Anger flared in his eyes and he went for his gun, but he was not fast enough. Bruno drew and fired. The scar-faced man had also gone for his gun, but before he could clear leather he was looking down the barrel of Bruno's gun.

"I wouldn't do that if I were you!"

The man froze and slowly raised his hands. Dropping to the floor beside Ben, Bruno rolled him over but it was clear that it was too late to help him. From somewhere behind him a gun roared and the scar-faced man spun around and fell against the bar, his gun falling from his hand, blood oozing from a wound in the shoulder.

Bruno leaped to his feet and grabbed him by the neck and lifted him off the floor. He slapped him across the face. "There's nothin' I hate worse than a back-shooter and for two cents I'd teach you a lesson you will never forget. What's your name?"

Moving his hand up to his bleeding shoulder, the man tried to stop the trickle of blood. "Let go of me. Do you want me to bleed to death?"

"You aren't going to bleed to death from that little nick and I asked you a question. What's your name?"

"I don't have to tell you nothin'."

Bruno back-handed him again. "You better answer me, because I'm running out of patience."

He raised his fist to strike, but the man put up his hand. "OK, OK, you made your point. My name is Stewart Hall and you better get your hands off me."

Bruno held him for a moment longer before he set him down. "Ben's not going to be able to help me anymore so it's up to you to do some answering for him. He has a lot of money that belongs to me and I want to know where it is."

"I don't know nothin' about any money. We were just havin' a drink together. I hardly even knowed em."

Bruno glared at the man. "That's not good enough. You'd better talk."

The man looked around for some support but found none.

Turning back he shrugged, "OK, you win. I met him playing poker. He wasn't very good at it, but he was a good loser. He acted like a man who had a lot of money, so we did a little drinking together. I was just trying to find out a little more about him and how he come across all that money he was losin'. If he stole money from you, I think you can just forget it. I think he was about tapped out."

"Is that all you know?"

"That's all. There's one more thing you need to know. Nobody treats Stew Hall the way you just done and gets away with it. You better watch your back trail, because this isn't over." With that he turned and walked away.

Clay stepped up and waved his hand indifferently at the man. "If you think you are going to get anything out of that one, you are spittin' into the wind. He's just a no account that was milkin' the situation for what it was worth. I probably should have killed him."

"I figured that. Maybe his brother can give us a little information about him. I heard he has a mine around here somewhere."

Clay shook his head. "I don't think you want to see him. He's one of three brothers that are pretty close. When he hears about this you can bet he will come gunnin' for you. He ain't likely to let this lay."

"You let me worry about that. Let's get out of here."

"Excuse me, Mister. I'd like a word with you."

Turning, Bruno found his way blocked by a woman who did not seem to fit these surroundings. The dress she wore looked more like it was suited for a Sunday meeting, but the Colt she wore did not. There was a no-nonsense attitude about her that demanded respect and Bruno could see she was not a woman to be ignored.

"What can I do for you, Little Lady?"

Before she spoke, she looked toward the door. "I think you are about to make acquaintance with our marshal. You don't need to worry though, I saw the whole thing. I'll handle it for you."

Stopping by the trio, the Marshal looked down at the body. Then he looked up at Bruno. "You responsible for this?"

"You can relax, Marshal," the woman said. "The man was a troublemaker and he just picked on the wrong man."

"Is that the way it was, Mr.?"

"The man owed me a lot of money and I came here to collect. He tried to get tough with me and he came up short."

"It was a clear-cut case of self-defense," the woman said. "Come on, Billy, don't make a big deal out of this. The man started a fight and he lost. That's all there is to it."

He looked at her quickly. "That may be, Kate, but when Dan hears about this, there is going to be trouble. He's a pretty steady man, but those brothers are pretty close. We could end up with another shooting."

Bruno turned like a rattler ready to strike. "Marshal, I came here for the purpose of getting back some money that was stolen from me and it looks like the matter is settled. I'm a peaceful man and there is no reason for you to worry about me. I'll be leaving town very soon."

The Marshal looked at the man lying on the floor. He had heard of the activities of this man through the grapevine and none of the things had been good. He was a troublemaker and Central City was better off without men like that. He had enough things to deal with, without running this one through the courts and this man was a stranger.

"OK, Kate. This one is on me, but you owe me a favor." Turning to Bruno he looked up at him. "As for you, I don't want to have anymore trouble from you. I'm going to give you a pass on this one, but you have used up all your hole cards." Turning, he walked out the door.

Bruno turned to the woman and nodded. "Ma'am. It's been a pleasure." He turned toward the door.

"Wait, Mr., I want to have a word with you." She hesitated a minute. "My name is Kate Bartholomew and I own the place. And you are?"

"Bruno Turnbull. I'm sorry I caused you trouble, but it is over now, so if you will excuse me?"

"I hope that's not true," she said with a smile. "I'd like to offer you a job if you are interested."

He smiled back at her. "I'm not a bartender, so I'm afraid I can't help you very much. Thanks just the same."

"I wasn't thinking of that. What I had in mind is more along the lines of bodyguard, and bouncer. Would you be interested?"

He paused for a minute. "I don't think that would make the marshal very happy."

"Don't worry about Billy. He's an old friend of mine and we have done a lot of business in the past. I think he would be relieved to have someone to take care of some of the trouble for him. I've been doing more of the dirty work around here than I care to and you have a knack for it. I'll pay you top dollar."

Bruno thought for a minute. "I do need a job and that is a mighty tempting offer. You give me free range to take care of things my own way. I won't tolerate anyone cutting in on me."

"You take care of the job and you won't have any trouble from me."

"You got yourself a hand. I'll start tomorrow."

"Good enough. I'll see you then."

Bruno tipped his hat. "Come on, Clay."

When they were outside, Clay looked concerned. "Weren't you a little sudden taking that job? You don't strike me as a lawman type."

"The job isn't for a lawman."

Clay stepped in front of him and stopped. "I can offer you a better job than that if you are interested."

"Shoot."

He looked up and down the street. "You probably think I'm down here looking for a job, but I'm not. I represent a man who is putting together a band of men that are going to make more money than any of these tinhorn miners. With all this gold and silver coming out of the ground, there is lots of it just lying around and we plan to stake a claim on it. Would you be interested in throwing in with us?"

Bruno chuckled. "You mean become an outlaw?"

Clay's eyes narrowed. "Let me put it to you this way. You lost a lot of money back there and my guess is you had put it together for some kind of a future you had all figured out. Am I right?"

"Keep talkin'"

"How long do you think it will take to get to that kind of money being a bouncer in a saloon?"

Bruno was silent.

"I happen to know there is a mine down in the San

Juan Mountains that is shipping $10,000 worth of ore every week and they're just askin' for someone to come along and pick it off. That's just one setup. These mountains are full of opportunities like that and you are the kind of man we need to pull it off. What do you say?"

"I appreciate the offer," Bruno replied quietly. "But I don't cotton to stealing. I tried it when I was a younker and it doesn't pay. I'm sure you won't have any trouble finding men that would jump at a chance like that. I'm afraid I'm not your man."

Clay looked at him and shook his head. "It's too bad you feel that way. The offer's still open if you change your mind."

"I won't."

Clay looked up at him and shook his head. Turning, he walked away.

CHAPTER 2

The sun was already high in the sky when the young woman stepped into the street. The trip to Denver had been an arduous one, but it was a small price to pay for the new life that lay before her. It was the first time she had seen a city and she was anxious to explore this new world. She had come from the wilderness of western Colorado, and Denver was much different than the life she had known. In her life towns had been a rare sight, but she was ready for the changes that this new place would bring.

Kitty Duncan was tall for her times and had a figure any woman would be proud of. She wore a red crimson vest over a simple white blouse and a flat-crowned hat that enhanced the freshness of her youth. In spite of her country-girl appearance there was a presence about her that lent an air of inner strength and mystery. The city was new to her, but she was not going to be intimidated by it and there was a determination in her step that revealed a spirit eager to take on the new challenges.

She had been born in Boston, but had been too young to remember the short time she had lived there. Her mother had died the day she was born and that tragedy was the turning point that had changed her and her father's lives forever.

Her father had never really liked the crowded cities of the East and he had felt like a prisoner in a foreign land. All through his youth he had dreamed of a life in the wild western lands and lived for the day he could make those dreams come true. He had married young and it was only after the marriage that he learned his new bride would never consider leaving the comforts of the city to move to a country that, as she had said, 'was only fit for Indians and other savages'. There were many discussions about it, but it was clear that there would be no compromise. Zeb settled into a life of tedium and stress and tried to adjust himself to a world that imprisoned his freedom-loving soul.

When Mary died, his grief was tempered by the fact that he had been given another chance. If he was going to go west, this was the time. He knew he could not take on that life of hardships and danger alone and with a new daughter; he was going to need help. And then he had met Hattie.

Hattie Sanford was unlike any woman he had ever known. Although she was in her declining years she had the spirit of a pioneer and the fight that it would take to start a new life. She had come from Georgia when her family had been sold to another plantation. Finding herself alone, she began looking for a way to escape the miseries of the life she was forced to endure. She found her chance in the company of a small group of slaves that were planning to escape. Most of them had been captured before they had gone far, but Hattie had eluded pursuit. The trip had been one of hardship and danger but she had managed to make her way to Boston. She was hungry and living on the street when Zeb found her. When he discovered she had no home or means to take care of herself, he offered her the position of nanny and housekeeper. She jumped at the chance and quickly proved her worth. Zeb knew he had found a woman with a mother's heart. Kitty accepted the new surrogate mother and grew to love her. With the addition to the family Zeb was given the freedom he needed to build a future none of them could have had on their own.

When he introduced the idea of moving west and starting a ranch it had not taken long for Hattie to warm to the idea. Life in the city had offered her no future and the pioneer spirit inside her overcame the concerns she had entertained. In the spring of 1855, they set out for the western land and had established a ranch on the western flanks of the San Juan Mountains. It had been a tough 23 years, but the ranch had finally flourished; it had become the finest ranch in that part of the state.

Today's task was one that Kitty wished she could avoid. She had promised her father she would check in with a pastor he had known in Denver and she was not a woman to break her promise. Zeb had told her the story many times of how on a trip to Denver he had met the pastor. Being new to the city, Pastor John had offered to show him around and helped him find bargains on things he had come to buy. In gratitude Zeb had taken him to the Denver House for dinner. In the course of the meal the subject of religion came up and the pastor had challenged him to become a Christian. Christianity was a subject that Zeb had never had the time to look into, but when the pastor showed him his need of a Savior with sound scripture and logic, he had decided the only rational path to take was to become one. They had bowed their heads and Zeb had received the Lord as his Savior. Before the day was out the pastor had given the new convert a sound orientation in his new faith and by the time he left Denver, his life was completely changed.

When he returned to the ranch, he was a man that Kitty did not recognize. He had explained to her what had happened, but it was obvious that she was not as enthused with this new change as he was. He had had the good sense to realize that this was something that was going to take some time for her to understand, so he backed off and began to pray for her. In the years to come, his life had changed as he continued to grow in his faith.

Kitty had assumed that it was a just a new fad that would blow over, but as time went by it became evident that it was more than that. He had invited her to join him in his morning Bible reading, but she had respectfully refused. The changes in his life became so pervasive that she had begun to wonder if he had developed some kind of a mental illness. He had always been a drinker and early on that habit disappeared. The foul language he had always used began to clean up and even when a word slipped out, he had apologized to her for his carelessness. She loved her father with all her heart, but the feeling began to grow inside of her that something or someone had put a wall between them that she could not tear down. The thought had crossed her mind that maybe he really had found something of value, but she quickly put that thought away. How could the scribbling someone had put in a book thousands of years ago be relevant to these times? Dealing with the problems that a ranch faced was entirely different. The Israelis had never had to deal with armed rustlers or bands of angry Utes. It was a mental sickness and the whole idea was just too crazy to even consider.

Yet she still loved her father and it pained her to see the gap between them grow. Finally she had all she could take and made plans to get away for a while. She had never known anything but the life on the ranch and there had to be more than that. It would be good to go to a place where there were people and life was more exiting. When they had moved into the territory, Denver did not exist but she had heard that it was now a thriving city. Maybe a little time there would open new prospects and there would be a way to build a life that offered more. It was time to spread her wings and show the world what she could do. When she told her father, he was greatly disappointed and told her there were many dangers in the city that she had never faced before. It would be a place that could lead her into a life of compromised values and he could not be there to protect her. It was a difficult subject for him to deal with, but in the end he had given his consent and told her his prayers would go with her.

A large oak door appeared before her and the thought went through her mind to run. The whole idea of getting help from a total stranger was foolish, if not dangerous. After all, this was a part of her father's life, not hers. The whole idea was a waste of time and there were more important things to do. There was a danger in dealing with people like this. They had corrupted her father and she wanted no part of it. Yet she had made a promise and to break her word was not an option. After all, there was nothing to lose. All she had to do was be polite and listen to the man. Her obligation would be satisfied. Everyone would be happy and she could move on.

The man who answered her knock was not what she had anticipated. Far from the skinny little man she had expected a preacher to be, this man was a magnificent specimen. Standing head and shoulders above her, he was a powerfully built man. From his handlebar mustache to his shiny boots, he was a man that would cause any woman to take a second look. His broad shoulders filled the doorway and the set of his jaw suggested a man who was able to handle anything that came his way. Yet the eyes were gentle and spoke of a heart that could be trusted.

"May I help you?"

"I'm looking for Reverend Hollister."

The man smiled. "I'm John Hollister. How can I be of assistance?"

Standing up straight, the girl looked him in the eye. "I am Kitty Duncan and I am here at the request of my father Zeb Duncan."

He looked puzzled. "Zeb Duncan? I don't recall anyone by that name."

"You made his acquaintance a few years ago, when he was in town on a trip to purchase a few things. He speaks very highly of you and he wanted me to check in with you as soon as I got into town."

The man's face brightened and he snapped his fingers. "Zeb. Yes, now I recall. And you must be his daughter. Please come in! I'm afraid I'm not being a very good host, leaving you out on the doorstep. How is Zeb doing? I haven't seen him since that day so long ago." Swinging the door wide, he stepped aside. "Please come in. I would be pleased to hear how things are going."

Kitty eyed the man skeptically. "I only have a few minutes, as I have other things to do today. I'm sure you will understand."

"Of course, I understand, but I would be a poor host if I didn't offer you a cup off coffee and maybe a few words of advice that you might find helpful. Please come in and Mrs. Hollister will make a little something to brace you against the day."

"I wouldn't want to put her out."

"It's no bother, she will be glad to meet you. Come on in."

Stepping inside, the girl relaxed a bit. "I am afraid my father is concerned that I will be in danger in such a big city. This is my first trip away from the ranch and things are a bit new to me."

Leading her to the dining room, the man pointed her to a chair. "I'm afraid you will find Denver a big change from the life you have had on the ranch. There are many dangers here if you are not prepared for them. Have you found a suitable place to stay yet?"

"Yes. I have taken a room at Ma Higgins place. I'll make out all right there."

"And have you found a place to attend church yet?"

The rattle of a serving tray came from the hall and Jaime Hollister appeared, carrying a tray filled with pastries and a serving set. She set it on the table. Turning, the pastor put his hand on her arm. "Miss Duncan, I'd like to present Jaime Hollister, the love of my life. Jaime, I would like you to meet Kitty Duncan."

The woman curtsied. "I'm glad to make your acquaintance. Now, you just help yourself to some of these buns, they are fresh from the oven."

Kitty looked at the woman and forced a smile. "No, thank you. I don't care much for treats."

Jaime smiled. "Well, if you change your mind there is plenty."

Kitty manufactured a smile and turned to the pastor. "In answer to your question, no, I have not found a church and I am really not much of a church girl. On the ranch, there were no churches and we made out without them. To be real honest, Father took care of that part of our lives and I really did not feel the need for it."

The pastor's face grew very serious. "I am surprised to hear you say that. Your father felt quite strongly about serving the Lord and I am sure he would be pleased if you could share that part of his life."

The smile faded from Kitty's face. "I'm sorry if I have disappointed you, but I don't see his religion in the same way you do. I'll give it to you straight, Mr. Hollister, my father and I had a wonderful relationship before he took on this extra baggage and I do not understand why God would want to take my father away from me when I needed him. His religion has caused me a great deal of pain and the last thing I would want to do is follow a God that would do something like that."

For a few moments, no one spoke. Then with a tender voice, the pastor said. "I'm very sorry to hear that you feel that way. Have you ever tried to talk to Zeb and work the problem out with him? He's a good man and I am sure he would never do anything to hurt you."

Suddenly, the room grew very small and Kitty jumped to

her feet. "I'm sorry I brought this up, Pastor. I had no right to burden you with our family problems and I think I'd better go now. I'm sure you have many more important things to attend to."

Crossing the room, Jaime touched the girl's shoulder. "Wait. You don't understand. You are not a burden to us; we are here to help you. Please sit down and let us. We want to be your friend and in this place you will need all the friends you can find. I am sure you can spare a few minutes for someone who can make the way a little easier for you."

Kitty turned to the woman. The smile had vanished, but there was warmth in her eyes. "Please stay for just a little while. We just met you and we'd like to get to know you a little better. I am sure your father would not want you to run off like this. Please give us a chance."

Sheepishly, the girl sat back down. "I'm sorry, but religion is a sore spot for me. It cost me my father and he means all the world to me."

The pastor folded his hands on the table and leaned forward. "I think you have a misunderstanding about what happened to your father. You see, he didn't get religion. Religion doesn't work, because it is a system where men try to find a way to work their way into God's good graces and we can never do that. We just aren't good enough. What your father has is not religion, but a personal relationship with Jesus. When he gave his life to Him, that did not mean that you became less important to him. Quite the contrary. Jesus does not take things way from us, He enhances them. You still have the same place in Zeb's heart that you did before, only now he is better equipped to love you than he ever was before.

Somehow, a misunderstanding got in the way and that has hurt you very deeply."

"I don't know how you can know that because you haven't been around him for years."

"I don't have to be around him. I know what happens in a man's heart when he becomes a Christian. It changes his whole life. The Bible says, "Therefore, if any man be in Christ, he is a new creature: old things are passed away; behold all things are become new."[1] You see, your dad is a new person and that probably confused you."

"But I don't want a new person; I want my old father back!"

"Listen Kitty, that old father that you knew is dead and he is never coming back. There is a solution to the problem though. You need to ask Jesus into your heart like your dad has and then you will understand what has happened to him. We can help you do that."

Kitty's eyes hardened. "You must be crazy. I don't want to be like him. It just wouldn't work for me. I'm still young and I want to live my life before I take on a set of rules I can't live up to. Surely, you understand that."

"I understand your logic, but you are wrong."

"Well, that is the way it is going to have to be. Right now, I am more concerned about finding a job than I am in dealing with these things and I think I had better get going. I appreciate your hospitality and I don't want to take advantage of you."

Standing she walked to the door. "I will let my Father know that I found you and that you are well."

Standing to his feet, the pastor followed her to the door. "Wait, I think I can help you in the job department. There is a man who goes to our church and works at the Palace Hotel; if he doesn't have a job for you, he will be able to point you in the right direction. His name is Powder House Willy or just plain Willy. He likes the longer name, because he used to work in the mines. Just tell him that I recommended you for a job."

"I suppose he is a Christian, too."

"As a matter of fact, he is and you will love him. He is very colorful and he has a heart of gold."

"I will look him up. Thank you for your help."

The Palace Hotel was a magnificent structure and would have impressed the most sophisticated traveler. To Kitty, it was a place of wonder and she had never in her wildest dreams imagined there could be such a magnificent place. The white marble and lava-stone building stood six stories high, with cupolas fringed with elegant wrought iron railings at each corner. Massive stone porte-cocheres with stone lampposts were at each of the corners and faced the street. The enclosure was large enough to accommodate two carriages at a time. Each lamppost was equipped with four burners that were lit even though the day was sunny. The entrance door was constructed of black walnut and stood 15 feet above the stones of the roadway. Two bellmen stood ready to assist travelers at a moment's notice.

Stepping into the massive lobby, Kitty was met with even greater wonders. The floors were black and white marble and from the 30-foot ceiling hung a large and elaborately decorated crystal chandelier. Great marble columns lined the walls and between them great paintings of mountain scenes were set in elegant frames. On the side of the lobby, a small door opened onto a side street with a sign that read "Lady's Entrance." The front desk was a great expanse of mahogany and several clerks waited on the diamond-studded travelers.

Kitty motioned to one of the clerks and asked where she should go to inquire about a job. She was directed to a door that opened into a hallway that meandered through the building until it ended at a door in the rear of the building. The sign on it said "William Duff manager." Tapping lightly, she was met by a booming voice bidding her enter.

When she entered the room, the large, bearded man behind a desk stood and extended his hand. "My name is Willy, what can I do for you?"

Putting on her best smile, Kitty took the hand and shook it vigorously. "Kitty Duncan. I'm looking for a job and Pastor Hollister said you might be able to help me."

Returning the smile, the man motioned her to a chair. "Have a seat, Miss Kitty. How is it that you know John Hollister?"

"He is a friend of my Father. They met on a business trip my father made to Denver several years ago."

Willy chuckled. "John's a good one for making friends with people that are new in town. I'll bet he had him in that church before he left. What kind of business is your father in?"

"He's a rancher."

"And that would make you a rancher's daughter. Tell me, why would a girl with your background want a job in a hotel?"

"Mr. Duff,"

The man put up his hand. "Call me Willy. Mr. Duff is my dad."

"Very well, Willy, I am here because it is time for me to

make my own way in the world. I have lived in the mountains all my life and I wanted to find out what it is like to live in a city. To be around people and to broaden myself. I like people, Mr. Duff … Willy, and I believe I can be a great help to you and this hotel. All I need is a chance and I will show you what I can do."

"It's easy to make a claim like that, but why should I believe you? This is a very classy hotel and I need classy people to run it. This is a lot different than chasing cows or mending fences. There is a lot of ground between the ranch life and what we would expect of you here."

Reaching over, Kitty straightened up the ink well on the corner of the desk and turned back to the man. "To be real honest with you, sir there were many problems to solve on the ranch that were not much different than the things you have to deal with here. These problems have one thing in common. It requires a person with lots of imagination and ingenuity to solve them. I am a woman that can do that and you can be sure that I will prove to you that it was a very wise decision you made the day you hired me. If you give me a chance, I will make you look very good to the owners or whoever your bosses are."

Willy studied the girl for a moment and then stood to his feet. "I'll give you credit for one thing, Kitty, you're not bashful and if you are as good as you think you are, you are going to have a dynamite future. I want you to take a walk with me."

A short walk brought them to the kitchen. The room was filled with busy people in white uniforms and the air was filled with the alluring aroma of food in various stages of preparation. On one wall was a row of stoves that were being tended by several men and the counters behind them were lined with people preparing platters of appetizing foods of various types.

Picking up a pastry, Willy popped it in his mouth and offered one to Kitty which she declined. "No sweet tooth? That's too bad, because this is the best food in Denver. We always have need for people who can cook. Are you a good cook, Kitty?"

She frowned. "I can hold my own on the ranch, but that is not what you are looking for. Besides, you wouldn't waste me on some boring job in the kitchen when I can be of much greater help to you in dealing with the people. Is this a test?"

Willy laughed. "No, I just want to show you what it is we do here. Come on and I will show you the dining room."

The dining room proved to be as elegant as the lobby. Two stories high with wainscoting that reached five feet above the floor. The walls above were decorated with massive paintings of aristocratic people enjoying elegant gardens and mazes surrounded by Grecian-styled buildings and palaces. The tables were set with the finest silver, crystal ware and fine linen. The whole scene took Kitty's breath away. Not wanting to appear as a country bumpkin, she hid her feelings. Even though she had never seen anything so elegant, her host was not going to know.

From there Willy guided her through the lobby to the saloon that adjoined the dining room. A mahogany bar ran the full length of the room and several bartenders with white shirts and bow ties were engaged in serving the fashionably dressed patrons.

Despite her efforts to hide her feelings, Kitty could not repress the impact of the spectacle. Trying not to be too obvious with her emotions, she smiled. "If you are trying to impress me with all of this, you have succeeded. I am not one that can be backed down by all of this and the things that I told you still hold true. I can fit into this and I can make you proud of me."

Willy took her arm and guided her back into the lobby. "I can see that, and I am sure you can fit in. But there is more. The rooms above are also decorated as nice and the fourth floor has apartments for the really wealthy people. Above that there is a floor for servants and other people that are needed to cater to the needs of people that are used to the best. The top floor is one that we don't talk about, but it is a service that we like to maintain for men that have special needs. To put it in plain words, it is a cat house. Is that going to be a problem for you?"

"Not as long as I don't have to work there."

Tipping his head back, Willy roared with laughter. "No, you won't have to do that. I think we can put you to better use. Kitty, I think you may be the kind of girl that we can use. I have a job for someone that can fill in different places where I need someone and I believe you might have the versatility to do that. Do you think you could handle the job?"

"I know I can."

"If I hire you, I will expect you to do everything from wait tables to work the front desk. As you learn the ropes, I would expect you to handle some of the difficulties that come up with spoiled people that have had it too good all of their lives. We are ..."

Turning toward the front door, Willy hesitated for a moment. Coming toward them was a large man who stood out from the crowd. His striped trousers were tucked in black boots which had been polished to a dazzling finish.

The broadcloth coat he wore was set off by a diamond stud pin that held his shirt at the neck. With the exception of the mutton chop side burns, he was clean shaven and his hair was neatly plastered down and smooth enough to reflect the light from the chandelier. Beneath his coat were two pearl-handled pistols in smartly hand-tooled holsters that were strapped to a silver-studded belt. Even in this elegantly dressed crowd he stood out with all of his brash and showy finery.

Taking a deep breath, Willy smiled and turned to meet the man. "Studs, you are early today. What brings you in at this hour?"

Ignoring the man, Studs' eyes brightened as he noticed Kitty. "Nothing special. I'm glad I did though or I might have missed meeting this lovely young woman. Aren't you going to introduce us?"

Willy's lips tightened. "Of course. Kitty Duncan, I'd like you to meet Studs McCain. He is the owner of the hotel."

Smiling, Kitty extended a hand and the man bowed and kissed it. "Charmed. What brings you to our fine city?"

"I'm looking for a job and this strikes me as a wonderful place to work."

"That is wonderful. I am glad you chose our hotel and I am sure you will be a great asset." Turning to Willy, he winked. "I am sure Willy will have just the job for you. When he is finished with you, why don't you stop by my office? I'd like to know a little more about you." Turning to a large mirror, he adjusted his stick pin and disappeared down a hall.

The couple stood in silence and watched him disappear. Turning to the girl, Willy shook his head. "There goes what will probably be your biggest headache. He's a one of a kind and the kind I can do without. Welcome to the hotel."

"You mean I have the job?"

"If you want it. It is plain to see that Studs wants you on the staff and I learned long ago not to stand in the way of what he wants. We are going to have to do something about that outfit, though. This is not the ranch anymore and people will expect you to look the part. I am going to send you to housekeeping and they will help you with that. I would like you to be here bright and early tomorrow morning to begin. I will see you then."

When Kitty stepped into the big office, a feeling of apprehension was growing in her heart and her senses were telling her to turn and run. Pushing them aside, her confidence began to rise. She had handled everything that ranch life could throw at her and this would be no different.

The room she had entered was a reflection of the man who sat behind the big desk. It was hard for her to believe that a normal person could have dreamed this up. It reflected a world that she had never conceived of and the gaudy display of wealth was almost laughable. From the massive wooden beams that stretched across the ceiling to the thick red carpets on the floor, the room screamed to be noticed. All of the furniture was trimmed in gold and plush red fabric covered the overstuffed seats. Several paintings of wild party scenes were mounted between the elegant mahogany book cases that lined the walls. On the desk was an ink pot set in a large piece of intricately carved silver.

The man behind the desk stood and with a sweep of his arm gestured to the garish display. "Welcome to my little piece of the world, Miss Kitty. Won't you have a seat?"

"Thank you, but I don't want to take up your time. I have many things to do and I am sure you do too."

Coming around the desk, Studs pulled out a chair and gestured for her to be seated. "Nonsense, I always have time for our new employees and especially for one as lovely as you, my dear. Please make yourself comfortable."

Cautiously, Kitty slid into the chair. "I really don't want to take up your time. I have some shopping to do so I will look my best for you when I start tomorrow."

"There will be plenty of time for that later," he leered at her as he reached down and squeezed her shoulder. "I'd really like to …"

Leaping to her feet, Kitty spun around and faced the man. "Sir, I am afraid you have the wrong impression of me. I came here looking for a job in the hotel and that's all. If you have any other ideas, you have been misled."

"Now, now, there is no reason to be alarmed. We are all friends in this business and this could be a big opportunity for you if you play your cards right."

She rushed to the door and paused with her hand on the knob. "I'm sorry, Mr. Studs, but I think you have somehow gotten the wrong impression of me. All I want is a job, nothing more."

He slipped up beside her and smiled broadly "But I can offer you a great deal more than that if you will only…"

"I'm sorry, Mr. Studs, but I have to go!" With that she slipped through the door and disappeared.

The next morning found Kitty in Willy's office. The new dress she had purchased was neat and trim and Willy was pleased. With the pressure of the job hunt over, Kitty was more relaxed and ready to learn the ropes of her new job. It was a world she knew nothing about and she was eager to meet the people she would be working with.

Willy quickly picked up on the new, fresh attitude and his approval showed on his face. "Nice dress. Did housekeeping pick that out for you?"

"No, I found a little dress shop down the street from where I live. I'd never seen so many beautiful dresses in one place. It was very hard to choose only one. I hope you like this one."

"It is very attractive and I can see that you have excellent taste in dresses. Now if you will have a seat, I can help you get started."

Willy stood and gathered his thoughts. "Kitty, the reason I hired you is because I could see that you are a special person. I have hired many young women to work in this hotel, but none have impressed me with their native ability and charm as much as you have. These things won't be enough, however, to make you a success. You need to know what kind of people you will be working with in the hotel and how to handle our guests. Are you a quick learner?"

She smiled sweetly. "You don't need to worry about that. There were many tough things to deal with on the ranch, too and we always found a way. I know how to solve problems and it doesn't matter to me if I am wearing denim or lace. All I needed was a chance to prove it."

"That's good, but you will find this job quite a bit different than the ranch. Sometimes we have guests that can be pretty tough and you may have to deal with that all by yourself. What would you do if a guest challenged you and you were all alone?"

Kitty became serious. "It would not be the first time that

has happened to me. We had a cowhand working for us that tried that. He thought we had a gold mine on the ranch. One day when I was riding alone he cornered me and tried to make me tell him where it was. That turned out to be a bad day for him. I flattened his head with my rifle and put him afoot. It took him until the next day to walk back to the house and my father was waiting for him. He fired him on the spot and that was the end of it. I am quite able to take care of myself."

Willy smiled. "It's not likely that you are going to have to do that here, but there are some pretty tough characters that stay here. You will have to spend quite a bit of time in the bar and there will be times when you will have to deal with the situation when there is no one else to do it. We often have problems with drunks and that can come up anywhere Do you have any problems with that?"

"No."

"If you can handle drunks, I doubt if there is anything that will bother you. Maybe you have some questions that you would like to ask."

"Yes, I have a big one. Yesterday when I went into Mr. Studs' office, he made a pass at me. Am I expected to welcome that kind of treatment?

For a few moments Willy was silent. When he looked up, his face was grave. "I suspected that when I saw him looking you over. That has been an ongoing problem here at the hotel and it is hard to do much about it when he is the owner."

"Are you telling me that I have to put up with that?"

"No, no, of course not. It's just that most of the girls in the past have let him get away with it or quit. Those aren't very good options."

Kitty's face became grim and she leaned forward in her

chair. "Where I come from, the men in the family protect their women folk whenever they can. When someone shows us anything less than respect, they are given an education. My father's not here to look out for me, but I can promise you one thing, Willy, if that man ever lays a hand on me again, I'm going to forget I'm a lady. By the time I am through with him, his manhood may be a memory."

A hint of a smile touched the corners of Willy's mouth. "Easy now, I understand your feelings and I don't blame you. I would suggest you make an effort to stay out of Studs' way. He is not a gentleman."

A little embarrassed, she leaned back in the chair. "I'm sorry, Willy, but I am not used to being treated that way. I just wanted to warn you ahead of time that if he insists on taking liberties with me, there will be consequences."

"And I will be on your side if I can. Just be sure you have good cause or no one will be able to help you. I think there are some things about Studs that you need to know. He's not a Westerner. He came from the East and his family has a lot of money. That is how he managed to build this hotel. He's about as sensitive as an avalanche and the way he dresses is an embarrassment to most of us. To be quite honest, I have considered quitting myself, but I have a pretty good job here and jobs like this are hard to come by."

"Maybe you are the one that needs to put him in his place."

"You could be right, but so far he had not made a pass at me. Let's forget about Studs for a minute and move on. Are there any other questions you have about this place?"

"Just one thing that I am curious about. Do you mind personal questions?"

"Shoot."

"I was wondering how you got the name 'Powder House Willy'. It doesn't seem to fit you."

Willy's eyes focused on the ink well on the desk as he gathered his thoughts. "That goes back a few years. I had found a rich mine up by Nevadaville, but it was more work than I could handle by myself so I took on a partner. Johnnie Gifford was his name and in the beginning things were working out pretty well. Apparently it was paying off too well because one day Johnnie decided he didn't want to share the mine with me anymore. I had gone to town for supplies and some of my load was dynamite. When I arrived at the mine, Johnnie was nowhere in sight, so I went ahead and unpacked the mules. I was putting the dynamite in the powder magazine when he took a shot at me. He didn't actually shoot at me, because that would have got him hung for sure. Instead he targeted a box of dynamite that was just outside of the door. Fortunately, it was only a partial box that I had taken outside so I could put it on top of the other cases. When it went off, I was on the other side of the mule and I am afraid the mule took the worst of it. When Johnnie came over to make sure I was dead, I plugged him. I was very fortunate to survive that explosion and if it had set off the powder magazine, I am afraid I would not be here to tell the story. All I got out of it was a bum leg which still causes me a bit of trouble. I decided that was enough of the mining business for me and I sold out.

When I came to Denver, I met John Hollister and he helped me get back on my feet. The best part is he explained to me what would have happened if I had been killed. To make a long story short, I became a Christian and that was when things started getting better. I got a job in another hotel and when they heard the story of how I got this limp, they gave me that name. The name followed me to this job and it looks like I'm stuck with it."

Kitty frowned. "It sounds like that preacher really gets around. That is where I came from before I came over here yesterday."

"Then you got a chance to meet him. That is good. Are you planning to go to his church?"

"Mr. Duff, I will give it to you straight. This religion thing is the source of most of my problems and I have no intention of going to his church or any one else's. Now if you don't mind, I would like you to show me what you want me to do."

CHAPTER 3

The sun was just slipping behind the distant hills as Bruno stepped into the street. It had been a long, busy winter and one that had brought many changes to the man. Not all had been good, but all had been necessary and he had learned his lessons well. Violence and bloodshed had been his teachers and it had been learn or die. He had discovered the role of the peacemaker and when that didn't work, how to control his temper and think clearly. His wisdom had grown with his diplomatic skills, which taught him how to make sound judgments quickly. Lives had been spared by avoiding unnecessary gunplay. His experiences in California had prepared him for the work in the saloon and there was very little that could catch him off guard.

He had not been in the town long when stories began to drift in of his exploits in the West. After being told around a few campfires the stories had taken on a life of their own. The reputation he was gaining as a gunfighter had its advantages, but it also brought with it some risks. When a man is known to be good with his fists and a gun, it brings a breed of trouble that he had not looked for or wanted. Still, it came with the territory. Like it or not, he accepted it as part of the life he had chosen.

Most of the problems had been with local miners and drunken boomers looking for trouble. Most of the regulars at the Shoo Fly were locals who were regular 'meat and potatoes' people, but there was the occasional drifter that came looking for trouble. They were the dangerous ones.

His skills with a gun and fists were becoming well known in the area. Few would be foolish enough to challenge him when it came to gunplay. He knew he was good, had grit and was fast. He had never feared any man, but the life of a gunman was never very long. Time and the odds were not on his side. Now his reputation had followed him to Colorado. He had never backed down from any man and his nerves were like steel, but that was not enough. It was not the men with reputations that he feared. Men like that knew how the game worked. The ones that managed to live long had learned to avoid the notoriety and limelight. Yet there were men like Bill Hickok that had stayed too long and got caught with their guard down. How long would it be until he made a fatal mistake? Even the most cautious man has blind spots. His jaw tightened. It was foolish to think that way. He knew he was the best of the best and no one was going to catch him with his guard down. After all, he was just a bouncer in a saloon. Who would come to a place like Central City to build a reputation? If he just kept a low profile and did his job, the world would forget about him. Then he could move on before that reputation got him into real trouble. In any case, this was not the time to worry about it, he had a job to do and those problems would have to wait.

One night as he approached the Shoo Fly, he spotted a small group of people engaged in a heated argument. In the middle of the group were two women who seemed to be the center of the argument. Recognizing the smaller woman, he stepped up to her side. "Lizzie,[2] what seems to be the trouble? Are these men bothering you?"

"No, it isn't them; it's this so-called lady that came looking for trouble. These miners thought I needed help, but I can take care of myself."

"What seems to be the problem?"

"The problem is I was about to go into the Shoo Fly and this woman made a remark that I didn't like and I told her so."

Bruno pushed back his hat. "And what was that remark?"

With fire in her eyes she turned to the woman. "She said I was a hussy and didn't deserve to be treated like a lady!"

"Is that right, Ma'am?"

The woman lifted her chin defiantly. "Not exactly. What I said is that this is no place for a lady and if she persisted in going in there she deserved whatever treatment she got from the decent people of the town."

Bruno frowned. "I'm just curious, what business is it of yours where she goes?"

"It's my business to know. Perhaps I should introduce myself. I am Lucy Stone. I am a member of the Woman's Suffrage Movement and we are concerned with the morals of this community. This woman is corrupting the image of women and we resent it. Look at her! She is wearing miners' clothing and she is going into an establishment where no respectable woman would go. She has been working in her husband's mine and she has even gone to the bank to borrow money to start a new shaft against her husband's wishes. I have heard she plays poker and even drinks whiskey with some of the men from their mine. Now it would appear that she is planning to frequent the saloons and bring further shame to the women of this community. Someone needs to say something."

Bruno was quiet for a moment, recognizing the awkward position he had placed himself in. "I think you should be happy with what she is doing. She is taking back ground the men have stolen from you. It looks to me like she is blazing a trail for the rest of you."

"Quite the contrary, Mr. Turnbull. We intend to make advances for the rights of women, but we do not want to lose our dignity in the process. This woman is damaging the image of women and we can never gain the respect we deserve if she sets this kind of an example for the men to see. To think of a woman going into a saloon to drink like a common …"

"Now you hold it right there, Little Miss Nosy!" Lizzie flared, "I am not going in there to drink anything. I am seeking a part in the play that is being given and did not have time to change my clothes. Who are you to tell me what I can or can't do with my life! If I decide to go in there and have a drink with the boys, it is none of your business. I suggest you go back to your little group of busy bodies and leave me alone."

Lucy's smile was cold. "It is clear to me that you have no regard for your own reputation, but you have a responsibility to uphold a respectable image for other women. Perhaps you should allow the men to take care of their own businesses and spend more of your efforts making a home to raise children in. After all, 'the woman's place is in the …'"

"You've said enough," Lizzie shouted, doubling up her fists, "And if you don't shut up I'm going to …"

Bruno stepped between the women just in time to prevent the first swing. "Easy now. Let's just back up a minute before you do something you will be sorry for, Mrs. Stone. I think you have made your point and we all appreciate your concern, but I think you can see this is not going to be settled here in the street."

"Oh, yes it can!" Lizzie snapped, as she pushed against him in an attempt to get at the woman. "I have just the cure for an attitude like that and if you would get out of my way!"

He grabbed her arm and gently pulled her into the doorway. "I've got an idea. Why don't you let me buy you a drink and we can work this thing out together." He smiled at Lucy and tipped his hat, "Good night, Mrs. Stone. If you will excuse us we have some business upstairs."

At the top of the stairs Bruno released his grip and looked down at the woman. "I'm sorry I had to do that. It wouldn't have done your reputation any good if you had laid her out on the street, now would it?"

Lizzie's face relaxed a little and finally she smiled. "You're right, but she was getting under my skin. I'd let you buy me a drink, but I am afraid I have already given the ladies enough ammunition for one day."

Pausing for a moment, she scanned the room. On the stage several young women were attempting to entertain the crowd while defending themselves from grasping hands. The mahogany bar was lined with miners, assorted boomers and other men in search of an evening of adventure. It was a scene of uncontrolled bedlam and chaos.

Turning toward her friend, Lizzie looked into his face. "I really do appreciate what you did for me and if it hadn't been for you I would have probably gotten myself into deeper trouble with the ladies than I already am."

"My pleasure."

"Bruno, there is something I need to tell you. Some riders came into town today that you might be interested in. One of them is Stew Hall and I think he is here to settle that business you had with him last spring. He's got some men with him and I heard they were brothers of the man you killed."

"Where'd you hear that?"

"Word gets around fast here and I think you had better talk to the marshal."

He frowned, "No sense in getting him all upset. I'll take care of it myself. Thanks for the tip."

"I'm serious, Bruno. One of the men is Tray Allison and he has sworn to kill you. He's a very bad man and he won't stop until one of you is dead."

"Lizzie, I have to go, but thanks again. And don't worry about me, I will be alright. Now if you will excuse me, I see someone I need to talk to."

"I'm serious Bruno. He's a dangerous man."

"So am I. Excuse me."

Working his way through the crowd, he stepped up to a man at the bar and put his hand on his shoulder. "Hello, Clay. It's been a long time."

Recognizing his friend, Clay's face brightened. "Bruno. You're a sight for sore eyes. I thought for sure you would have gotten yourself shot or in jail by now. Let me buy you a drink."

"Not this time, I'm on duty. What brings you back to Central?"

"I just needed a little time away from things and this is as good a place as any. Besides, I wanted to check up on you and see if you were tired of this job yet."

"Not yet. It keeps me in biscuits and beans and that's good enough for now."

Clay reached for the bottle and poured himself another drink. "I know where you can do better than this. Of course it might put us on opposite sides of the law, but I think we can work that out. As a matter of fact, you have been requested for the job."

"Like I told you, I'm not looking for a job."

"This one's different. Leadville is looking for a Marshal and I think you are the man who can do it. Last week, Marshal Lynch got himself killed and they want a good man to fill his shoes. Lynch had heard the stories about you and before he died, he recommended you for the job."

"I've heard stories about Leadville. A lot of men get killed up there. It sounds like a place to stay away from."

"If you were the law you could change that."

Bruno frowned, "Never thought about being a law man. I'm usually crosswise of the law and can't imagine anyone wanting me to take that job."

"Maybe you should think about it. I spend a lot of time in Leadville and I'd rather have you be the law than someone I couldn't trust. They need a tough man up there and you could handle it."

"I'll study on it some." Motioning to the bartender for a

glass, he poured himself a drink. "I'll have to admit it might be fun to be on the right side of the law for a change."

For several moments neither man spoke as they thought about what had been said. Finally, Bruno pushed the glass away. "You still tied up with that outfit you told me about?"

"We're making a little money on some business I have set up. We could still use a good man though, especially if he was the Marshal. You could make a big difference in the take. You interested in joining up?"

"Just curious. I like to keep my options open."

"You don't want to wait too long. The opportunities won't be there forever."

"I'll give it some thought. I don't like to jump into things without thinking about it."

"We can sure use you."

"I said I'd think about it."

Clay studied his glass. "There is one other thing you should know about. When you killed Ben last year, you took on a whole peck of trouble. Tray is one of Ben's brothers and he is comin' to pay you a visit. He's a bad one, Bruno, and a pretty good gun hand too. Stew told him about what happened and he has sworn to take you down. Dan will throw in with him. He is the other brother and he's a real hothead. Tray and Stew are in the Leadville gang and I won't be able to help you on this one."

"Took an awful long time to get mad didn't he?"

"He ain't around people much. When he's not on a job, he disappears into the mountains, sometimes for weeks at a time. Gil has been using him for some other business down Santa Fe way and he didn't hear about it until last week when he came to Leadville. I told him it was a drifter that killed Ben and that held him off for a while. Last week, Stew filled him in on what really happened. Them Allison's is real clannish and they're a bad lot when they get their hackles up. You better round up some help before they get here."

"Who's Gil?"

"He's the head of the outfit."

"Thanks for the tip, Clay. I won't forget this." Stepping away from the bar, he scanned the room. "Talk to you later, Pal."

Making his way through the crowd, he headed for the back door. The back of the saloon was off limits to the drinking crowd and the hall that led to the changing rooms was empty. This part of the building was dark and the back door at the end of the hallway was never used. Stepping through the door, Bruno found himself alone in a dark street. Leaning up against the building, he built a smoke and lit it. This part of the town was quiet and he let his mind relax and enjoy the stillness of the night. His thoughts drifted back to the day he had come into town and how drastically his life had changed. The killing of Ben was an unwanted memory and he had put it out of his mind. There had been no way to know what events that fight would set in motion. He had let his rage rule his actions and it was not over yet. Still, if he had it to do over, he could see no way he could have changed it. He had always been good at getting himself into trouble and had always found a way out of it. He hoped this time would be no different.

The moon was rising over the mountain and a dark cloud drifted across its face as if to send a threat of impending doom. He watched the display for a moment and turned away. He told himself he did not believe in omens and he would not be intimidated by anything so foolish. He believed in his ability with the gun and nothing else. Then he thought of the men that stayed in this business until the odds caught up with them. It didn't matter how good they were, there was always a time when their draw was a little too slow or something came up that they could not have counted on. Maybe Clay was right. Maybe this was the time to move on. After a year on this job, things were getting pretty dull. It would be nice to have a change of scenery. The Bartholomews had been good people to work with and they had backed him in his play without cramping his style. The reputation that he had built had proved to be a mixed blessing. It could be a great help as a marshal. Leadville was a rising star and maybe that is where he could fit in. One thing was sure; he would never get his ranch working in a job like this. Leadville was a rich silver camp and maybe the opportunity he was looking for could be found there.

This was not the time to think about things like that. There were more pressing problems to deal with and first things first. Crushing out his cigarette, he slipped back into the building.

As he moved up the hallway he heard the sound of tables and chairs being thrown about. Hurrying into the saloon, he saw three men were facing Clay and one of them had squared off with him. They were now circling each other in the space they had cleared. Recognizing Stew, Bruno stepped between them.

"Boys, I don't know what this little quarrel is about, but you are not going to settle it here. Clay, why don't you go back to the bar and get yourself a drink and I'll take care of this."

No one moved. Recognizing the intruder, Stew's hand inched toward his gun. "You're in my way Bruno. We got some business to settle and then I will get to you when I am finished."

"Get your hand away from that gun. We're going to keep this nice and peaceful. Why don't you and your friends come have a drink with me and let's talk this over?"

Stew's face darkened. "I don't drink with the likes of you. We come here to settle accounts for Ben once and for all. This is as good a time as any."

"That business with Ben was between him and me and you have no part of it. I don't want anyone to get hurt here, so why don't you let me buy you a drink."

"There ain't going to be no drinking. If you got the guts, make your play."

Bruno spoke quietly, "I don't want to kill you Stew, and this isn't your fight. He looked to the men beside him. "If you boys have something you want to settle, I will be happy to oblige you, but if you want to see the sun rise tomorrow you'll just forget it and go on home. Ben was a good man but he made the mistake of stealing my gold. Then he made another mistake by pulling a gun on me and he came up short. I would have settled for the gold, but he gave me no choice. I had to kill him."

Suddenly fire flared in Stew's eyes. "Enough talk! Kill him!" He pulled his gun, but before he could fire Bruno brought his gun down on the man's head. Out of the corner of his eye he saw Tray's gun coming up and he put an elbow into his ribs, causing his shot to go wild. With his free hand he punched him in the face, knocking him to the floor. Dan's gun had just cleared his holster when Bruno turned and fired. The force of the bullet drove him back against the wall, where he crumpled to the floor. Silence filled the room as the gun smoke began to clear.

Tray quickly regained his feet, his face a mass of blood.

Bruno looked at him with contempt in his eyes. For a split second the urge to fire crossed his mind but he ignored it. Slowly he holstered his gun. "Is that enough for you or do you want to take this outside where we can finish up?"

Stew was just starting to get up and his eyes were beginning to focus. Bruno grabbed him by the shirt front and jerked him to his feet. "You don't learn very good, do you? I'm going to tell you one more time. This is not your fight and if you ever come looking for trouble again, I'll kill you. Now get out of town before I finish this!"

Shoving him back he turned to Tray. "That goes for you too. This business about Ben is closed and if you don't want to join him you better let it lay. Now it looks like Dan's mine is going to need somebody to work it. My advice to you is to go on up and do some honest work. A little hard work would be good for both of you, because neither one of you is very good at the business you're in now."

Tray's face twisted into a snarl as he wiped the blood from his mouth. "You talk mighty big for one man alone. You won this round, but there will be another time. Nobody treats me this way and gets away with it. Come on, Stew, let's get out of here."

There was an unnatural stillness in the room as the men left. The threats they had made did not fall on deaf ears and Bruno knew that the fight was not over. An unnatural rage continued to burn inside of him and in spite of himself, he knew he looked forward to a final resolution to this fight. Where there should have been fear or concern, there was anticipation that he did not understand. It was not something that he need be concerned with for now. Reluctantly, he pushed those thoughts from his mind.

"Looks to me like they didn't learn anything," said Clay as he joined his friend. "You should have finished the job while you had the chance."

Bruno scowled. "Little men like that don't scare me. It's the back shooters you have to worry about."

"What makes you think they're not?"

"I know they're not that kind. They like to play the part of a big man and neither one of them measure up. They were only brave because they thought they knew how this fight was going to end. Now they know better and they will think twice before they try again."

Clay shook his head. "I think you are wrong. I know these men and they are bad ones. Tray is a hothead and you have shamed him. I've known him for a long time and he will kill you if he ever gets the chance. Stew will only be a threat if his friends are behind him. That's pretty often because he is seldom alone."

"I'm not worried about it. At least it's over for now. What was that big argument about?"

"Not much. Stew thought I had come down here to warn you that they were coming."

"Did you?"

"Of course. I want to keep you alive so you can come up to Leadville. We need a good man like you up there. That's where the action is."

Bruno looked at the blood stain on the wall. When Dan had slid down the wall the blood had smeared, forming an arrow that pointed to where he lay. Was it a warning to him from beyond the curtain of death? Was some spirit trying to warn him of things to come? He pushed the thought from his mind. Maybe it was time for a change. He surely wasn't making any progress toward getting his ranch here. Could Leadville be his land of opportunity?

"You heading back to Leadville?"

"In the morning."

"I'll be seeing you then."

For Kitty, it had been a busy year. Life in the city was much different than ranch life, but she had adjusted to this new world. There were many shops to explore and with money to spend she enjoyed adding new things to her wardrobe. It was a treat to be able to go to the cafes and restaurants and order meals she did not have to prepare. Many of the foods she had never seen and were only known to her by the books she had read.

At the hotel there was much to learn and she had been quick to pick up the routine. She had found the staff very friendly and helpful, with many suggestions that had made her job easier. Willy had in part filled the hole left by her father's absence with his colorful stories and sage advice about how to survive in the city. As she became accustomed to the job, he had let her take on better, more responsible assignments. She had shown a natural gift for dealing with people who found Denver very different from the cities in the East. Much of her time was spent at the front desk, where those skills were put to good use. She learned to enjoy every part of the business with the exception of the brothel on the sixth floor. The very thought of such an operation was revolting to her, but she believed in the 'live and let live' philosophy. Yet her curiosity about such women had led her to develop friendships with some of the girls.

One of these girls was Connie Fletcher and the two women

developed a relationship that was special. If it had not been for Connie's help in the early days, Kitty might not have even stayed at the hotel. She had coached her in the area of dealing with aggressive men and that had pulled her out of a few delicate situations when Studs had tried to force his attentions on her. She had hoped that with time his interest would fade, but it had become a crusade to add a rancher's daughter to his collection of conquests. Gradually Connie's friendship became the only place where she could go to share her feelings with another woman. Unfortunately their chances to talk were quite rare, as Connie was a virtual prisoner of the sixth floor. It was a place that Kitty rarely visited. She knew she could talk to Willy, but somehow that was not the same.

One day when she had finished a particularly difficult shift, Studs appeared before her. It had already been a taxing day and she was in no mood to deal with what was sure to come.

"Kitty, you are just the person I was looking for. Can I have a minute of your time?"

Taking a deep breath, she forced a smile on her face. "Of course, what can I do for you?"

"I have a group of special guests coming in from Boston that are going to require some companions for the evening. I am going to take them out to do the town and I will need a date. I would very much like for you to join our party. Of course, I would pay you a little extra for your company."

A feeling of disgust rose within her, but she refused to let it show. "Mr. McCain, you know I can't do that. There are lots of girl on the sixth floor who would be thrilled to go with you. Why don't you ask one of them?"

"Kitty, this situation calls for a lady of grace and charm

and familiarity with the ways of the world. I have watched you grow over the last year and you have turned into just such a woman. None of the girls up there fits that description, but you fit it to a "T." There is just no one else who will do."

"Mr. McCain, what you are proposing would ruin my reputation and I am not going to be one of your 'soiled doves'. I was not hired for that kind of work and that is not the kind of woman I am. Now if you will excuse me, I have to go."

Before she could move, the man stepped in her way. "You could be making life more difficult for yourself with this attitude. You know how I feel about you. Why don't you come along? I promise, you will have a great time and I will be a perfect gentleman."

"I'm sorry, Mr. McCain. I am afraid I am not your girl." Pushing past him, she hurried down the hall.

The next morning Kitty arrived at work early and headed for the sixth floor and knocked on Connies's door. Connie was still in her nightgown, but smiled and invited Kitty into her room. Kitty stepped in and managed a brief smile, but her voice was anxious, "Connie, can we talk. I think I need your advice."

"The first thing we need is a cup of coffee. I'm no good without my coffee in the morning. It is one of the few pleasures we are allowed here."

"You won't be expecting any visitors, will you?"

She laughed. "No, this is the quiet time of day. Most of our business is in the evening." Crossing the room, she picked up a cup and brought it to her guest. "What's on your mind that is so important that you would visit me this time of day?"

"It's Studs again. I'm just about at my wit's end on what to do about him. Last night, he stopped me in the hall and wanted me to be his date for an evening with some guests who are coming in from Boston. In the past he has tried to get me alone in his office, but this time he tried to make it part of my job. He's really pressing me and I don't want to lose my job over it, but right now I'm about ready to quit. I turned him down last night, but he will try again. It could end up costing me my job if I don't give in."

Taking the coffee pot, Connie filled their cups. "I doubt you need to worry about losing your job. He wants you too bad to fire you. Quitting might be the only thing you can do."

"But I don't want to quit. I like it here and I have worked hard to have what I've got. This is the best hotel in town and I don't want to go to some of those other flea traps. There must be something else I can do."

Walking over to the window, Connie looked down at the busy street. "Kitty, you are very lucky. In just a year's time you have worked yourself up to one of the best jobs in Denver for a woman. You should be glad that you are not in my position. I'm practically a prisoner here in a job that has no future. When women like me lose their looks and grace we are thrown into the street. That is the ones that can survive this kind of a life, and when that happens there is no one that wants you. Life is over. Not many men would have a woman like that. Many of those women commit suicide or turn to drugs when it becomes too much to bear. About the only other options we have is to be a washer woman or scrub floors somewhere. I'd give everything I have to be in your position."

"I'm sorry, Connie; I didn't mean to bring that up in you. I just thought you might have some advice for me."

Turning away from the window, she smiled. "No need to be; I shouldn't have laid that on you. That's what happens when you don't have many friends to talk to." She paused for a moment and turned her eyes to the ceiling. "If I were in your position, I would give some serious thought to moving to Leadville."

"Leadville? What's so special about Leadville?"

"Leadville has many advantages. The silver boom is beginning to produce new millionaires and most of them are very lonely men. You might want to stake a claim of your own. There are also a few hotels and the way they are growing there will be plenty of jobs. You need to face it, Kitty, you are a country girl and you don't belong in a city like Denver. You are young and beautiful and you have a great future ahead of you. You asked me for my advice and that is what I think. Take a chance and try something new."

"I'll give it some thought."

"You might try talking to Willy. He knows about Studs and might be able to help."

Kitty frowned. "After last night he might want to fire me. I think he believes in letting sleeping dogs lie and last night I kicked the big one. Wish me luck."

Willy was deep in thought when Kitty walked into his office. Without looking up, he motioned her to a chair. Seating herself she took a few moments to gather her thoughts. She knew she had put Willy in a bad position and she regretted that, but that was the only regret she had. He would just have to live with it.

When he finally looked up his face was somber. "I understand you had a little run in with Studs last night. Want to tell me about it?"

"There's not much to tell. He offered me a job as his private escort service and I turned him down."

"That might not have been the best choice you could have made. He can make life pretty tough for you if you don't play along."

"Listen Willy, when I took this job, I said I was not going to be one of the girls in his stable and I meant it. When I go out with someone it is a person that I choose and I certainly am not going to do it for money. The truth is, I don't even like the man and I'm not going to spend the evening with someone I don't like. If you want to fire me for that, then that is the way it will have to be."

Willy leaned back in his chair and smiled. "That's what I figured you would say and I don't blame you. Unfortunately, I am caught in the middle of this and Studs asked me to talk to you. I'm going to suggest that you go along with him just this one time and maybe you can work out your differences. You don't have to worry about your honor; I am sure he will not make any demands you can't handle."

Kitty leaped to her feet. "And if you are wrong, what then? You do not have to deal with him the way I do. I carry a gun, Willy, and I will use it if I need to. Can you imagine what the laws would do to me if I shot him! I don't want to find out and he is just going to have to find another girl."

"It's all right, Kitty, just calm down now. I'll talk to him and see what I can do. There will be a way to work this out. Why don't you go to work and I'll take care of it."

Kitty glared at the man for a moment and then her face softened. "I'm sorry, Willy. I'm not mad at you and I apologize for putting you in the spot you're in. I have my standards, though and Studs doesn't meet any of them. If I'm going to work here, you are going to have to tell him to stay away from me or I will take matters into my own hands."

Stepping into the hallway, she turned toward the lobby and froze in her tracks. Before her stood Studs McCain.

CHAPTER 4

The morning was crisp and clear with a few lingering stars hanging above the mountains. Hawk was anxious for the trail and he tossed his head in anticipation. He had always been a good traveling horse and his most satisfying times were when he was on the trail. He lived for the smell of fresh air of the trail and the pine scent of the mountains. He had spent far too much time in the stable lately.

Bruno too was anticipating the excitement of new places. A feeling of relief filled his spirit as he saddled up and strapped on his gear. He had grown in the year he had spent in Central City, but he was anxious to put it behind him. It represented the loss of the dream that had motivated him since he had left New York so many years ago. Now it was time to push on to a future that the Shoo Fly could not give him. He had learned his lessons too well to make the same mistakes in Leadville. It was a place of dreams that would give him a fresh start. He was no longer satisfied with just a warm meal and a place to sleep. In his time in Central City, he had been lulled into a lack-luster life of just getting by. Now was the time to get that place of his own and maybe even a woman who would stand by him on the tough road that lay ahead. He had never met a woman like that and the years were slipping away. Were there any women with sand left in the world? He had not yet given up hope. At least he had a good horse, but there were needs in his heart that a horse could not fill.

Clay's arrival interrupted his thoughts. "It's going to be very chilly in the high country," said Clay, as he looked to the high peaks. "I hope you have some cold weather gear in that pack."

"You don't need to worry about me, I always come prepared."

"I haven't seen hide or hair of the boys since last night. Do you think they left town?"

Bruno looked across his saddle. "Don't know. Don't care. As long as they stay out of my way, I'm satisfied." He tugged on the cinch. "Maybe the marshal put them in jail for vagrancy. That's where they belong. My guess is we have seen the last of them."

"I wouldn't count on that. I know those men and this isn't over. Next time they won't play fair. They want you dead and neither one of them will quit until you are."

Bruno frowned. "Those boys opened the ball, but I'm the one that will call the tune. I'm willing to let it ride, but if they push it they'll answer for what they do."

"You don't know these men like I do."

"Don't have to. I've dealt with men like that before and I can handle any kind of game they want to play. They got off easy this time and if they are smart they'll let it ride. It's their choice."

"Their friends are some pretty bad hombres."

Bruno swung into the saddle. "I've got better things to think about right now. Let's ride."

The streets were beginning to fill with miners as the men rode out of town. The night crews had just gotten off and were standing in groups, exchanging information with the crew that was going on. It was a sight that Bruno was all too familiar with and it reminded him of the days in California. When he walked out of the mines he swore he would never enter them again and he never had. It was a relief when the town disappeared behind them and the sight of Virginia Canyon came into view. Hawk recognized the trail and tossed his head excitedly as they pushed forward.

Crossing over a saddle, they descended into Idaho City.[3] In the beginning it had been called Jackson's Diggings but had undergone several name changes. It was the place where the gold excitement had begun when Jackson had dipped his pan into the creek and found color. The excitement had crossed the hills and when John Gregory had found gold on a placer bar on Clear Creek, Central City was born. Idaho City was still holding its own as a mining town and many of the early pioneers had become financially comfortable from the mines they had developed.

When they reached the town, Clay turned his horse west up the creek into the narrow mountain valley. The wagon track could hardly be called a road with its ruts and wash outs and it was evident very little traffic came this way. As they ascended the rocky valley several small mines appeared along the side of the mountain. Soon even they disappeared as the undisturbed wilderness closed in around them. It was a relief to the men when the sun rose over the eastern horizon, warming the air to a comfortable temperature. With the increasing elevation the Pinyon forests gave way to great stands of ponderosa pines and douglas fir. As the temperature rose, the ground began to thaw causing the trail to become muddy. Often the horses slipped on the treacherous path, but as they gained elevation the mud disappeared.

Finally the trail turned to the south and angled its way up the steep mountain slope. Their assent was rapid for several miles and gradually the trail became frozen ground again. Bruno glanced at the high peaks and shivered. The timber was giving way to the raw-backed ridges that ran up the mountain where large patches of ice and snow still clung to the rocky ground. In the distance a saddle appeared.

When Bruno had had enough he pulled Hawk to a stop and stepped down from the saddle. "We're taking a break. These horses can't keep up with this."

Clay looked over his shoulder. "We don't have time for that. If we are going to make camp on the other side we need to keep moving. It's not far to the pass and then we can give the horses a break there."

"We'll do it now or you will find yourself afoot."

Clay shook his head and stepped down. "Suit yourself."

Looking across the rocky snow-covered slope, Bruno scratched his head. "I find it hard to believe this is the best way to Leadville. No pilgrim is going to handle this."

"Most don't come this way. There is a stage route over Wesson Pass, but that is south of Leadville and it is too far to go. It's quite a bit lower than this route and much easier."

"I'll take your word for it. This is an awful lot like the

Sierras in California. There were lots of people that didn't make them either."

"You mean like the Donner party?"

"You know about them?"

"Everybody knows about the hard times they went through."

Bruno frowned. "Pilgrims. Let's mount up."

When they gained the pass, they gave the horses a chance to blow and sat their saddles looking over the country. Off to the left ran the majestic peaks of the Continental Divide. Much of the snow had been blown from their rocky slopes by the high wind that was now blowing delicate fingers of snow from the summits. In the distance was the Snake River Basin and beyond was some of the most magnificent country Bruno had ever seen. Below them the twisted trees of timberline gave way to the sub-alpine fir that worked their way down toward the mountain valley. Far below could be seen groves of aspen which were just now putting out the rich green colors of spring. The valley floor was covered with a dense pine forest that was divided by a mighty, rushing river, still swollen by the melting snows of winter.

For a few minutes the men sat in silence. Finally Clay whispered in awe, "I told you to be ready for some real country. And we're not done yet."

Bruno looked perplexed. "It is beautiful, but where are we?"

"Close to the headwaters of the Snake River and we need to be in the bottom of that basin before the sun goes down. It gets mighty cold up here at night. You think that horse of yours is up to it?"

Bruno scowled." You don't need to worry about this horse.

He'll carry me down this mountain and you too if need be. We'd better get moving, we're burnin' daylight."

Clay turned away and smiled. Pointing his horse toward the trail, he led off. As they moved, the wind began to rise. It was a cold wind that chilled a man to the bone and they picked up their pace. Hunched over in the saddles to shield themselves from the wind, they threaded their way through the clumps of ground fir and broken rocks until they reached the timber. Entering the pines the winds continued to whine like a disembodied spirit while the sky became overcast. Huddling against the horses, the men pushed on until they were deep in the tall timber. As they moved through the trees a light rain began to fall and lightning streaked across the sky. As the rain picked up, thunder crashed across the valley until it sounded like it would split the tops of the trees. Then as quickly as it had come it was over. By the time they reached the valley floor the winds had stopped and the sun came out.

The valley was covered with a forest of towering Ponderosa pines. Scattered through the forest were the skeletons of many dead trees mixed with small groves of aspen. Rising out of the trees was a massive ridge of rock that increased in size as it went south, becoming a series of tall peaks that divided the basin into two separate valleys. When they reached the river the horses balked and refused to cross the swollen waters. Reluctantly the men dismounted and lead them into the rushing water. The water was cold and swift with a current that threatened to drag them downstream into a rocky gorge below them. It was a fight to keep the horses moving but in the end they won. Soaked and exhausted, they dragged themselves out of the water on the other side. It was a short ride to the stream that came down from the far side of the ridge. Turning their horses to the south, they followed the stream up the valley. In many places the trees had fallen across the path, forcing them to detour through dense undergrowth that tore at their clothes and made progress difficult. Here there were signs of a forest fire that had destroyed the pine forest many years ago. The space the fire had left had been taken over by the aspen and now some of the pines were coming back. Many of these tender young trees had been freshly stripped of bark, suggesting that it had been a tough winter for the deer.

They rode on through the heavily timbered country. As they moved through the forest the path disappeared into a tangle of fire-scarred trees that had fallen in a great jumble of broken logs. Many of the downed trees, suggesting the bones of long-dead monsters, blocked the way.

"I thought you said this was the trail to Leadville," Bruno growled. "This is worse than a pig trail. Are you sure you aren't lost?"

"There is an easier way, but it takes longer. Don't worry, it will get better. Not many people come this way, you know. "

There was nothing to be gained by talking about it so Clay urged his horse forward. The men were seasoned mountain travelers and knew that all trails improve with time.

Bravely the horses went on until the mountain ridge to the west ended abruptly in a small mountain park. Here they were given a rest while the men considered their next course of action. From the west a stream emerged from behind a ridge; Clay turned and followed the narrow path that paralleled it.

The sun was sinking below the jagged ridges, painting the mountains with gold and crimson when they turned their horses to the south again. Following the western side of the ridge, the men pushed on until the darkness made progress impossible. Suddenly the distant flicker of a campfire caught Bruno's eye and he pulled up. Quietly they dismounted and walked their horses forward. A horse nickered and the men stopped.

"Hello the camp," Bruno called out. "We could use a cup of coffee."

The man by the fire leaped to his feet and leveled a Winchester in their direction. "Who are ya?"

The men stepped out of the brush. "A couple of men looking for a warm fire and some conversation. Can we come in?"

"Come on in, but keep your hands where I can see them."

Carefully the men eased their way into the firelight. "No need for that shootin' iron, Partner, we're friendly."

Cautiously, the man lowered the gun. "Can't be none too careful these days. The whole world's gone crazy and you don't know who you're going to run into. Where are you comin' from?"

"Central City. Headed for Leadville to see what all the fuss is about."

"More boomers, aye. Set yourself down and help yourself to a cup of coffee."

Moving over to the horses, Clay tied them to a deadfall and returned with cups. Squatting by the fire he filled them. "We appreciate the hospitality of your fire, Neighbor. You comin' down from Leadville?"

"That's right. Lyle Jenkins is the name. Who are you?"

"Names Coffin, Clay Coffin and my friend is Bruno Turnbull. We're headed for Leadville to try our luck."

The man shook his head. "Hope you got plenty of it, cuz

you're going to need it. There's so many men coming into town lately that you might have to stake a claim just to have a place to sleep." Picking up his cup he smiled. "You don't look to me like miners. What kind of business you in?"

"Just seemed like the place to be," said Clay. "Things are happening there."

"You said a mouthful there. There's been so many shootings going on that it is hard to keep track of it all. A while back the marshal was killed and that really stirred things up."

Bruno set down his cup. "You mean Otto Lynch?"

"That's him. You a friend of his?"

"Know of him."

"He was a good man, but he sure didn't last long on that job. Only five weeks and he was killed."

"Did they get the hombre that killed him?"

The man was silent for a few moments. "That depends on how you look at it. The town's still wondering who done it, but when they find out they're in for a shock."

Bruno looked straight at the man. "You think you know who did it?"

The man shifted nervously. "I think I have said too much already. I don't want to get in any trouble over it. Besides what difference does it make? They got a new marshal and in a few weeks he will probably be dead. Nobody will give a hoot."

Bruno shot a glance at Clay and winked. "You're right, it probably doesn't matter." Dumping out his cup, he frowned. "I think I have had enough of this coffee and I think we can do better than that. Clay, you want to get that jug of red eye out of my saddle bag. It would be only fair if we paid our friend back for his hospitality."

Moving to the horses, Clay returned with the bottle

"Nothing like a little something to warm your insides on a chilly night. Will you have a shot, Lyle?"

The man extended his cup with a happy grin and for the next hour they swapped lies while they finished the bottle.

Finally Bruno set the bottle down and turned to the man. "Tell me, Lyle, how did you manage to find out so much about this business with Lynch. Did you know him well?"

"Me? I knowed Otto ever since I came to Leadville," he said with a crooked smile. "I was almost one of his deputies. "I would have been too, if it weren't for that smart-aleckey deputy of his. He told Otto I was a drunk and that just wasn't true. I might have had a little snort now and then, but I was no drunk. If he had give me a chance I would have…"

"What was the deputy's name?"

"Tex Bloodson," he said, as he waved his cup around, spilling the contents. "If I wanted to, I could really fix his wagon. If I told what I know about him, he'd be swingin' from the end of a rope before the sun went down. Should be anyway, for what he done."

Bruno put his arm on his shoulder. "He killed your friend, didn't he?"

"You're darn tootin' he did. I seen him take him down by some of them mine dumps on Poverty Flats on a wild goose chase. When he came back he was alone. They found Otto the next morning with a bullet in the back of the head."

"Why didn't you say something?"

"Cuz nobody would have believed me. And when they made Tex marshal. I knew he would find a way to get me too. I left because I knew it was only a matter of time before he done me in. You ain't going to say nothin' about this, are you?"

"No. I'm thinking about taking a job as one of his deputies

myself. Sounds to me like he needs someone to look after him."

"Raising his cup to his lips Lyle emptied the last few drops. Looking around for the bottle he tipped it up and found it empty. In disgust he threw it in the fire. "Looks like the well went dry. You got any more of that stuff?"

"That's all there is. You better have yourself a cup of coffee."

"Coffee! This is no time for a cup of coffee."

Reaching for the pot, Bruno poured a cup and handed it to him. "I'm afraid that is all we have left."

Taking the cup, he set it on a rock and looked back at Bruno. "Take a word of advice from me, son. You don't want to be no deputy. You'd be safer in front of his guns than you would be behind them."

"I appreciate your warning, but I can take care of myself. You better turn in, Old Pal. We've all got a long ride ahead of us in the morning. Come on, Clay, let's tend to the horses."

When they reached the horses, Bruno turned to Clay. "I thought you said they were looking for a marshal. Did you know anything about this story?"

"No, this is news to me. I had heard that Lyle wanted the deputy's job, but he was a drunk and Lynch wouldn't take him on. When he was shot, it was anybody's guess what had happened. Who knows, maybe his story is true. You still want that job?"

"That's why we're going up there."

"I can still make you a better deal than that."

"You mean to be an outlaw?"

"I think your chances of staying alive are better as an outlaw than being the marshal in Leadville. Gil Davis is the honcho of the outfit and he thinks pretty good. He can make you a rich man."

Bruno unhooked the cinch and pulled the saddle off the horse. "I've seen my share of outlaws when I was in the mining camps in California and take my word for it, you will never get rich riding the owl hoot trail."

"If you go after that marshal's job, the deck is stacked against you."

"You just let me worry about that. You better turn in now; we got a long way to go in the morning."

For a moment Kitty stood frozen in her tracks looking for an exit, but there was none. Trying another tactic, she smiled up at the man. "Excuse me, Mr. McCain; I don't have time to talk right now."

Retuning the smile, he continued to bar the way. "I'm sure you have a minute for me. As a matter of fact, I was about to come looking for you. I wanted to confirm our date for tonight."

"I never said I was going to go out with you and if you think you can get Willy to change my mind, you are mistaken. Now, if you will excuse me, I really have to go."

The smile disappeared. "I don't think you understand the situation. When I asked you to be my date I was trying to be polite, but the truth is I wasn't prepared to take no for an answer."

Kitty's face flashed with anger. "No, I think you are the one that doesn't understand. I told Willy when I came here that I was not going to be one of his soiled doves and I haven't changed my mind. My responsibilities end when I walk out that door. I am the one that chooses who I wish to go out with. You had better get yourself another girl."

Studs face darkened. "You better understand this. If you want to continue to work here you had better put on your party dress, because we are going out tonight and you don't have anything to say about it!"

Before he could say anymore, Kitty pushed against the big man in an effort to get by him but he grabbed her and pulled her back. When he opened his mouth to speak, she slapped his face so hard that it spun his head and he released his hold. Before she could move, he grabbed her again and tried to draw her into a bear hug, but she brought her knee up into his groin doubling him over. With all her strength Kitty slapped him on both cheeks, bringing a stunned look to his face. Before he could focus on what had happened, she delivered her best kick to his shins knocking him to the floor. Stepping past him, she turned and glared down at him. "You may consider that my official resignation." Turning, she marched through the lobby and into the street.

By the time she reached her room her anger had subsided and reality set in. The feeling of satisfaction she was enjoying was slowly replaced with concern for her future. She was a single girl far from home and she was not the kind to call on her friends for help. That is, if she had any. There was always Connie, but the idea of returning to the hotel was not one that she cared to face. Just the thought of it fired the anger in her heart. She had walked through the doors of that place for the last time. There would be another way to go, as there always had been. She didn't need any help to find it. There was still the ranch and her dad would be very happy to have her home, but that situation would not have changed. By now he probably had built a church and was inviting anyone that he could find to attend. She was not prepared to face that again.

She had not thought of her father for a long time now and the thought of him brought a tear to her eye. She still loved him with all of her heart and it made her mad to think that something as foolish as religion could come between them. All her life she had known him as a very lonely man. There was an empty place in his heart that even she could not fill. Her mother had died giving her life and he had never fully recovered from that. It was when he got religion that he had changed into a person that she did not recognize. Since that day he had begun to change and he had never looked back. He was happier than she had ever known him to be, but there was something in that change that had separated him from her. She would give anything to go back to the way things had been, but that was gone forever. She knew it was time for her to make a new life and maybe Denver was not the place to live it. Maybe Connie was right and Leadville was where her future lay.

There was a knock at the door. When she opened it, Willy was standing there. Swinging the door wide, she invited him in.

He grinned at her. It was that same comical grin he would put on his face just before he told one of his hilarious stories. "I was hoping I would catch you at home. Have you got a minute?"

"I've always got a minute for you. Come on in and have a cup of coffee."

Gently he laid an envelope on the table. "I have a little money here for you. I figured you wouldn't be coming back and I thought I would just drop it off."

"Thanks."

Willy fidgeted nervously. Kitty could see that there was something on his mind, but he was unsure how to get it out. An awkward silence followed. "Willy, I can see you have something on your mind. Why don't you just spit it out?"

He grinned sheepishly. "You left quite an impression on Studs when you left. He is vowing that will never work in Denver again and he's got the connections to pull that off. Have you made any plans on what you are going to do?"

"I hadn't thought about it much. I hear things are really popping in Leadville and I thought I might try that."

Willy nodded his head. "I am sure there will be lots to do for a pretty girl like you. It's a very dangerous place though and I have spent a lot of time in camps like that. You might need a friend or two to help you get started. I know a preacher up there that would be glad to help you. His name is Parson Tom Uzzell and he will know the ropes."

Kitty frowned and set her coffee down. "Another preacher? No thanks. Preachers have messed up my life and I have no intention to talk to another one. I'll make out on my own."

"Kitty, can I talk to you frankly?"

"Of course."

"I've been watching you for the past year and you have really grown up in that time. You have come from a wide-eyed country girl into a woman that can handle most of the difficult problems that life can throw at you. I've invited you to church several times, but you have never taken me up on it. I've talked to Pastor John about you and we have both done a good bit of praying for you."

Kitty looked up and their eyes met. He smiled and her lips thinned to a hard line. "I appreciate what you are trying to do for me, Willy, but to be real honest, you are wasting your time praying for me. My father used to tell me about prayer and I told him what I'll tell you. You can't change anything by saying a few words. You have to do something. It caused some real problems with father and me and it is part of the reason I left home."

"I know about that situation with your dad and I know it breaks your heart to be away from him. It wasn't prayer that caused the problem. To be quite frank, I believe the only way you are ever going to get that problem fixed is for you to become a Christian like he did. If you would do that you would have a relationship that would go beyond anything you have known in the past. There are lots of people all around you that would be glad to help you if you would only let us."

Kitty put up her hand. "Wait just a minute. Before you go any further, I want you to know that I had already made up my mind about religion a long time ago. I'm not the religious type and if you think that is going to change, you are spitting into the wind."

"Listen to me, Kitty. This might be my last chance to talk to you and I owe it to you for all that you have done for me. There is a verse in the Bible that says 'For God so loved the world that he gave His only begotten Son, that whosoever believeth in Him should not perish, but have everlasting Life.'[4] That is what your dad did. He gave his life to Jesus and that is why he is changed."

Kitty leaped to her feet, spilling her coffee on the floor. "Willy, you should know better than that. Those are just some words that were written down a long time ago and they have nothing to do with my life. I don't think they work for everyone."

"But they do work for everyone. There are many changed lives that prove they are true. Your dad is one of them. He is not the same man that raised you. The man you use to love is dead and in his place is a new man that is better. He can love you more now than he ever could before. There is nothing that would make him happier than for you to ask Jesus into your heart. If you will do that, you will have an understanding of him that you can never have if you go on like this. Now, I've said enough. I hope I am still your friend, but even if I'm not, I am willing to gamble our friendship to give you a chance to have eternal life. Are we still friends?"

Kitty was silent for a moment and then she smiled. "Of course we are friends, Willy. We may disagree on a few things, but you will always be my friend. I owe you too much to be mad at you."

Willy stood to his feet and opened the door. "I'm glad to hear you say that and I feel the same way. You will always be in my heart and prayers."

Turning, he stepped through the door and disappeared into the street. For a long minute Kitty stood there looking out at the high peaks in the distance. Willy had been a good friend and now there was a danger of losing that friendship. Denver was becoming a dead end and there was still a pull in her heart for that western country. Her mind was made up. Her future lay in Leadville and she could not wait for the adventure to begin.

The sun was still high in the sky when the men arrived in Leadville. Pulling up at the end of the street, they took a moment to assess the situation. The city was set in a wide valley surrounded by great snow-covered peaks glistening in the light of the sun. In contrast to their splendor were the slopes surrounding the town. Stripped of their trees, the stumps were all that remained. Scattered among the stumps were many dingy cabins and shacks.

Chestnut Street, which was the main street, was filled with a jostling crowd of men of all types from miners to drummers and all in a hurry to get somewhere. The false-front buildings that lined the street were similar in appearance, but offered a variety of services. Dance halls, variety theaters, saloons and other businesses filled the needs of the miners. Several recently-built hotels rose above the single story buildings, setting a standard for the future. A bank was receiving its first coat of white paint and the smell of money was in the air.

A drunken miner stumbled into Hawk, startling him and causing him to sidestep. Regaining control, Bruno shot a glance at his companion. "I thought you said this place was nice and peaceful. This is no better than the old mining camps in California."

"I never said that. If you want peace and quiet go back to New York."

Bruno scowled. "Very funny."

They rode on, doing their best to avoid the jostling crowd. The sounds of laughter filled the air and from somewhere came the sound of gunfire. From the doorway of a saloon could be heard the lively strains of a piano hammering out a tune that sounded more like a war dance than music. Large ore wagons lumbered down the street, accompanied by the crack of the whip and curses of the teamsters urging the oxen on. In the middle of the street a man was viciously whipping a horse, but no one seemed concerned. It was a dog-eat-dog world and it was every man for himself.

Looking about, Bruno searched for a place to begin. The scene was very familiar to him and it brought back memories of his days in Bodie. The shootings, the fights and the endless array of saloons and pleasure palaces filled with men drinking away their hard-earned wages. Anger rose up in him when he recalled those days and the loss of the savings that had taken many years to gather. This time it would be different. There was money to be made and he intended to get his share. He was older and wiser now and no man would catch him off guard again. This time it was his turn.

"Where do you want to start?" Clay asked. "The marshals office is just a ways up the street."

"The best place to start would be with the man that gave him the job."

"That would be Horace Tabor. He is the latest flash in the pan and the man that calls the shots. I don't know if he will do you any good though. He's already hired his man."

"I came here for the marshal's job and I mean to have it. You just show me where this Tabor fella is and I'll take it from there."

Clay shook his head. "The only way you are going to be a law man here is to talk to Bloodson. He's the law now and he's the man you have to convince."

Bruno was quiet for a moment. "I have a plan and it doesn't include Bloodson. Why don't you go and get yourself a beer while I take care of it."

Urging Hawk forward, Bruno moved up the street. Hurrying to catch up, Clay came abreast of him. "You ain't getting' rid of me that easy. I got a piece of this and I want to see what you're gonna do. Tabor runs a general store up in California Gulch and that would be the best place to catch him. He's a pretty tough customer and you ain't likely to push him around."

"You let me worry about Tabor. Just show me where he lives and I'll take it from there."

"Suit yourself."

When they reached the edge of town the men pointed their horses up through the gulch that led to Tabor's store. Here the hillsides were dotted with mines and prospect holes in various stages of development. To the left rose Carbonate and Iron Hill. Their slopes had been stripped of all signs of the lush forest that had once covered the land. In their place were mine tailings that were being hauled out, forming small platforms of broken rock. From the mine portals flowed the foul, sulphur-tainted water that drained down the slopes like a festering sore, forming streams of foul-smelling water. Beyond was the old town of Oro where the Tabor store stood.

Standing behind the counter was a distinguished man in his middle years. His face showed the signs of many years of struggle and work. Yet there was warmth in the eyes that gave evidence of a man who had endured the years without surrendering to the trials they had brought.

When he had finished with the customer, he turned to the men. "Can I help you gentlemen?"

Bruno waited until the customer had left before he spoke. "Is there somewhere we can speak in private? It's about the marshal's job."

"You have a complaint about the marshal?"

"You might say that. I came up here to get that job. From what I know about Bloodson, you made a mistake when you hired him."

Horace grinned. "I'll admit the man's not perfect, but

what gives you the idea that you can do a better job than he can?"

Irritation appeared on Bruno's face. "Because you got a tough town here and you need someone that can stand up to what has to be done. Bloodson is not up to it. He will get himself killed before the month is out. I don't have time to wait for that."

Horace looked at him cynically. "And what makes you think you can do a better job?"

"By what I've heard about him. I've handled tough characters from the Comstock to Bodie and lately Central City. Leadville will be no different."

"Maybe it would help if you knew who you are dealing with," Clay broke in. "This is Bruno Turnbull."

Horace's face brightened. "Well now, that puts a different light on things. I've heard of you. You have made quite a name for yourself. It's just too bad you weren't here when Marshal Lynch was murdered. We might have been able to use you. Unfortunately, the job was given to the deputy and I have no intention of firing him. If you think you are a better man, then maybe you should go down and talk to him. He might put you on as his deputy."

Bruno frowned. "That doesn't sound like a very good idea. The people that work for him have a habit of getting killed. I don't intend to be one of them."

Horace closed the ledger that lay before him. "Unfortunately, that is all I can offer you right now."

"Maybe you could do a little more if I told you what I know about the Lynch murder. There is more to that than you know."

"What do you mean?"

"I know who killed him."

His eyes narrowed. "Who?"

"I can't tell you that but I can put him in jail if you give me the job."

"Mr. Turnbull, I will admit that we need a man like you for the job, but I can't fire Bloodson for no reason. I know he is not well liked, but that is not enough reason to fire him. I would like to clear up that murder, but I am not going to pay the ransom of the marshal's job to do it. I just don't work that way. Now if you will excuse me I have work to do." Turning, he went into the back room and closed the door.

"Looks like that is that," said Clay. "What are you going to do now?"

Bruno turned toward the door. "I'm going to do what I came here to do."

"But he said he wasn't going to get rid of Bloodson."

"Then I guess I will have to do it for him."

CHAPTER 5

The marshal's office proved to be a very unimpressive building. Sitting in the middle of a large vacant lot, it was constructed of rough-cut lumber with a small window on each side. Behind the small building stood a log jail that, in spite of its simple design, appeared to be very sturdy and secure. The interior of the office was very plain and sitting in the middle of the room was a sheet-iron stove with a fire-blackened coffee pot on top of it. The only furniture was a large desk. Behind it sat a man of about thirty-five years, with a thin, angular face, set off by jug-handle ears and the stubble of a beard. Atop his narrow, rounded shoulders was a long neck with a dominant Adam's apple, giving the appearance of a vulture ready to strike.

When the men appeared before his desk, his long, thin fingers curled into fists and he shifted nervously in the chair. "What can I do for you boys?" He mumbled.

Bruno considered the man before him and his face showed the disgust he felt. "Are you Tex Bloodson?"

"I am."

"Then you can start by getting out of my chair."

Tex leaned back in the chair and smiled. "What gives you the idea that this chair is yours?"

"Because I'm the new marshal and I don't want anyone else sitting in my chair, especially you. I know all about you and I know how you got that job. You don't deserve it and in my opinion you need your scrawny neck stretched. Now get out of my chair."

Tex leaned forward. "That's a pretty strong opinion coming from someone that doesn't know me. What makes you think I should have my neck stretched?"

"For murder. I know what happened to Marshal Lynch and you figure in it pretty prominently. If you play along with me, I'll let you get off with your life, but if you give me any trouble, I'll hang you myself. Now what's it going to be?"

The man's shifted uncomfortably. "Mr., I don't know where you got a story like that, but somebody has been feeding you a pack of lies. The marshal was killed by some unknown party and the city council voted me in to take his place. Somebody has been giving you some bad information. If you tell me who it is, I'll get them straightened out."

Bruno leaned forward onto the desk. "It's none of your business where I get my information and I'm running out of patience with you. Are you going to get out of my chair or do I have to help you?"

Tex's chin lifted defiantly as he looked up at the man. "Mr. I told you that someone has given you a bum steer and if you don't get out of my office right now, I am going to lock you up. Have I made myself clear?"

Reaching out, Bruno grabbed the man by the front of his shirt and jerked him across the desk, lifting him in the air until his feet were dangling. "I'm afraid you are the one that doesn't understand. Now, what I need from you is a letter of resignation and your promise that you will get out of Leadville as quickly as you can. Now do you think you can handle that?"

Gasping for breath, the man's face was turning blue. "Let me down, you big piece of gristle."

Delivering a slap on each cheek, Bruno threw the man into the stove, turning it over and inundating him with an avalanche of stove pipes and soot. Grabbing him by the collar, he dragged him over to the desk and leaned him against it. Rummaging through the drawers, he produced a piece of paper and a pen which he put in front of him.

"Now write this down:

'I, Tex Bloodson, have decided that I am no longer able to fulfill the duties of this office. As of today, I officially resign and recommend that you appoint Bruno Turnbull to take my place.'

When you get that written and sign it you can go. I will deliver it to Mr. Tabor myself."

For a moment he sat there trying to put together what had just happened. As the fog began to clear he looked up. "I've heard of you, Turnbull and you don't scare me. I'm not going to write that and you can't make me."

Jerking the man up from his knees, Bruno slapped him again. "You had better write it and be quick about it. You are going to leave town today and it's your choice if you will be setting up in the saddle or draped over it. Now what will it be?"

With no friends in the room, the man gave in to the only choice he had. With an expression of disgust he took the pen in his shaky hand and scratched out the note. Handing it to Bruno, his face twisted into a snarl. "You got your way this time, Mr., but I will be back."

"You won't be back. Not if you want to live."

"You don't scare me, Turnbull. You're not as tough as you think you are and when I come back we will settle this business. You're going to wish you had never met me."

"That'll be the day. Now there's the door. You better get yourself through it before I take you over my knee. Now scat!"

Watching him go, Clay shook his head. "There goes an unhappy man. Do you think he is going to cause trouble?"

"Don't know. Don't care. He's just another scared little weasel trying to take on more than he can handle. I got more important things to worry about than him. Are you coming with me?"

"Where are we going?"

"To see Tabor. We need to let him know that I am on the payroll."

When they arrived at Tabor's store they were met by Augusta, his wife. When they explained what they wanted, she ushered them into the back room. The room was filled with boxes, shipping crates and appeared to be a storeroom/office combination. The room was lit by a large window that gave an excellent view of the town. The only piece of furniture in the room was a large desk that sat in front of the window. Behind it was Horace Tabor, deeply involved in the paperwork before him. It was a few moments before he looked up. Recognizing his guest, he smiled.

"Bruno, what can I do for you?"

Spotting a badge lying on the desk he pointed at it. "I came for that."

Glancing at the badge, Horace's chin lifted. "I thought we already talked about that. Bloodson is taking care of all our law enforcement and he handles the hiring. You go on and talk to him."

Picking up the badge, Bruno pinned it on his shirt and threw the note on the desk. "Not any more. He just quit. I just came over to let you know what is going on and if you need to swear me in or anything, let's get it done. I got a job to do."

Horace's face flushed angrily. "Now hold on. You can't just come in here and declare yourself marshal. That job was filled by the town board and they won't be meeting for another week. I told you if you wanted a deputy job, you needed to talk to Bloodson. You better take this up with him."

"You better read that note. Bloodson quit and he recommended me for the job. He's already left town, so I'll be taking care of the business of the marshals office. I will pick my own deputies if I think I need them."

Glancing at the note, Horace's lips moved as he read the message. Looking up, he frowned. "This is awful sudden. What does it mean he can't fulfill his duties?"

"Just what it says. I told him I knew who killed Lynch and I was going to hang him. Then with a little more persuading he decided to call it quits."

"And who did you tell him killed the Marshal?"

"I didn't have to tell him because he knew."

"Who was it?"

"Bloodson. He knew the jig was up and I told him to get out of town. He took my advice."

Horace studied the note for a moment to give himself time to think. "That puts a different light on things." He looked up. "I don't have the authority to swear you in until the town board makes the decision. They will decide if they want you to have the job."

"And that means for a week you will have no law in town. You can't afford to take that chance. Not in a town like Leadville."

Horace looked unsure. "I suppose I can give you the job temporarily, but it won't be official until the board meets."

"That's fine, but I have some requirements that you will have to meet. I will be in charge of law enforcement and what I say goes. That means I don't want any interference from you or the board. The second thing I want is to build a better jail. Not out of logs, but stone and steel. I am going to be needing it and the sooner you get started on it the better."

"But we just built that jail."

"That jail is only good for drunks and miners getting into trouble. I plan to put some people in there that are going to have help from outside and the jail you have now is just not strong enough for that. I'm only going to need one deputy and that will be Clay. I want someone I can trust. Are you going to have any trouble with that?"

Silence filled the room. Finally, Horace stood to his feet casting a glance in Clay's direction. "I'm not sure I agree with your choice of deputies, but for a week I will let it ride. After that it will be up to the board. You can consider yourself sworn in and you start right away."

When they were outside Clay began to mutter under his

breath. Finally he looked up. "Seems to me you were a little quick to volunteer me for deputy. We didn't talk about that."

"Needed someone I could trust and you know the town. What's the matter, can't you handle a job like that."

"You know I'm an outlaw and so does Tabor. He also knows about some of the business we are involved in. How's that going to look when the board looks you over."

"You let me worry about the board. You offered me jobs one time and I owed you. If you don't want the job, I will still need someone to back me up. You cover my back and I will take care of you. Now you have a friend in the Marshals office. You said we could make a lot of money here and now I can help you. Of course it won't be free. How does that sound to you?"

Clay chuckled. "I think that will work and Gil will be pleased. We might need some help in the courts, too. Are you going to be able to do anything about that?"

"Where is this Gil?"

"He's at the hideout. We have a nice little place down in the San Juans. We have a lot of things going on and he runs the operation from there."

"When do I meet him?"

"You probably won't. He doesn't come up this way because he has other things to deal with. I handle things here."

Bruno nodded his head. "As long as he stays there, we will be all right. All my dealings are going to be with you. If any problems come up with the courts, we'll deal with it.

Clay's eyes glinted with satisfaction. "That sounds good to me. Have we got a deal?"

"Deal."

Early the next morning Bruno arrived at the office. To

have his own office was a new experience for him and he leaned back in the chair and surveyed his new domain. The chance he needed had finally come and he was not going to miss this opportunity to cash in. There was money to be had and he was going to get his share. This time around, he was going to be the big winner and he would do whatever it took. Whatever the price for success, he was willing to pay.

While he was occupied with these thoughts, the door opened and Clay stepped into the room. Taking the room in at a glance, he leaned his rifle against the desk. Gesturing toward the empty room he smiled. "You better get a chair or two in here if you expect anyone to come callin'. I've seen mountain camps that had more furniture than this."

"If you need a place to set, bring your own chair. I'm not running a hotel."

"I got some news you might be interested in. You won't need to worry about Bloodson anymore. He's dead."

Bruno shook his head. "That doesn't surprise me. He needed killing."

"You must have convinced him that he needed to get out of town, because he was in such a hurry he stole a horse. He made a big mistake though because the horse belonged to Billy Sharp. He is about the best shot I know of and he let him make a half a block before he shot him out of the saddle. He didn't live long enough to apologize."

He paused for a moment to see what effect the news would have, but Bruno looked unimpressed. "I just stopped by to tell you so you wouldn't be worrying about him. You ain't going to arrest Billy are you?"

"I don't arrest people for doing the community a service. If he hadn't done it, someone else would have."

"Well, I just wanted to be sure you got the right story on it. Billy's a friend of mine and I wouldn't want to see something happen to him."

Bruno stood to his feet. "He won't get any trouble from me. I'm going to take a walk around. You want to come along?"

"No thanks. I got some business to take care of. Besides we shouldn't be seen together too much. I'll talk to you later."

After Clay had gone, Bruno stepped into the street and took a moment to study the scene before him. Life had taught him to always be aware of what was happening around him and there had been many times that lesson had saved his life. The street was quiet; it appeared as if the town was giving him a pass while he adjusted to his new job. He would need to spend the first few days learning the town and getting the feel of things. News would travel fast on Chestnut Avenue and everyone would soon know who the new marshal was. Many were familiar with his reputation and that was a mixed blessing. With the reputation came respect, but also an element of danger. He was good and his confidence came from deep down inside of him. He had confidence in his natural ability and there had been many along the way that had tried their luck. There would always be someone out there who thought he was better and maybe one day they would meet. Unfortunately, he had very little control over when that day would come and it was not his concern. He pushed those thoughts from his mind.

Bruno had also learned a few things about the circuit judge and how his courts were run. Clay had filled him in on how the system worked. He told him stories of rulings the judge had given on cases where there was a question of who had rights to the lands where claims overlapped. Word had it that the owner who could pay the biggest kickback always won the case.

He had also filled him in on what his men were involved in. They had discovered there was much high-grading going on in the mines and they had tapped into that resource. When the thieves were threatened with exposure, they found it easier to pay the blackmail the gang demanded than go to jail. If a miner resisted, an accident was arranged that left the miner alive, but more willing to cooperate. In a short time word got around and the kickbacks were seldom challenged.

When Bruno asked how the gang had gotten started Clay was happy to fill him in. Gilbert Davis had organized a small gang of outlaws that had begun by robbing stage coaches and freight wagons traveling the old Santa Fe Trail. From there they had branched out to routes of travel in Colorado. Early on, they had set up a hideout that was centrally located in their field of operations that offered a place to drop out of sight when the need arose. Gil had discovered the old cliff dwelling when he had worked on a ranch in the Mesa Verde country. It was located in a remote canyon close to the Mancos River. There was an ancient Indian ruin and a spring there and he had stored its location in his mind for later use. When the outlaws took it over, they added corrals with sheds for the horses and lookout posts at the end of the canyon.

When the silver boom erupted in Leadville, he had sent Clay and some of the men up to look for a way to make a profit from the mines. They had started by the high-grading operations. Now with the vast quantities of silver coming out of the mines it was time to enlarge the operation. With Bruno working with them in the marshal's office, there was no limit to the money that could be made.

Leadville was much larger than Central City and a very busy town. On the hill could be seen the smoke stacks of many smelters pouring great clouds of smoke into the clear mountain air. The sound of the steam engines that drove the pumps and compressors could be heard running day and night. Adding to the din were the sounds of gaiety and laughter coming from the saloons and gambling halls. From somewhere up the street a banjo was playing a lively version of *"Little Brown Jug"* and from the wagon shop came the ring of the blacksmith's hammer.

Suddenly, shots rang out. It came from the direction of a large saloon at the end of the street and Bruno quickened his pace. When he stepped inside the saloon, he stopped just inside and took in the scene before him. The Bon Ton was one of the most popular watering holes in Leadville and it was crowded with thirsty miners. The piano player was banging out a lively version of *"Oh, Susanna"*, while a bunch of miners gathered around a roulette wheel, intently watching the bouncing ball. At the bar stood two tough-looking men who had a drummer backed up against the wall. The larger man of the two glanced toward the door and spotted Bruno. He curled his lip and whispered something to his companion, who laughed. Recognizing Tray, he stepped up to the bar and shouldered his way in between the two men.

Angrily they turned to the intruder, but before they could respond he spoke. "If you boys have had your drink, you better move on. I don't take kindly to troublemakers, so you had better pull in your horns before you get yourself into some real trouble."

Tray's eyes darkened and he reached for the bottle in front of him. "I heard you took over the job of marshalin', but I didn't believe it. Leadville must be getting hard up for lawmen to hire a discard from Central City." He turned to the bartender. "Ben, why don't you set this man up with a sarsaparilla before he leaves?"

Reaching over, Bruno grabbed the bottle and twisted it out of the man's hand. "Tray, if you are hunting trouble with me, I'll be glad to oblige you. I'm the law here now and things are going to be different. You already got one strike against you, so my advice is do your drinking someplace else if you can't stay out of trouble. I'm not in any mood to be hurrahed by a saddle tramp like you. I thought you learned your lesson in Central City, but I might have been wrong. This is a new day and if you can't go by the rules here, I'll run you out of this town too."

A wolfish grin appeared on Tray's face. "Turnbull, we got a score to settle with you and I'm bound to make you pay. You're a coward that shoots helpless young men and you're not going to get away with it. You killed my brothers in cold blood and your time has come. Now, why don't you have your last drink before I kill you?"

Bruno stepped back from the bar and faced the man. He was relaxed and sure of himself and it felt good. A surge of excitement welled up inside of him and he felt that old urge to kill. He fought it down and looked into Tray's face. "I don't drink with a polecat like you, so as soon as you apologize to that man I'll let you go. If you can't handle that, you better drag iron right now."

Riveted to the spot, Tray's face went white. Suddenly he felt uncertain and the confidence he had felt disappeared. He glancing at the batwing doors. There was a clear path for his retreat if he wanted to take it. Deep inside he knew that was not an option. If he turned yellow now, he would be finished. He hesitated for a moment as his nervous fingers hovered above his gun. "I don't take my orders from you or anyone else. I ain't afraid of you."

"Just remember, Tray, this time you are drawing against the law. If I kill you, there will be no questions asked."

Tray looked about for support, but there was none. Sweat broke out on his forehead when he turned to face the man. "You might be Marshal now, but you're not going to push your weight around here and get away with it. You're just trying to prod me into drawing on you so you can shoot me down."

"You are the one that started this dance when you picked on that drummer."

Tray's hand trembled as he measured his chances. "I know your tricks and that ain't going to work. I think you are a yellow-bellied coward that hides behind that gun."

Reaching over, Bruno laid the gun on the bar. "If this gun is bothering you, I'll make it easy for you. Now what's it going to be. Are you leaving here peaceful or do you need a little help?"

Tray shifted uncomfortably and he glanced at his partner. "Billy, it looks like we're going to hold school here. We got us a man that is on the prod and I think he needs a lesson. Marshal, I been waiting for this for a long ..."

Reaching out, Bruno grabbed a handful of shirt and jerked the man off the floor, slapping him across the face. Before he could recover, he threw him into Billy and they both hit the floor. Recovering quickly, Tray began to circle in an attempt to get the lawman between himself and Billy. As he did, Billy moved in and took a swing which Bruno ducked while he back-heeled him, knocking him to the floor.

He jumped up and threw a punch, but as he stepped forward there was a moment when his foot was off the ground. With a quick kick, Bruno knocked his leg out from under him and he went down again.

Without turning his head, he snapped, "Billy, you better stay out of this, it doesn't concern you." Ignoring the warning, Billy got up and picked up a chair and swung it, smashing it on the big man's back. Spinning around, Bruno grabbed a falling leg and brought it down with a resounding thud on his head. Billy dropped like a pole-axed steer.

In the meantime, Tray had regained his feet and charged. Bruno swung and caught him on the jaw, stopping him in his tracks. Recovering quickly, he took a swing which Bruno ducked and drove his head against his chest. Jerking his head up, he smashed his head against his jaw with a brain rattling "Liverpool Kiss." Tray's head snapped back and Bruno followed with a right and a left to the body.

Staggering back it took Tray a moment to regain his balance. Then he sprang forward, swinging with both fists. Several of the blows landed before Bruno could block them and he countered with a solid right to the jaw. The punch staggered the big man and he fell against the bar. Before he could recover he took another blow to the stomach and another to the solar plexus. Toppling to the floor, he made an effort to rise but fell back again gasping for breath.

Reaching down Bruno grabbed both men by the collars and picked them up. Turning to the drummer who was squeezed against the wall, he shook Tray until he raised his head. "Now I want you to apologize to this nice man for the inconvenience you caused him."

Muttering incoherently, Tray made an effort to comply.

Turning, Bruno dragged the men to the door and threw them into the street. "Boys, that is the last warning you are going to get from me. I don't want to see you in town until you can behave yourselves." Without answering, the men staggered down the street and disappeared.

The crack of the whip cut the air and the coach jerked into motion, setting Kitty back in the seat. Rearranging herself, she watched as the stage station disappeared from view. It was a relief to be on the move and she anticipated the new life that lay ahead. The year she had spent in Denver had been exciting, but that part of her life was over for keeps. There was a bright future ahead for her in Leadville if she played it smart. It was a great relief to be away from the confines of the city and into a world that she had missed. There had been times when she had wondered if it had been wise to leave the ranch, but that part of her life was over too. She missed her dad terribly, but there was no going back. Still, there were times when she found herself longing for that peaceful, uncomplicated life she had left behind.

The wheels of the coach rumbling over the stones in the road had a tranquilizing effect on her and she was carried back to the days when she was a little girl. She remembered the stories her dad had told of the early days when he had started the ranch. It had been a struggle in the beginning. He had found a ranch in New Mexico that had sold him a few head of cattle that had given him a start. With only fifty cows and one good bull, it had taken years to build up the herd. He had been fortunate to settle in a basin with good water and lush grass with practically unlimited range. The winters had been harsh, but that came with the mountain country that surrounded their home. The mountains had also provided the seclusion that he had sought and it was in this land that he had decided to live out his life. Over the years they had built up a herd until it was the largest in the area. He had fought the heat of the summer and the cold of the winter. He had won the war against predators both wild and human, which had proven he was man enough to hold the land. No one was going to take from him the paradise he had created.

Looking out the window, she watched the country go by. The hills rose from the plains as they ascended into the hills that were covered with the lush new greens of early spring. Tall, rocky escarpments rose along the edge of the rushing waters of the creek. Sagebrush and juniper gradually gave way to slopes covered with Douglas fir and mountain mahogany.

She still carried the fond memories of her teen years, when she had worked side by side with her father. There were times when the money was in short supply and they could not hire extra hands. In those times they had mended fences and worked the cattle from 'can't see' to 'can't see'. It was hard for a young girl, but she had learned the lessons that came from building a dream. She knew dreams did not come for free. She remembered that first trip into the mountains with her father and how she had loved the fresh breezes that blew across the face of the mountain. She also remembered the great sweeping views of the ranch from their vantage point high above it. It had been a prospecting trip and they had carried great hopes of finding a rich claim. If they were lucky, a rich strike could make the difference between a hard, back-breaking life and one of prosperity. It was one of many trips they had taken together, but they had never found the rich vein they had sought. The real treasure had been the chance to spend time with her father and get to know him in a way that she had not known him before. She treasured those memories.

It had all been so wonderful, until he spoiled it by becoming religious. At first it seemed like a new idea for him to explore, but he had taken it seriously. The changes in his life had been dramatic and she no longer recognized this new man. Over the years the new ideas had taken over his life until she had no choice but to leave. She had seen the same symptoms in the preacher in Denver, but you could expect that in a preacher. But Willy was not a preacher and he was just like them. Could they know something that she didn't know? Had they really discovered the secret of life or was it just some hare-brained idea?"

"Beautiful country isn't it"

"Excuse me?"

"I said, 'Beautiful country'. It is a land that God has poured out His special favor upon."

"I suppose you could say that. My name is Kitty Duncan. Who are you?"

"Lucinda Clark. It's going to be a long ride and I thought you might like to have a friend for the journey."

Kitty considered the woman for a moment. She was beautiful by anyone's standards. Dressed in the latest Denver fashion, the dress enhanced her figure without flaunting it. Her hair was golden and set off by deep blue eyes and an unblemished completion that was highlighted by an attractive smile. She appeared to be a woman who had learned the secrets of being a lady and knew how to present herself without being pretentious.

"And what kind of business are you in?"

"I have been working in a dry goods store in Denver and

was asked to go up to Leadville and help out in the new store. The man that runs that store is my bosses' brother and they are trying to expand their operation there and get in on the silver boom."

Kitty smiled. "I don't want to be presumptuous, but you don't look like the kind of a girl that will fit in a town like Leadville. I hear it is a pretty rough and ready town."

Lucinda smiled sweetly. "Don't let my appearance fool you; I have handled some pretty rough characters in my time. I used to work on Holladay Street and there isn't much that I haven't seen."

The smile disappeared. "You must be kidding. The only kind of women that worked down there that I know of were…"

"Harlots, I know. That's what I use to be."

Kitty raised an eyebrow. "You are kidding, of course."

"No, I'm not. That all ended when I became a Christian and left that life behind. With the Lord's help, I have been able to build a new life. I will be forever in His debt."

Caught by surprise, Kitty sat in silence for a few moments. It was happening again. Just when she had thought she had left this crazy religious stuff behind, it was following her into the mountains. What would it take to leave this annoyance in her life behind? Maybe a straight-forward response would bring the answer.

"If you are a Christian, maybe you can help me out. My father became a Christian a few years ago and it has caused a few problems in our relationship. So much so that it caused me to leave home. If Christianity is so great, why is it ruining my life?"

"It can't ruin your life unless you let it. Can I be frank?"

"Sure."

"Before your dad became a Christian, you were both in the devil's camp. He had you both, so there was no reason to bother you. When your dad became a Christian, he became a member of the family of God. That made him an enemy of the devil and a war began. If you refuse to be a Christian you will still be in the enemy camp. Even though your father still loves you, there is a barrier between the two of you that you will never be able to cross. Even though you still love each other, there are now basic differences in your lives. You will never really understand him until you become a Christian too."

"But I don't want to be a Christian. I just want to live my life and be left alone."

"You could do that and live your life out settling for second best. Your relationship with your father will never be what it once was and when you get to the end of your life you will have to answer to God for your sins. The wages of sin is death [5] and we are all guilty of sin.[6] The only way you are going to restore that relationship with your father and God is to ask Jesus into your heart. If you do that, He will come in and change your life. Then you will understand what has happened to your father. I can help you if you would like to."

Kitty looked out the window in silence. Was this some kind of a conspiracy? Her dad had said the same things and she knew she could never make the changes her father had. The offer was tempting if it was real, but would it restore that old relationship with her father? It would never work for her. Yet she had seen changes in her father that she would have never believed possible. His language had cleaned up and the whiskey bottles he had kept in the pantry had disappeared. He had developed a joy in his life that she had not seen before and his love for her had never been more genuine. No, she could never change that much, but he had.

"I could never make those changes in my life. The changes in my father's life were like night and day and I could never do that."

"Kitty, you don't understand. I was like you and there was no way I was going to be able to change my life either. The Bible says 'I can do all things through Christ which strengthens me.'[7] No one can do it by themselves. If you mean business with the Lord, He will help you. He will never let you down. Would you like to pray with me?"

Kitty grinned sheepishly. "I'm sorry, but I'm afraid I'm just not ready for that. I'm glad that you were able to come out of your old life, but not everyone can do that. Maybe when I am old I will give it some thought. For now I have too much I want to do and I am afraid religion will just get in the way."

"I'm sorry to hear that," Lucinda said gently. "Just remember what I said and one day maybe you will see the truth in it and your life will change. Don't wait too long, though. We are living in dangerous times and Leadville will not make that decision any easier."

"I will admit it sounds like a great life, but there is no way I can do that right now. I appreciate your concern, but if you don't mind I'd rather not talk right now." Turning back to the window, Kitty struggled to regain her composure.

"If that's what you really want. Just remember, I'll be praying for you."

Kitty remained silent as she watched the scenery go by. She could not stop the tear that ran down her cheek.

CHAPTER 6

When the stage rolled into Leadville, Kitty knew that she had been mislead. Instead of the bustling new city she had expected, she was met with dusty streets lined with boardwalks, hitching rails and false-front buildings that barely concealed the log cabins that they had intended to hide. Several hotels could be seen rising above the single-story buildings, but they did not compare to even the simplest hotels in Denver.

It was clear this was going to be a new challenge for her, but new challenges had never stopped her before nor would they stop her now. She had been through the fire in Denver, so this was just another problem she would have to solve. Her head began to fill with ideas of how her experience could be put to use. There would be a place that she would fit and she would find it. All she needed was a chance. Her opportunity had to be here, but where? Her mind was made up and 'come hell or high water' she was going to find a way in this strange place. She was better prepared now and she was ready for the demands this new life would bring.

At the end of the street stood the stage station. Stepping down from the coach, Kitty straightened her dress and looked around. Beside the weather-beaten old building was a corral that held several horses. Pieces of old harnesses hung on the fence and scattered about were parts of a broken wagon. A wheel leaned against the building. On the hills to the east, she could see many mine dumps and shacks scattered across the barren hillside. A few small trees still stood on the slopes. Stripped of their boughs, they appeared to be monuments to the decimated forest that had once covered the land. Sadly, she turned away. It was a world that had been destroyed by greed and if she was to make it here she would have to accept things as they were.

The driver handed down her bag and she following Lucinda inside. The man at the counter greeted them with a pleasant smile.

"Welcome to Leadville, Ladies," he said. "If you will wait a minute Tom will get the rest of your luggage and we can make arrangements to take them to the hotel."

Lucinda glanced up the street and shook her head. "That won't be necessary. I have some one coming for them. If I could just leave them here for a while, I would appreciate it."

"Ma'am, I can't be responsible for any bags left here. This is not a town you want to leave things lying about in."

"They will be fine and someone will be here for them in a little bit."

The man glanced at the bags and raised an eyebrow. "I'll

set them behind the counter for you. They should be safe there."

Kitty crossed to the door and looked up the busy street. This was going to be much different than Denver, but she knew she could adjust. Men were the same no matter where they were and men were her business. It didn't matter if they wore the fine clothes of a gentleman or the rags of a miner. Inside their desires were the same and she was a beautiful woman. She had learned how to use that to her advantage at the Palace and it would be the same in this outpost of civilization.

"Kitty, do you have a place to stay?" Lucinda asked, drawing her back from her reverie. "I have been told it is hard to get a room in the hotels and there aren't many other options available. Would you be interested in sharing my room above the store until you can get situated? It would be nice to have a little company in a place that is strange to both of us."

"Thank you, but I will be fine."

"You're sure?"

"Yes, but thank you for the offer."

Picking up her small bag, she smiled. "If you change your mind I will be at Barnaby's dry goods store. Don't be bashful. You will be very welcome there." She turned toward the street and was gone.

When she was gone Kitty breathed a sigh of relief. Lucinda was a nice lady, but she could never really feel comfortable around her. It didn't matter now, she had left and it was time to explore her new world. Just up the street was the Grand Hotel and that was as good a place as any to start. The lobby had a high ceiling, but was much smaller that she had expected. On the walls were mounted heads of elk and deer and the only furniture were a few chairs lined up along the wall. The man at the desk was polite, but there were no rooms available.

Her next stop was the Clarendon, with the same results. The story was the same at the Winsor and it began to look like the livery stable was the only option left. Reluctantly, she remembered Lucinda's offer. She was not thrilled with the prospect, but she had to admit she was running out of options.

With great reluctance she headed for the store. Delighted to see her new friend, Lucinda invited her in and in no time they had made a comfortable space in her room. The room faced the street which offered a grand view of what was going on in the town. Kitty was relieved when a customer called her friend away and she got a chance to relax a little and formulate some kind of a plan. Things were not turning out the way she had hoped. It went against her grain to accept the hospitality of people she hardly knew, but she would have to endure it for a little while. She would have to get something going for herself very quickly.

At daybreak she was up. Being careful not to awaken Lucinda, she slipped out of the room and down the stairs. A small kitchen had been set up in the back of the store, but she resisted the temptation of a hot cup of coffee and quietly left the store.

It had become clear that Leadville would not be able to offer her the kind of a job she had in Denver, so lowering her sights she headed for the Clarendon. The hotel was a two-story structure that had been hastily put together. The interior was quite old-fashioned and the rotunda was lavishly decorated with large paintings and tapestries. The floor was set with colored tiles and two massive walnut staircases led to the upper floor. By Denver standards it was quite provincial, but it offered hospitality that was more suitable to the business crowd that could afford more comfortable surroundings. It was the best hotel in town and she would show them what a city girl could do. When she asked for the manager she was ushered into a small office in the back of the house. Behind a large desk sat a middle-aged man with a neatly trimmed beard and handlebar mustache His suit was well-tailored and he had the look of a man who knew what he was about. He introduced himself as Mr. Bush and invited the young woman to have a seat. Kitty was well-prepared for this moment, but in spite of her best efforts to charm the man into giving her a job the answer was 'no'.

Undaunted by the failure, she moved on to the Winsor, but the results were the same. Lowering her sights again she went to the Grand, which also proved to be a waste of time. A change in strategy was needed. There were many stores along the street, but being a clerk was out of the question. The next best opportunity would have to be the saloons. After all, the town was filled with them and much money was being spent there. The Pioneer looked like as good a place to start as any, so she took a deep breath and pushed her way into the crowded saloon. The large smoke-filled room was filled with men involved in the various forms of amusement. Along one wall was a bar; Gambling was the main attraction here and the room was filled with poker tables, three-card monte and other games of chance. In the rear was a stage with a small dance floor. The place had promise, but she was disappointed to find that the upper floor was a brothel. She moved on. The next stop was the Keystone which was also a waste of time. Pap

Wyman's place showed some promise, but he had no openings at the moment.

By this time the day was far spent and discouragement was beginning to creep into her heart. Most of the saloons that were left were very crude affairs and they would be a waste of time. The only real possibility left was the Bon Ton. If there was no job there, she did not know what she would do. For the first time she was beginning to question the wisdom of coming to this place.

The Bon Ton was a combination saloon and billiard hall and was one of the busiest watering holes in town. At the bar Kitty introduced herself to the bartender and told him she was looking for a job. Excusing himself, he disappearing into the back room. He returned with a man who introduced himself as Mr. Nye. He escorted her to a table in the corner and motioned for her to have a seat.

After a quick appraisal of the woman he smiled. "Bill told me there was a beautiful young woman who wanted to see me and I couldn't pass up an opportunity like that. What can I do for you, Miss …?"

"Kitty Duncan. I just arrived from Denver and was hoping I could find a job in your saloon."

The man sat back in his chair and studied her. "You want a job here?"

"Yes; I have a lot of experience in working with people and I can do just about anything. I worked at the Palace Hotel in Denver and I have lots of experience in this kind of work."

"Young lady, let me give you a piece of advice. Save yourself a lot of trouble and take the next stage back to Denver. I don't think you would like working here. This is nothing like Denver and we get a pretty rough crowd. You don't strike me as a person that can handle that. Most of these men put in a hard days work in the mines and when they get off they are looking for some action. You might find yourself in a situation you can't get yourself out of."

Irritation appeared on Kitty's face. "Mr. Nye, you underestimate me. I can handle anything this place can throw at me. If you will give me a chance, I can prove to you that I can deal with anything these men can put out. I'll even wash dishes to start, if that's what it takes to show you how badly I want this job. All I need is a chance."

Standing to his feet the man's face grew serious. "I'm sorry, Miss Kitty, but I am afraid I can't use you. Better take my advice and go back down to Denver. I wouldn't want to be responsible for getting you hurt."

Leaping to her feet, Kitty grabbed his arm. "Mr. Nye, you are making a mistake. I can handle this crowd if you will just give me a chance to prove it. My mind is made up to stay in Leadville and I really need this job. I'll do anything you ask me to."

"Girl, you really don't understand the situation here. There isn't a job for you and I doubt if you can even find a place to stay. In some of the saloons men are sleeping on the floors because there just aren't any rooms. What chance do you think a young woman like you would have? You had better take my advice and go back to Denver. Now if you will excuse me, I have some business I have to attend to. "

Her eyes flashed anger as she watching him go. Being taken as a tenderfoot made her mad and she was running out of patience with people who treated her that way. She would have to change her image if she was going to make it in this town, but how could she do that?

"Missy, don't you believe that. I know a place where you can stay and it will be free."

Kitty turned to see who had spoken. Unlike most of the men in the saloon, this man stood out from the crowd. Wearing a Prince Albert coat and a planter's hat, he showed a touch of class. From his highly polished boots to the diamond stick pin, he was a portrait of style. He looked like he had just stepped out of the bar in the Palace Hotel.

It didn't matter. Kitty was in no mood to deal with some tin horn and she threw him an angry glance as she tried to get past him. Blocking the way, he smiled broadly, "Missy, I made you an offer and you're not showing much appreciation. Why don't we sit down and talk this over. You will really like me once you get to know me."

"I'm not interested in knowing you. Now get out of my way!"

Pushing against the man, Kitty made another effort to pass, but was blocked. With all her strength she shoved against his chest, but he refused to budge. A fierce anger began to rise in her and she delivered a vicious kick to his shin. Caught off guard, he fell to the floor dragging her with him. Rolling over, the man's face filled with anger and he swung his fist, catching Kitty on the side of the head with a glancing blow.

"Why, you little tramp, I'm going to teach you a lesson you'll never forget."

Grabbing her by the hair he dragged her to her feet. Pulling back his fist he took another swing but she ducked. Before he could swing again, she pulled a derringer from the folds of her dress and pointed it at him.

"Mr., you better back off or I'm going to kill you. I'm not kidding!"

Looking at the gun, his lip curled. "You little tramp, you wouldn't dare. Now give me that gun." With a lunge he grabbed for the gun, but he was too slow. Kitty shoved the gun into his stomach and pulled the trigger. The man stopped in his tracks. Shock registered on his face when he looked at the enlarging spot of red that had appeared on his shirt. His face darkened with rage.

"Mr., you stop right there or I'm going to put the next one were it counts."

Ignoring the warning, the man lunged and Kitty fired. The .44 caliber slug entered his neck just above the Adams apple and he dropped to the floor.

In shock, Kitty stared down at the body. The room had grown quiet and when she looked up, a circle of men had formed around her. She pointed the gun at the crowd, her eyes blazing with fury. "You people stay back. Or I'll give you some of what he got. Now get out of my way."

A pathway opened in the crowd and she moved toward the door. Before she could reach it a big man appeared. In a glance he summed up the situation and he turned to the girl. When she looked up their eyes met and for a long moment they held. He reached out his hand. "I'll take that gun, Miss."

Kitty stood unmoved. "Get out of my way or I'll give you what he got."

Taking the gun gently, Bruno looked down at her. "Not with this gun. It only holds two shots. Now, tell me what happened."

"This man attacked me and I had to defend myself. He gave me no choice but to shoot him."

"That's right, Marshal," said a tall miner. "The man

grabbed her and she was just defending herself. I'll be glad to testify for her."

Bruno looked around. "Is that right?"

A ripple of agreement went through the crowd. Bruno looked at the man who had spoken. "I will need you to come down to the office and fill out a paper testifying to what you saw." Turning to Kitty, he spoke gently. "You need to come with me."

"You heard what he said, Marshal, I was just defending myself. You can't arrest me for that."

"I'm not arresting you; I'm taking you in for questioning. It won't take very long and we can get this thing straightened out."

Unhappily the girl fell in step beside him and they made their way to the office. Inside, he offered her a seat and placed a sheet of paper before her. Pointing at it, he handed her a pencil. "I want you to write down exactly what happened and don't leave anything out."

She nodded. "I hope this isn't going to take too long; I have other things I have to do today."

Bruno settled back in his chair. "I'm afraid you are going to have to put them off until tomorrow. I am going to hold you overnight."

The pencil froze in the air. "What did you say?"

"I said I am going to hold you overnight. It's standard procedure when there is a death involved."

"You can't be serious."

"I'm afraid I am. If it's any comfort to you, I will be staying here too. It wouldn't be safe to leave you by yourself."

"All of this for a simple case of self defense?"

Bruno shrugged his shoulder. "I wish I could change it, but that is what the law says."

She bit her lip and looked toward the jail in the back. "I certainly wouldn't want to break the law. Who's going to protect me from you?"

"You don't need to worry about me, Ma'am. My appearance can be deceiving. I'm really a gentle man and I will do anything I can to keep you safe."

He smiled and Kitty was amazed at the way it lit up his face. She could see he was a man who rarely smiled. "Maybe I should introduce myself. I'm Kitty Duncan. Who are you?"

"Bruno Turnbull and I would be glad to protect you even if I wasn't the marshal."

Startled by that answer, a slight smile appeared on her face. "What makes you think I am a girl that needs protecting?"

Bruno hesitated a moment. She was so lovely to look at it caught his tongue. "Because I believe that beneath that tough-girl image you put on back there in the saloon, there is a sensitive young woman. Given the chance you could make a man willing to move the earth to make you happy. Whoever that man is he will be very lucky to find you. I wish it was me."

Surprised, Kitty looked up into his face. There was a loneliness there that had etched itself into his features. Years of being alone had taken the tenderness from his face and left a hardness that did not seem natural to the man. Yet there was nothing in those features that invited sympathy and she knew he was a man who did not share his feelings easily.

Their eyes met and for a long moment they held. When she spoke there was a quality of uncertainty in her voice. "You don't strike me as a man that would want to settle down with a woman."

"Why not? I'm like any man. No one wants to spend their life alone. I'll bet you're not planning on doing that."

"That's different. I'm a woman."

"There's no difference. You are a beautiful woman and you could have any man you wanted, but you are still alone. You are no different than me."

She shook her head, puzzled at what she had heard. "I've never met anyone that I trusted enough to share my life with. Not to mention my feelings. That kind of a man is hard to find. Are you that kind of a man?"

"I'm a man that has spent most of my life alone. Who would want to share their feelings with a man like that?"

"I would, if he loved me."

For a moment they were quiet. No words of love had been spoken, yet there was an understanding that did not require words. There was something happening between them that he had not expected and he was not sure he understood it. He had known a few women in his life, but this one was different. The nervousness that he usually felt had not surfaced. There was no need for the defenses he normally put up. The feelings that were stirring were something he had not prepared for, but he would not deny them. How should he deal with the feelings she had generated in him?

"Do you plan to be a marshal all your life?"

"No. I have other plans, but I doubt a pretty girl like you would be interested in hearing about them."

"Try me."

"I have plans to one day have a ranch where I can build a large herd of cattle and raise horses. If I was really lucky I would find a woman like you to share it with. Do you know anything about ranching?"

"Are you kidding? I was raised on a ranch. My father has a ranch west of the San Juans. Until I went to Denver it was the only life I knew."

"Why did you leave?"

Kitty frowned. "It wasn't because I didn't like living on a ranch. It was because my father got religion. After a while, it became just too much for me to handle. I had to get away from it. I needed a change of life and I thought I would try my luck in Denver."

"So what brought you here?"

"I had a boss that was making life miserable for me. I heard Leadville was starting to blossom into a new city and it sounded like it might be a place I could find a future. So far it hasn't worked out."

Bruno's voice was tender. "You know what I think. I think you have the same dream as me and I think together we could make it work. You are the woman I have been looking for."

A questioning look appeared as she studied his face. "You don't even know me. What makes you think we have anything in common?"

"You handle yourself just like I do, only you do it like a lady. We both have the same dream and we are both alone. How many people do you know that have that much in common?"

Kitty considered that. In a strange way he reminded her of something she had seen in her father's manner when she was a little girl. Was she looking for that quality in this man? Was she looking for something that wasn't there? She spoke quietly. "It takes a lot more than that to make a life."

"That's right, it takes courage. How brave are you?"

Her chin rose, "I'm brave enough. I am also smart enough to know that it isn't wise to rush into something like you are proposing, with my eyes shut. I will admit it is a tempting idea, but I don't see any future in it. Now, if I have to stay here tonight maybe you had better show me to a room where I will be safe."

Bruno reached into the desk drawer and produced a set of keys. "Suit yourself. Just remember what I said. I think if you sleep on it, you might see the logic in what I said."

"There's one other thing. You didn't tell me what you are charging me with."

"I don't have to charge you to hold you overnight."

"If you don't charge me with something it is false arrest."

Bruno scowled. "We'll try vagrancy for now."

"Vagrancy?"

"That's right. You don't have a job and I see no visible means of support. You have no husband and that makes you a vagrant. Now I'm going to have to search you before I lock you up."

She turned sharply. "Search me? You've got to be kidding! I'm in here because a man tried to put his hands on me. What makes a search any different?"

He grinned at her. "I've already taken one gun off of you. How do I know you don't have a hideout gun or a knife somewhere? I have to protect myself."

"I don't have any more weapons. Where would I hide them?"

Spreading out her skirt Kitty turned around. "See, there is no place where I could hide a weapon."

Noticing a small pocket in the folds of the skirt Bruno pointed at it. "What is that?"

"That is where I carry my Derringer. It wouldn't be right for a lady to wear a holster. I sewed it in there myself. Is that against the law?"

Looking the skirt over carefully, he couldn't resist a smile. "How do I know if you aren't hiding another gun somewhere else?"

"You are going to have to trust me on that. Do you want me to turn my pocket inside out?"

He shot a glance at her. "That won't be necessary. If you give me your word that you have no more weapons, I'll let it ride."

"You have my word."

"Good. Now, if you will come with me, I'll get you settled in."

The log jail was primitive in its appearance, but sturdily constructed. Inside were four small cubicles with a narrow passage that divided the room. Selecting the cleanest one, Bruno opened the door. Stepping inside, Kitty inspected her new surroundings. There was one small cot on the wall with a thin mattress and a slop bucket in the corner. She looked at it in disgust. "You don't believe in elaborate accommodations, do you? What am I suppose to do if nature calls? I'm not going to use that."

"Just give me a call and we'll take care of it. I will be in this cell next to you. You make yourself at home and I will be back a little later."

When Bruno returned later that night, the woman appeared to be asleep. Careful not to make any noise, he opened the adjoining cell and slipped inside. Silently he lay down and folded his arms behind his head. Things had been moving pretty fast since he left Central City. There had been little time to think about what was developing in his life. He was grateful for the tranquility the jail offered away from the excitement of the city. Being the marshal was something he had not thought much about, but he was beginning to see the possibilities that were unfolding. For the first time since he had left California he was in a position to make some real money and the law was on his side. Now, he was not only in charge of the law, but he had control of the outlaws as well. If Clay wanted his help, he would have to dance to his tune. It was going to cost him too. This time he would get a piece of the pie and he would decide how much. This time the law was going to work for him and the town would have to fall in line with his plans. For the first time he had the leverage he needed to get what he wanted.

It was very quiet and somewhere a tin bucket rattled. Down the street a dog barked. He turned his eyes and looked at the sleeping woman. For the first time in his life he had a woman to think about. Was he really ready for that? Women had always been a diversion to him and not to be taken seriously. Whenever the need arose there were always the cribs. The idea of having a woman of his own was not something that he had given much thought to. He had always tried to ignore loneliness in his life, but Kitty had forced him to deal with it. He had always figured on having a wife someday, but that would be later on, when he was ready. A woman would need the security of a home, which he could not give right now. Yet this woman had stirred something inside of him that he had never felt before. Was that love? Did he even know what love was? One thing was sure, she had created new feelings inside that he had never felt before. If that was love, he was not going to miss it. It may never come again.

Somewhere a screen door banged and Kitty turned in her sleep. He looked at her sleeping form. Even in the dark she stirred his passion. He had never trusted his feelings when it came to women. For the first time in his life a woman had lit a fire he was not sure he could control. That made him a little nervous, but like a man is drawn to wild country, he could not walk away. He had always kept his emotions to himself, but this was different. In his business, to share too much of yourself was a dangerous thing. He had always protected himself when his emotions were involved. This time it was different.

"Bruno, are you awake?"

"Yes."

There was a long moment of silence. "Did you really mean the things you said about wanting me?"

"I meant every word."

"I have been lying here, trying to think about what it would be like being married to you. I really don't know much about you."

Bruno sat up on the bunk and looked into her face. "If I tell you the truth, it might scare you off."

"Try me."

Moonlight filtered in to the cell through the barred window and for a moment it highlighted the finely sculptured lines of the woman's face. For a moment, Bruno wondered at the sight. Regaining his focus, he took a moment to gather his thoughts. "I grew up in New York, but I came west to find my fortune. Something was happening here and I wanted to be a part of it. I worked around mining camps for years. When I was in California, I discovered I was pretty good with a gun and I liked the idea of making a living with one. It got me out of the mines and I will not go back. It makes me a pretty good living and for now that is what I have to do. Does that bother you?"

"Have you ever killed anyone?"

"Yes. It comes with the job"

"I guess that was a dumb question." Kitty's voice was unemotional as she considered the new thought. "Is that the way you want to live?"

"It's not my choice, but that's the way it has to be right now. We live in a time when many differences are settled with a gun and being able to use one well is power. Right now I am on the side of the law, but that could change. I have a dream and I will do whatever it takes to make it come true. I want you to be part of that dream. I want to make your dreams come true and they are the same as mine."

Kitty thought on that for a moment. "You don't know what my dreams are."

"Yes, I do and I will make them come true. I want to protect you for the rest of your life. Together we can build that ranch we want."

"And in the meantime, what happens to me if someone comes along that is faster than you?"

"That is a risk you will have to take. Like any wife, you need to stand with your man through whatever comes. I'm not as well known as Wes Harden or Clay Allison and I'd like to keep it that way. I have a few things planned that will get me out of this business soon. Then we can build a ranch before my reputation catches up with me."

Kitty sat up. "How soon?"

"Soon enough. Now you had better get some sleep. We can talk about this later."

At daybreak, Bruno was up and at the hotel. A hallway led to the kitchen, where he was met with the inviting aroma of breakfast being prepared. The cook was filling plates with the delicious steaming food. Bruno snatched a sausage from the stove and popped it in his mouth. "I need you to make me two breakfasts just like those and a pot of coffee. You can put it on the city's bill."

The cook looked at him cynically. "That's a lot of food for one man. Is the city trying to fatten you up?"

"Got a prisoner to feed. I just elected you to be the official cook. If the city has a problem with that, send them to me and I'll take care of it."

The man opened his mouth to speak, but the marshal's stern expression changed his mind. "It will be a few minutes. I got a full dining room this morning. You go sign the ticket at the front desk and I'll send a boy around with the food as soon as it's ready."

Bruno nodded and headed for the dining room. When he reached the jail, Clay was waiting for him.

"One day on the job and you are already filling the jail. You keep this up and you won't have a place to sleep."

Bruno nodded. "Just doing my job. What's on your mind?"

"The circuit judge is going to be here in a few days and I need to fill you in on what's going to happen. With you as marshal, you can help us with a little problem we are having with the judge. The district has brought in a new judge that is probably not going to see things our way. You are going to have to help us out. We have some business going with Joe Growler over at the Emperor Mine. He uncovered a rich vein where it joins the property of the Poker Chip. I'm afraid we can't depend on the judge to see things our way. We need you to convince him that it would not be smart to make a ruling against Joe. The boys will back you up on whatever you decide to do, but we need a good ruling on this one. If he wins we get a share of the silver coming out of that mine and I will see that you make out all right. Do you think you can handle that?"

Bruno leaned back in his chair and folded his hands behind his head. "How have you been handling it in the past?"

"We had a judge that did just what we wanted as long as he got his share. The district office shipped him out when they suspected he was taking money under the table. This guy they sent up from Denver to replace him is hopelessly honest. We tried to make a deal with him and he threatened to put us in jail. When Lynch was killed we thought you might be able to help. You are the kind of a man that can get the job done. All you have to do is convince the judge that Joe has a valid claim and everything will be fine."

Bruno stared at him for a moment. "I can handle that, but there is something I need from you. I got a prisoner back there that will need a place to live. You've been around here for a while and I want you to find something for her. She will be going up before the same judge and when she is cleared, she will need a place."

Clay raised an eyebrow. "I heard about that gal and she just moved in at that new dry goods store. What's wrong with that?"

"I want something better for her."

"I don't know if there is anything better. Places to stay are pretty hard to find."

Bruno's eyes narrowed. "I'm not asking a favor, Clay. I want a place for her and if you don't get it I'll take yours."

Clay looked at him and it was plain that he was not kidding. He shrugged his shoulders. "I'll see what I can do."

When the food arrived, Bruno invited Kitty to join him in the office. Setting the tray in front of her, he looked for a smile of approval. "I didn't know what you wanted, so I let the cook figure that one out. It's pretty hard to mess up breakfast."

"This will be fine," Kitty poked at the plate with her fork. "I appreciate your efforts to take care of me, but I need to know how long you plan to keep me here."

"I'm working on that. I heard you were staying at that new dry goods store. Do you know the people there?"

"Not really. I met a lady on the stage who offered me a place until I could get situated. I didn't have much choice, so I took her up on it."

Bruno reached over and filled her mug with coffee. "I'm afraid I'm going to have to hold you for a few days until the judge gets here, or I could…"

Kitty leaped to her feet. "You can't hold me here for shooting that gorilla. It was self-defense, plain and simple. You should give me a reward for getting him off the streets!"

"I wasn't finished. The best I can do is ask you to give me your word that you won't leave town. If you do that, I will release you in the custody of that woman. That is, if she agrees to it."

Kitty relaxed a little. "I'm sure she will be happy to have me stay. It has to be better than that dungeon back there. What happens when I go to court?"

"You don't need to worry about that, it's just a formality. I'll be glad to testify for you and I promise you, no judge is going to convict you of anything."

Kitty smiled. "Is that part of your plan to take care of me for the rest of my life?"

"Something like that. There is one thing I would like you to do."

"Name it."

"I'd like to take you out to eat. It is part of my rehabilitation program. Very few prisoners qualify for it. Are you game?"

"That sounds like an interesting offer. It's the best one I've had yet."

"Is that a 'yes'?"

"You've got a date."

CHAPTER 7

The sun was just setting over the mountains when Bruno escorted Kitty to the hotel. Inside, they stopped for a moment to look over the people who had gathered for supper. It was an old habit that Bruno had formed over the years and one that was necessary for a man who made a living with the gun. Unlike the saloons, the folks here were dressed in their best. It was not a crowd that Bruno felt comfortable with, but he made an effort to relax and fit in. Most of the people were mine owners, business men and other people who rarely got their hands dirty. None of them were people that Bruno knew. Selecting a table near the front, he was satisfied that he could see who entered the restaurant and at the same time watch what was happening on the street.

Making one final check of the room, Bruno seated his guest. "I know you are probably used to classier places than this, but this is the best the town has to offer. Leadville is just getting started and it will be a while before they can catch up with Denver."

Kitty smiled. "This will be fine. I'm more interested in the company than I am in the decor."

"I'll second that. Did you talk to Lucinda about staying there for a while?"

"There was no need for that, as Lucinda had already invited me. She is a nice lady and means well, but I would rather spend my time with you. She is a little too religious for me. In that way she reminds me of my father."

"I have never been around religious people much," said Bruno, "and I don't know a lot about them. I met a preacher when I was in Bodie and he seemed like a nice guy. He had his work cut out for him though. God left Bodie long before he got there and I don't think He was planning to come back. Are you going to be able to handle living with Lucinda?"

"I can deal with her. I had a lot of experience with my dad and I don't plan on being there too long."

"I'll be able to help you with that. I'm making arrangements to get you a place and by the time you are done with the judge, you should be able to move right in."

Kitty's voice grew serious. "I appreciate your help, but it's not your job to take care of me. The things we talked about meant a lot to me, but I'm not your responsibility."

"Girl, I'm not very good at beating around the bush," Bruno explained patiently. "I'll give it to you straight. When I met you I was serious about wanting to marry you and I haven't changed my mind. I want to take care of you for the rest of your life, and unless I missed my guess, you feel the same way."

Before she could answer the waitress came to the table.

Recognizing Bruno, she smiled an embarrassed little smile. "Good evening, Marshal. What can I get for you tonight?"

"Two of your best steaks and a pot of coffee. Is there anything else you would like, Kitty?"

"No, that will be fine."

"Very good, Mr. Turnbull. They'll be coming right up."

She headed for the kitchen and Kitty watched her go. After taking a few moments to compose her thoughts, she turned to Bruno. "You are a very direct man, Bruno, and I guess you deserve an honest answer. I am attracted to you and I would marry you today, but we have to think about what that would mean. What kind of a future would we have together? There is no future in making a living with a gun."

"You don't need to worry about making a living; I'll take care of that. You said it yourself; you want a man that would love you. I'm that man. Just because I have a reputation of a gunslinger, doesn't mean I don't have feelings."

"I didn't mean that. The most important thing to me is not how you make a living. I just want a man that will love me."

"Don't let what you see fool you, Kitty. When I am on the street, I have a job to do. How I feel about it has nothing to do with it. When I met you, it was different. I found out there are feelings that I didn't know I had. Before you came along, I didn't believe in love at first sight. You changed all of that. Girl, I love you and I would devote my life to making you happy. I'm a man that gets things done and I'm declaring my love to you right now. You can wait and settle for second best with someone else, but I'm offering you a future and I will get that ranch you want. We'll live on it and raise lots of cattle and fat, happy kids. You're never going to get a better deal than that."

Kitty was silent for a few moments. "You know, if I go by

the rules I'm supposed to be shy and reserved and make you chase after me, so I can prove that I am a lady."

"I know about all of that, but this isn't some eastern city where they have the luxury of time on their side. Things move fast in the West and there is not time to court you like you deserve. If I had the time, I'd do it, but I don't. The only thing I care about right now is that you feel the same way I do."

She glanced at him for a moment. He was a picture of what she had always imagined a man would be. She knew there would never be another one like him. He had lit a fire in her that brought an excitement she had never felt before. He had awakened that desire that is in every woman's heart. How much could she share? Did she dare to open her heart to him? She had no experience to set a precedent, yet she wanted to tell him the things that were deep inside. Her instincts were telling her to be careful about what she said, but her heart wanted her to throw caution to the winds. She had never let fear govern her life before and she was not going to start now.

"Bruno, I do care for you and to deny that would be a lie. I really don't care what other people do when they fall in love. The only thing I care about is that you love me. If you do that I will ask nothing else."

"What about the way I make a living?"

"I have no problem with you being the marshal. You did make a promise to me that you were going to get out of this kind of business and I can wait. There is one more thing you need to know and that is, I am not going to be the wife of an outlaw. You are far too good a man to go down that road and if you do, I will do what I have to do."

Bruno tilted his head and studied her for a moment. All of his life he had been free to do what he wanted and the idea of a woman telling him what he could do with his life was a new thought. Yet, what she had said made sense and he could not deny it. The business with Clay was not going to last forever and then they could get on with their lives. If she could trust him for just a little while everything would be all right.

"Listen to me, Kitty, this is our time and you don't want to miss it. You are going to have to trust me for a little while and then we will be free to build that life we want. I am into something that I have to finish and I don't see any other choices. Can you live with that?"

For a moment, their eyes held and there was no hiding the feelings that were in her heart. She ached for the security and affection that she had known with her father and this man was offering it to her. Was the price too high? There was only one way to find out.

"Bruno, the feelings I have inside go against everything I have been taught. The funny thing is I don't even care. I just want you to be mine."

"I give you my word," he said softly. "I have made some commitments that I have to honor, but when I have done that we will get out of Leadville and I will get that ranch that we want. In the meantime, you will just have to trust me."

Before she could answer, the waitress appeared and set their steaks on the table. When she had gone, Kitty whispered. "I will take that as your solemn promise and I'm going to hold you to it. Now, eat your steak before it gets cold."

For the rest of the meal they talked of ranching and Kitty shared some of the fond memories of her childhood. When they left the restaurant, darkness had set in and the streets were filled with the usual crowd of carousers and drunks. For Kitty, it felt good to be with a man who could take care of her. She had always been able to do that for herself, but it was nice to know that he was protecting her from the dangers that lurked in these streets. In some ways, Bruno reminded her of the security she had known when she was with her father, but this was better. When they reached the store she drew a key from her pocket, but before she could use it Bruno took her hand. She turned to him and again she saw that expression of wonder that had touched her heart the first day she had met him. He drew her to himself and for a long moment they stood in silence, enjoying the intimacy.

Finally, she looked up and smiled. "I wish this could last forever, but I have to go in. You bring something out in me that my father would not approve of."

"He'd approve if we were married."

"Bruno, if I could..." Reaching down, he kissed her. Unsure of how to respond, she laid her cheek against his chest. When she finally looked up, she caught a glimpse of his face in the moonlight. In those features she saw a strength she had never seen in another man. It kindled a desire she had never felt before.

When she wrapped her arms around his shoulders the warmth of her body began to ignite a passion in Bruno he knew he could not give in to. For the first time in his life, he knew he was not in complete control of the situation. Tenderly, he pushed her away, bringing a puzzled look to her face.

He grinned sheepishly. "I think it is time you go in before I do something that I will regret."

"Did I do something wrong?"

"No. This is a first for me and I think I had better go."

"You mean kissing a woman?"

"It's something else. Something I'm not sure I understand.

133

Kitty, I love you so much I think I need to slow down. We need to get a handle on this before we mess it up."

"Don't tell me a big, tough gunfighter like you is afraid of a little woman."

Feeling his cheeks turning red, Bruno was grateful for the night. "Kitty, I could face a hundred guns and know what to do, and none of them could stir my feelings like you have. You are the only one that has ever done that and I'm not going to let you get away. When we finish our business with the judge, we are going to make some more permanent plans. Now, I'd better get going before your lady friend gets the wrong idea about you." Taking the key from her hand, he opened the door and let her inside, handing her the key. Then he slipped into the shadows and was gone.

For Bruno, the rest of the night was long and sleep would not come. He was up before the sun and this morning the coffee was especially inviting. For a long time, he sat at his desk nursing the cup while he tried to sort out the events of the evening. Kitty had stirred his heart more than he would believe possible and he knew his life had been changed. The idea of having his own woman was something he had not thought much about. The plans he had made did not allow for one at this stage of his life. He had planned to have a ranch all set up complete with a home that was suitable for a woman before he ever went shopping for one. Fate had taken a hand and those plans would have to be scrapped. When he thought of Kitty now, he was reminded of something he had heard from an old miner on the Comstock a long time ago. "For most men, there is only one ultimate woman," he had said. "And when she comes along he had better not pass her by. She is a rare treasure and a man would have to be a fool not to fight to get her." He knew that Kitty was that woman and he was not going to make that mistake. Like many lonely men, he knew the value of love and the rarity of it. His plans for a long and profitable relationship with the gang would have to be changed. Now there were new priorities.

Suddenly the door burst open and a boy raced into the office. "Marshal, you have to come quick. There is trouble at the Bon Ton and somebody is going to get killed. Hurry!"

When they reached the saloon, a gunshot rang out. Pushing through the doors, Bruno recognized the source of the trouble. Standing in the middle of the room was Tray with a smoking gun in his hand. On the floor was a bartender gripping a bleeding shoulder. Pulling his gun, Bruno leveled it at the man. "Tray! Put the gun down easy before you get hurt."

Turning slowly toward the voice, Tray continued to hold the gun. Bruno cocked his weapon. "Tray, I don't want to kill you, but if you don't put that gun down I will."

The bartender sat up and pointed across the room. "Everyone hold your fire. Tray, you had better do what the marshal said. Bruno, take a look over there."

Standing at the bar was Stew, holding a shotgun in his drunken hands. "That's good advice, Marshal, but you are the one that needs to get rid of the gun. Tray, collect his gun."

Bruno continued to hold the gun. "Stew, you better drop it. I can kill you both before you can pull that trigger, so put the gun down before I run out of patience. If you start this dance you are going to be the first to die. That goes for you too, Tray. Now what's it going to be?"

Stew continued to point the gun in Bruno's direction.

"Looks like we got a Mexican standoff, Marshal. We're just havin' a little fun and we don't need any help from you, so just back off."

Bruno turned the gun slightly until it was trained on Stew's belt buckle. With a cold stare, he looked him in the eye. For a moment their eyes held. "You better put it down right now. I can kill you and the law will be on my side."

White-faced, Stew shifted his eyes to his partner. "Come on, Tray, this is your play."

Tray backed up to the bar, sweat beading on his forehead. "We were just having a little fun with these miners and the barkeep pulled that scatter gun. All I did was defend myself. There's no law against that."

"Is that the way it was, Ben?"

"Not exactly. These tinhorns were bothering some of my customers, so I told them they had enough to drink. Then Tray pushed this man down the bar and reached for his drink. I pulled the shotgun out, but Stew grabbed it and pulled us both across the bar. Tray drew his gun and when I raised the shotgun he shot me. I want them arrested."

Bruno looked at Tray. "I'll make a deal with you. We put our guns away right now and if you think you can beat me to the draw, I'll give you the chance. That is, if you are man enough."

"I ain't putting my gun away."

"I'll make it easy for you," said Bruno as he holstered his gun. "I'm taking that gun away from you and if you shoot me they will hang you." He looked toward the end of the bar. "Ben, you put that gun away; I will take care of this."

When Tray turned toward the bar, Bruno leaped forward and twisted the gun from his hand. Caught by surprise, Tray's face blazed with fury and he took a swing. Bruno stepped inside and pounded a left and a right to his face. Staggered by the blows, Tray fell backward against the bar. Recovering quickly, he threw a punch which Bruno ducked and countered with a wicked blow to the midsection. Bellowing in anger, Tray lunged forward, striking Bruno in the ribs. Beside himself with fury, Bruno fired a smashing left to the mouth, splitting his lip. Clearly the blow had hurt the man and he swung again and missed, throwing himself off balance. Before he could regain his footing, Bruno grabbed him and threw him into Stew with a rolling hiplock. Both men went sprawling on the floor. In the confusion Bruno grabbed the shotgun and turned it toward the men.

"All right boys, on your feet."

Stew leaped up and grabbed the bartender by the arm and stuck a gun in his ribs. "You're not puttin' me in jail, Marshal. Now you back off before Ben gets hurt." He inched his way towards the door and the crowd moved out of the way. When he reached the door, he gave the man a shove and disappeared down the street.

Bruno had barely locked his prisoner in the cell when Clay came through the door. Pointing him toward a chair, he took his place behind his desk. Anger still showed on his face and he was muttering to himself. He had lost a prisoner and it went against his pride to admit it was his own fault. He was in no mood to deal with Clay.

"I see you're havin' a busy day," said Clay. "Have you forgotten about our little business deal?"

"If you're talking about Tray, that has nothing to do with what we agreed on. He broke the law and I had to arrest him.

You are going to have to keep your boys under control if you want to do business with me. If you can't do that, keep them out of town."

There was a harsh challenge in the words and Clay frowned. "I suppose that is a small point to consider, but you need to cut us a little slack. Don't forget where your money is coming from."

Bruno's lips tightened. "You're the one that better do some remembering. You're the one that asked me to come in on this deal and without me, you're spittin' in the wind. What your men do in town is my responsibility and I'm not going to put up with any problems they cause because they can't hold their liquor."

Clay paused for a moment. "We'll see what we can do about that. In the meantime, I want Tray out of jail. Gil is not going to take too kindly to you locking him up. He's a man you don't want to get on the bad side of."

"You tell him I'm running the show in Leadville," Bruno said stubbornly. "I have a tough town to keep the lid on and I'll decide how that is to be done. I'm going to be putting on a deputy to help me and he is going to be handling things the same way I do. If Gil doesn't like that, you can tell him to come and see me. That has nothing to do with our business deal."

Clay shot him a quick glance. "I'd be careful about crossing Gil if I were you. People that make him mad have a way of disappearing and nobody is stupid enough to ask any questions about it."

Bruno gave a wolfish grin. "You need to remember it was not Gil that got me this job and he is not in a position to know what has to be done. I'll handle my end and we will all make a lot of money. Are you going to have a problem with that, because if you do, let's get it taken care of right now."

Clay shifted nervously. "We'll let that one ride for now. I wanted to talk to you about the judge. You are going to have to talk to him about the Emperor Mine case. He's been filled in on how things were handled in the past, but that didn't set too well. You need to make him understand that we aren't going to put up with any trouble from him. There's a lot of money riding on this case. Stew has already talked to the owners of the mine and they have agreed to pay us a fat percentage on the take from that ground that the Poker Chip is claiming. We can't lose this one. I heard there are already over one hundred lawyers in town and every one of them would like to get their meat hooks on a deal like this. We are going to have to move fast or word will get out on what is going on. There is a lot of money in this for you if we can pull it off."

"You don't need to worry about the judge, I will take care of him, but Tray stays in jail."

Clay frowned. "You know he doesn't like you too much; this isn't going to help. I have some other business I need him for and I want him out."

Bruno was quiet for a moment. It went against his grain to change his mind, but he could not let pride stand in the way of business. What difference did it make anyway? "I can turn him loose in your custody, but I have to have your word that he will show up in court."

"It's a deal."

"Now I need something from you. I need a place for a woman to stay and I want you to get it for me before the judge comes to town. If that doesn't happen, the chances of you winning that case are going to be in trouble."

Clay pushed his hat back on his head. "That's a tough order. I told you before, it's hard to get a place in this town. I can't make a promise like that."

"Sure you can. I'll make it easy for you. If you don't find her a place, I'm going to put you and the boys in jail and take your cabin. Now, do you think you can find something?"

Clay leaped to his feet. "That's blackmail!"

Bruno leaned back in his chair and smiled. "That's right. Isn't that the business we're in? Let me know when the place is ready."

Clay opened his mouth to speak and hesitated. Thinking better of it, he relaxed and returned the smile. "I'll see what I can do."

The next day the streets were quiet. Bruno's reputation was already beginning to earn him a measure of respect from the wilder crowd. Word of his run-in with the outlaws got around fast and there were few in town who wanted to be on his bad side. With a little time on his hands, it was time to try his luck at a little poker. He had developed an interest in the game in his early days on the Comstock, but his inexperience had cost him a lot of money. Watching others play was free though, and he began to learn the secrets of the winners and the mistakes of the losers. As time went by, he picked up the basics of the game and when he tried again his luck had improved.

The first thing he had learned was: it was a game of skill. He became quite good at outguessing the other players and developed the skills that allowed him to fill in his hand with the cards he needed. He knew all the methods of cheating and was not above using that means of winning if necessary. He had a good memory for cards and knew the odds of wining with the hands that he held. He also knew when it was time to quit. Winning small amounts did not upset people and over the long run, the smaller pots added up.

Choosing a table away from the door, he began by losing a few hands. Soon the suspicion of the other players eased and he was able to win a few. He was just breaking even when Clay came through the door and signaled him. Reluctantly, he excused himself and joined him on the street. Clay was obviously pleased with himself, so Bruno waited until they were away from the crowd to see what it was all about.

"This better be important. I don't like being bothered when I am playing cards. Did you get my cabin yet?"

"Bruno," Clay spoke sharply. "I got a place all right, but it came with a bit of trouble. When I told the boys what you had said they were pretty upset. I explained to them how important it was that you worked with us and how you needed the place for a lady. I finally convinced them and they got another cabin. I'm afraid you have used up all your favors, though."

Bruno responded dryly. "This has nothing to do with favor. It's just a business deal. If you want me to work with you, I expect you to keep me happy. When can we move in?"

"I guess any time you want to. I'm giving you our cabin and Billy has already moved to the new place. You had better stay away from him, because he is pretty mad. Thanks to you, I had to send Stew back to the hideout and that will leave me short-handed. I don't know what I am going to do with Tray when he gets acquitted. He'll be mad enough to shoot you on sight. We're going to have to try to keep peace in the family or things aren't going to work out."

Keeping peace in the family was the last thing Bruno was concerned about, but he smiled and slapped Clay on the back.

"Don't worry Clay; I'll take care of you. If the boys are having trouble with me, just remind them of how much money I am going to make for them. After all, isn't that what we're here for?"

"Sometimes money isn't enough and after what you did to Tray, I'd watch my back. I'll do what I can to keep the peace, but you'd better watch your back. Tray's not too choosy about how he gets even."

Bruno had heard enough. "Just remember; I'm the law here and if Billy tries to pick a fight with me, I've got a free pass to take care of him and you might remind him of that. You know one day soon this town will settle down to a regular community with a court house and churches and real law. This is our time, so you keep those boys out of my hair. We've only got a short time to cash in and we can't afford to lose it by fighting amongst ourselves."

The logic of what he had said was clear. "You're right, of course, and you need to remember that yourself. Don't forget, you're not bullet-proof either."

It was a special occasion and Bruno was not going to let Kitty forget it. It was not every day that he was able to present a gift of this magnitude. For the occasion, he rented a buggy and drove it to the dry-goods store. Kitty was glad to see him and with great fanfare he steered her to the rig. Avoiding her questions, he drove to the lower part of town where the miner's axes had not yet destroyed the forest. Following a seldom-used road, they traveled through stands of virgin forest. It was a country that was wild and magnificent with trees that swept the sky with their great height. This forest lay down the valley from the camp and had already been gone over in the early days. A few old prospect holes gave evidence that the rich ore deposits had not been found in this area. The outlaws had chosen the location for its isolated setting and this part of the valley had been left in pristine condition.

The trail passed the base of a giant, lightning-scarred spruce and turned up the slope. Winding through a grove of tall trees, it entered an area of large, shattered rocks that ended in a small clearing. Covered with a growth of lush green grass and flowers, it was bathed in the warm sunlight that blanketed the side of the mountain. Barely visible through the trees was a cut in a ledge where water tumbled down over slabs of rock until it settled into a pleasant stream that flowed along the edge of the small meadow.

Proudly, Bruno helped Kitty down and gave her a moment to look over her new home. The cabin was built of country rock and topped with a steep roof of thick, pine shingles. Inside, it was divided into two rooms. On the far wall was a large fireplace with a table of split logs before it. On each side was a log bench and along one wall were bunks. The floor was hard-packed earth that someone had taken great care to level and remove all the stones. The front door was only a few yards from the stream which still ran clear in spite of the prospecting that had been done on the slopes above.

"For a town that has a housing shortage, you sure came up with a winner," Kitty said, with a confused look. "How did you manage it?"

"I have my ways. Does it suit you?"

Kitty's eyes swept the room visualizing the possibilities. "It's very nice, but it will need a woman's touch. With some curtains and a little furniture, it can be really nice. I couldn't pick a better place myself. How can I show you my gratitude?"

"You don't need to worry about that," Bruno said with a boyish grin. "I just want to be sure you are happy with it."

"Yes, I am, but it is quite a ways from town. That could be a problem when I get a job."

"You don't need to worry about that, either. As long as I'm around, you won't have to take a job. I'll bring you everything you need. Just tell me what you want and I'll get it."

Kitty looked out the door at the jagged peaks of the Continental Divide. Rising above the trees, it made a magnificent frame for this beautiful place. She had never seen such a lovely setting and it took her breath away. It was all so perfect, yet there was still that unanswered question.

"Do you remember the things we talked about in the jail?"

"Every word."

"There is one problem that still bothers me. I don't want to hear one day that you were shot down in the street in some meaningless gunfight by some drunken miner that just happened to get lucky. We both know that every day you walk those streets it is a roll of the dice. If you plan to continue to be the Marshal, it's going to catch up with you. Tell me something that will make me quit worrying about it."

Bruno reached down to kiss her, but she turned away.

"You know I can't give you any guarantees. It's part of my job. I thought we had this settled."

"How important is this marshaling job to you?"

"Why do you ask?"

"I just had an idea that I thought you might be interested in. What would you think of coming back to the ranch with me? There is more work there than my father can handle and you could help him."

Bruno shifted uncomfortably. "I thought you left the ranch because you wanted to get away from him. Why would you want to go back there now?"

"Because with you there, things would be different. When it was my father and I there was always that religion thing that got in the way. He didn't always talk about it, but when I was around him it just seemed to float in the air. I could never get comfortable with it. It made me spend more time alone than I wanted to. With you there, it would be different. We could be together and I wouldn't be so lonely."

He stared at the floor for a moment as he considered the possibility. His plans did not include working for another man and he had no taste for it. Answering to her father or anyone else went against the grain. On the other hand, he would be with Kitty and the danger of the life he was living would be gone. Could he answer to another man?

He stepped outside and gazed at the distant mountains. "I never thought about ranching for another man. That wasn't part of my plan."

Stepping up to him, Kitty slipped her arms around his waist and hugged him. "Remember what you said to me that night in the jail? You said you wanted to make my dreams come true. Did you really mean that?"

"You know I did."

"You also said our dreams were the same and I believed you. We both want to go ranching and we have one just waiting for us. My father is getting older and he won't be able to do all the things he did when he was younger. I believe he will be very happy to have you join us and we could build a future there. That is your dream too and we can make it work."

Bruno fidgeted. Had he trapped himself with his own words? Had he let his emotions lead him into a promise that he could not keep? One thing was sure; he was a man of his word and he was not going to change that now. A man must answer for his words and there could be no compromise. What she said was true and he could not deny it. Did that mean he had to compromise his dream? There had to be another way.

"Kitty, I meant every word that I said that night, but things aren't as simple as that. I do want to take care of you, but I have to do it my way. It will take a little longer, but I promise you I will get you a ranch and it will be ours alone. When this business is finished we will have the money to get it, but you have to let me have the time to work it out. I promise you it will be worth the wait. In the meantime, you can help me by trusting me to keep my word. Can you can do that?"

Kitty looked up at him with eyes that were full of love. Even when he was silent, she could feel the love that was in his heart. There was a communication in the spirit that went beyond words and she knew it was rare. She may never find it again. He was a special man, but was she letting her heart blind her to his dark side? Could he deliver that life that she longed for and did she even care?

"Bruno, if I was a smart woman I would turn and walk away from you. My father warned me about men like you, but I love you. That is the only thing that matters to me anymore. I didn't used to believe in love at first sight, but I have loved you ever since that first day I saw you. I knew the kind of man you were, but I believe your heart is good. I believe in you and my future is in your hands. I'm willing to wait."

When their eyes met he saw a trust and innocence that he had never seen before. In her innocence she had brought up strength inside of him that he did not know he had. With it came a commitment to do whatever it took to satisfy the desires of her heart. If it cost him his life, he would not fail her.

"Kitty, come hell or high water you have my word that I will not let you down. You are my woman and I cannot give you a more sacred vow than that."

She smiled sweetly. "Is that a statement of intent or a proposal of marriage?"

Bruno laughed. "When I propose marriage, you will not have to ask a question like that. Things are in motion and you will not have to wait long. That is all I can tell you right now. Now let's get back to town. We've got things to do."

CHAPTER 8

For Kitty, the night passed slowly. So much had changed in the past few days and for the first time in her life she had made a commitment that would change her destiny. Now she was committed and for better or worse, there was no going back. There was an excitement inside that brought an anticipation of what the future would bring. Finally, there was someone that she could share her most intimate feelings with. It was something that she had never had before, not even with her father, but there was also a feeling that restraint should be employed. Was fear creeping into her heart? She put those thoughts aside. She had made a commitment and she would stand by it with her life. She tossed and turned restlessly on the bed, but by three in the morning exhaustion overtook her and she did not awaken until the smell of fresh coffee drifted up from the kitchen. When she dressed and went down she found Lucinda pulling the coffee pot from the stove.

"Tough night?" she asked as she slid a steaming cup across the table. "I heard you moving all night and I thought you might have had a bad day."

"No, it wasn't that. There are just so many things happening right now, it is hard to keep up with it all."

"Is there something I can do?"

"No, it just takes me a little time to adjust to a new place. As a matter of fact I had a very good day." Raising the cup she tested the hot coffee and set it back down. "The marshal found me a place to stay so I will be moving out there today."

Crossing to a desk at the end of the counter, Lucinda produced a piece of paper. "Speaking of the marshal, he was here early this morning and left this for you. He said it was important and that you should read it right away."

Kitty looked puzzled. "That's strange, did he say anything else?"

"Not really. He did ask if I would help you and I can't tell you anymore than that until you read the note."

Kitty opened the note and read:

Please go down to the livery stable this morning. There is something waiting for you there.
I love you. Bruno.

"What's this all about?"

Lucinda shrugged her shoulders. "He didn't tell me. I guess you will have to go the livery stable to find out."

The hostler met them when they arrived at the livery. He greeted them with a smile and led them to the back of the building. Passing the large corral that held the horses for the stage, he led them to a small pen in the rear. Standing in the pen was the most beautiful Buckskin that Kitty had ever seen. With a questioning face she turned to the hostler.

"The horse is yours." He said with a smile of satisfaction. "The marshal bought him for you yesterday. He's a Morgan/ mustang mix and they're very rare in this country. His name is Buck. I have a saddle for him inside."

Unsure of what to say, Kitty turned to Lucinda who was watching the proceedings with a big smile. "Bruno asked me if I could let you keep him at the store until you get settled in the new place. I told him that would be just fine. He said he would bring him up this afternoon."

"You knew all about this."

"Bruno told me he wanted it to be a surprise. You must be pretty special to him."

"I wouldn't look a gift horse in the mouth if I were you." The hostler commented wryly. "This is a fine horse and you would have to look a long time to find a better one."

Walking back to the store, Kitty was silent. Her mind was full of questions that she could not answer. Everything seemed so perfect, yet there was uneasiness that she didn't understand. Was she getting cold feet? Was it a concern for Bruno? With the commitment she had made came a deeper concern about what he was doing. Whatever it was, she was now involved too. What were those "business deals" about that he refused to share with her? She knew it was a small step from marshal to outlaw and he may have already stepped across that line. Could she be the wife of an outlaw? It would certainly be more exciting than taking a job as a clerk in a dry goods store. In a town like Leadville there was very little law, so what difference did it make which side you were on? She was being foolish and she pushed these thoughts from her mind.

"Things are moving pretty fast for you, aren't they." said Lucinda. "Just in the few days I have known you I have seen a big change in you. Are you going to be all right?"

"I'm OK," she answered with a confidence she did not feel. "It's just that I'm facing so many new things in my life that it takes a little time to adjust."

"I don't want to push you, Kitty, but if there is anything I can do to help, I am here for you."

"I said I'll be fine," Kitty answered abruptly. "I can work this out by myself."

The women walked on through the crowded streets in silence. When the store came into sight, Lucinda turned to her companion. "Kitty, if you are going to be leaving soon I may not get a chance like this again. I am very concerned about you. I've been praying for you ever since we met and I believe this is the time you need to deal with what you are going to do with your life. This is a wild and Godless country we live in and you may never get another chance. You need to make a decision to give your life to the Lord while there is still time. I can help you with that."

Kitty sighed and shook her head. "I really appreciate your concern, but it isn't as easy as that. I could never make the changes my father made. I will admit that secretly I admired him for what he did, but his world is a lot different than mine. It would never work for me."

"That is exactly what I thought when I became a Christian. When I was working in that brothel I didn't think there was any hope for me, either. Then a strange thing happened. On a lark, I decided to go to church one Sunday. From that first Sunday I knew I had found something that I had not known even existed. Those people had a joy that just radiated from their faces and I had to find out if it was real. I began going every Sunday. I found that it was and I wanted some of that for myself."

"I'm not going to go to church. That is not my style."

"It's not about going to church. You could go to church all your life, but if that is all you did it wouldn't make any difference. It might make you a better person, but that is not enough. The thing that makes the difference is what you do with Jesus. I asked Him to be my Savior and He changed my life. I was like you; I didn't think I could ever make those changes either, but I began to read my Bible and gradually I found the answers to my questions. With the Lord's help, I was able to come out of that old life and make a new start. The Bible says 'Give your burdens to the Lord. He will carry them. He will not permit the godly to slip or fall.'[8] It is not your strength that will get you through, it is the Lord's. All you have to do is be willing."

Kitty was silent for a moment. Could she be right? Is that how her father had made those changes? She had not really seriously considered becoming a Christian in the past, as the whole idea seemed too idiotic to take seriously. What if she was right? She had heard the stories about Heaven and Hell, but had never really taken them for more than fairy tales for children to believe. When her father had mentioned those places, it had stirred her heart and she had not understood why. Could Hell be real? What would happen to her if it was?

"Do you believe there is a place like Hell?"

"Yes, and Heaven too. The Bible says, 'Don't be afraid of those who can kill only your bodies—but can't touch your souls! Fear only God, who can destroy both soul and body in Hell.'[9] It's a real place and you don't want to go there. You have a choice of going to either Heaven or Hell. Everyone makes that choice and you can't avoid it. What could be so important that could be worth missing Heaven over?"

"I don't know. I have never really thought seriously about it."

"Kitty, this is too important to put off. Is there any logical reason that you can think of that would keep you from making that decision right now? The Bible says 'now is the day of salvation.'[10]"

Kitty looked down the street at the scene of bedlam and dissipation. Was this the life she had chosen over the life her father was leading? There was some logic in what the woman had said. How could she argue with the Bible?

"Lucinda, I appreciate your concern for me and I promise I will give it some serious thought. Right now, I have some other things that need to be taken care of. Right now I'd like to get the stable ready for my horse."

A few days later the judge came up from Denver. When he arrived at the saloon the room was filled with a rowdy crowd, anxious to begin the proceedings. In the early days of the West the courts offered some of the best entertainment around and many people came to town just to see what would happen. This was a festive occasion and the town looked forward to it like a holiday. Only the Fourth of July was more exciting. Court was held in the Bon Ton because it was the largest building in town. Lake County had not yet built a courthouse.

Accompanying Bruno to the court was Brace Hawkins, the new deputy. A petty thief and bully he was well known around the town and most people avoided him. Clay had recommended him because he was a tough guy who could get things done. It mattered little to him if the job was legal or not and that was the kind of deputy Bruno wanted.

When the bailiff quieted the crowd the judge banged the gavel on the bar and declared the court open. The Emperor Mine verses the Poker Chip was the first case on the docket and the court recorder read the complaint to a packed room.

Satisfied with the reading, the judge sat back in his chair and surveyed the room. His face was sober as he addressed the crowd. "Friends, we are holding an informal hearing this morning to determine if this matter can be resolved without holding a formal trial. All statements will be sworn and we will try to determine the truth. Would the owner of the Poker Chip please take the stand."

The man crossed the room and seated himself in a chair that had been set up against the bar.

Producing a Bible, the bailiff held it in front of him. "Put your right hand on the Bible. Do you promise to tell the truth, the whole truth and nothing but the truth?"

"I do."

"Please state your name for the court."

"Mervin Flynn."

"Mr. Flynn, would you please tell the court the nature of the complaint."

"Yes, Sir. My property is adjacent to the Emperor mine and we have been mining in that section next to their mine for several months. We hit a very rich vein and followed it back into the mountain. Word got out of how rich the find was and Joe Growler decided he would cash in. He ran a drift off of his main entry and intersected the same vein and began taking silver out that was on my property. I went to see him and told him that he had crossed the property line and was mining my silver. He got mad and told me that the vein was on his claim and he could prove it. He showed me the map you have there and we went up to look at the claim markers. I had put those markers in long before Joe had even found his claim and I could see that they had been moved. When I told him, he got mad and ordered me off of my own property and said he would shoot me if I ever came back. Rather than starting a shooting war, I filed this case. If you will look at the map I brought, you will see where I marked the location of his drift. It is clearly on my property."

After looking the maps over the judge looked over to the table at Bruno. "Mr. Turnbull, who represents the Emperor Mine?"

"I do, Your Honor."

"Isn't it a little irregular for the marshal to act as council for a defendant?"

"The defendant asked me to handle this for him, so I am acting on his behalf. Is that against the law?"

The judge scowled. "No, it is not. Do you care to question the witness?"

"I do not."

"In that case the witness is excused. Mr. Growler, please take the stand."

With a confident smirk on his face the man crossed the room and slouched in the chair. When he was sworn in Bruno stepped up to the bar. "Tell me Joe, how long have you been mining that drift?"

"Since last March."

"And when did you stake that claim."

"Last winter."

"And who made that map you gave to the judge."

"I had it made by a mining engineer I know in Denver."

"Does it show that drift you are mining inside your claim markers?"

"It does."

With a crooked smile Bruno turned to the judge. "There you have it, Sir. Joe's map is a legal map and the one that Mr. Flynn gave you is a forgery. I suggest you throw the case out and let Joe get back to his mining."

Leaping to his feet the judge pointed the gavel at the marshal. "I'm the one who makes the rulings in this court, so you just get back to that table before I fine you for contempt of court."

Grudgingly Bruno returned to his table while the judge reseated himself. "If ever I have seen a case of forgery this is it. Mr. Growler, this is the worst attempt at drawing a map I have ever seen and I will not accept it as evidence. The legal map is the one Mr. Flynn brought and I am ruling in his favor. Mr. Growler, you will cease mining in the drift in question and you will pay Mr. Flynn a cash compensation for the ore you have removed. If you do not, your mine will be confiscated and sold to pay what you owe Mr. Flynn. This case is closed."

Rising, Bruno walked slowly across the room to stand in front of the judge. He knew the crowd was there for a show and he was not going to disappoint them. It was the first time he had ever been in this position and he was going to play it for all it was worth. There would be other cases like this one and it was time to set a precedent.

"Your Honor, I am afraid I am going to have to overrule your decision. I have checked those stakes myself and it is clear to see that they have been there for a long time. Mervin is the one that gave you a phony map and if it weren't for the fact that I don't want to feed him I would lock him up."

Leaping to his feet the judge's face turned red. "What do you mean you are going to overrule my decision? You have no power in this court and you have just overstepped your authority. Deputy, Arrest this man on the charge of barratry."

A twisted smile appeared on the deputy's face and he took a sideways glance in Bruno's direction. "Sorry, Judge. I don't take my orders from no jackleg lawyer like you. I answer to the marshal."

Before the judge could respond a cheer went up from the crowd. Encouraged by their support, Bruno took the judge by the arm and gently, but firmly, guided him across the room to a chair.

"Your honor, you have been overruled. Leadville is a mining camp and we don't need any law from Denver coming up here and telling us what to do. This camp will be run by mining law and you no longer have any authority here. Now you just sit here and we will show you how a court is to be run." Another ripple of approval went through the crowd and there were a few cheers. "I have decided that we will appoint our own judge and take care of our own affairs. Clay, you are going to be the new judge, so why don't you take your place and let's get on with it."

Caught by surprise, Clay quickly concealed it and walked over to the judge and pulled off his robe. While the crowd cheered he slipped it over his shoulders, stepped up to the bar and motioned for silence. "O.K., Boys, let's quiet down. Let's have a little respect for the dignity of the occasion. As your new judge I intend to uphold the laws of this community and this time we will have justice. For my first decision I will uphold the judgment of the Marshal, and we will rule that the claim boundaries are valid as shown by Mr. Growler's map. The fact that the marshal has personally inspected them is reason enough to recognize the boundaries that now exist. The next matter of business is the case against Kitty Duncan. I'd like her to take the stand."

Taking Bruno's arm, she was escorted to the chair. With a satisfied look on his face, Bruno turned to Clay. "Your honor, I know this defendant and I will swear by her word so we will dispense with the swearing in. You can taker her word for what she says."

"Agreed. Young Lady, would you kindly tell the court what happened the afternoon of the shooting."

"Certainly. I had just talked to Mr. Nye about getting a job in the Bon Ton and was leaving when this drummer got in my way. When I tried to go past him, he blocked my path, so I kicked him. Then he took a swing at me but missed. When he tried to hit me again, I shot him. I don't have to take that kind of treatment from anyone. Now can I go home?"

Clay paused for a moment as if weighing the testimony "Is there anyone here that can give testimony that what this young lady says is true?" A ripple of agreement went through the crowd and a few men who had been there confirmed that what she had said was true.

"Then it is the judgment of the court that this woman is innocent and acted in self defense. The case is dismissed. Young lady, you are free to go."

With a smile of relief, Kitty joined Bruno and they headed for the door. Puzzled, Clay called out, "Bruno, we got another case here to deal with; I'm going to need your help with that."

"You take care of it, Clay. Tray is your friend and you can decide what to do with him. Brace can take care of anything you need. I'll see you later when you are finished."

The next day was moving day for Kitty and when Lucinda volunteered to help she took her up on the offer. There was much to be done and she gladly accepted the offer of help. Besides, she was proud of the new cabin and wanted to show it off to her new friend. She had made a list of the things that it would take to make the cabin into a home and Lucinda helped her find the furniture, dishes, material for curtains and other essentials that it would take to give the place a woman's touch. By the middle of the afternoon the cabin had been transformed to a home that Kitty could be proud of. There were now curtains on the windows and cushions on the new chairs. New dishes filled the cupboards and copper pots hung by the fireplace. By the door was a full length mirror with hooks on each side for coats and a place for boots. She could not wait to show Bruno what she had accomplished in just one day. With the work done, Kitty stoked the fire under the coffee pot.

"I am sorry I can't offer you something to go with that coffee, but it will take me a little time to get the finishing touches in place," Kitty said, as she put the cups on the table.

"It certainly is an improvement from what you started with," said Lucinda. "I am sure Bruno will be pleased."

"I don't think it will take much to make him happy. He's been living at the jail and it won't take much to improve on that."

Lucinda was silent as Kitty poured the coffee. "I haven't had a real home since I left my father's ranch and I am very grateful to Bruno for getting me this place. I think he made some kind of an arrangement with Clay's friends to get it. Judging by the way they kept house it wasn't very important to them anyway.

"Now that you are all set up in your new home, I suppose the two of you are planning to tie the knot?"

Kitty looked a bit uncomfortable. "I'm not sure what the plans are in that department. Bruno hasn't said much about it."

Lucinda studied her cup for a moment as she searched for the right words. "Kitty, I have to talk to you straight about something that is on my mind."

Kitty settled herself in a chair. "If it's Bruno you are worried about, don't be. He has plans to leave the marshaling job soon. We want to go into ranching as soon as we can find a place and work out the details."

"That's not what I was thinking about. I'm concerned about the things we talked about at the store. With these new changes, things are going to be a bit more complicated for you. I'm afraid with Bruno in your life it's going to take your mind away from what's really important."

"What do you mean?"

"I mean, dealing with the spiritual need in your life. Have you thought about that since we talked?"

"Not really. At least not much."

"I'm going to give it to you straight. I believe this is the time that the Lord is calling to you to give your life to Him. It may never come again and you don't dare take a chance on missing it. Remember what I said, today is the day of salvation. You have no promise of tomorrow."

Kitty looked into Lucinda's face. Her smile had been replaced with a look of concern. It was clear that she was not going to let this thing go and she was going to have to deal with it. She knew what Lucinda had was real because she had seen that same look on her father's face. There was something very genuine there that ran deep and she knew the concern she showed was more than friendship. What would Bruno think if she made a decision like that? Would she lose the love that she had found? Was it important enough to risk that?"

"As long as we are being honest, I'll level with you too. When I first met you I didn't like you because you were too much like my father, but I will admit things have changed. If I were to become a Christian now I could lose Bruno and I don't know if I want to risk that. Men like that don't come along every day."

Lucinda nodded. "Yes, a good man is rare, but what standards are you using to call a man good? A good man is someone that wants the best for you and not just in this life, but forever. Bruno can't give you that. He is a gunfighter and he has chosen a path that will destroy both of your lives. If that happens, who will be there for you? I can't be sure it would be me and you could find yourself in a situation that is much worse than this. Besides, this isn't about Bruno, it's about you. It's about where you want to live forever and I think the time has come for you to decide. This is something you have to do for yourself."

Kitty could not avoid her questioning eyes and she shifted nervously. There was warmth there that reminded her of her father and it brought back memories of the times when he had shared his feelings with her. There was an unspoken love in that connection that she longed to find in her own heart, but it had never been there. It was a special channel of communication that she wanted and she knew she had to have it.

"I think you are right, but I don't know how to make that change. It's a pretty big decision. Maybe I should talk to Bruno and see what he thinks."

"Kitty, he is not going to understand this and he will try to talk you out of it. This is a personal decision and it does not involve Bruno."

"I'm not sure I'm strong enough to be a Christian."

"No one is. The Bible says He is your strength and your shield.[11] He will never leave you or forsake you.[12] It is not your strength that will get you through, it is the Lord's. Why don't you pray with me and get this thing settled once and for all?"

"How can I be sure it is the right thing to do? There are lots of religions in the world and I am sure each one thinks they have the answers. How did you know?"

Lucinda considered the question. "For me it was a matter of faith. I had tried lots of things in my life and none of them had really brought the satisfaction I was looking for. The Christians that I met were different. They weren't dependent on what other people thought of them. They just shared their love with me and asked for nothing in return. I had never known people like that before and I decided to take a chance. When I stepped thought that door, I never looked back because I discovered it was true. As I grew my heart began to change and now I know it is the love of Jesus that is in me. I could never have loved like that on my own. I needed Him to change me. I took a step of faith and I have never been sorry. "

"That must take a lot of faith."

"Don't worry about that. The Bible says when we are too weak to have any faith the Lord will help us.[13] He will go with you if you will just trust Him. You are in a position where there just isn't time to wait. You are living in a dangerous world and you have no guarantee of tomorrow. I can help you to become a Christian and then you will never be alone again. My Friend is only a prayer away. Is there any reason why you could not ask Jesus into your heart right now?"

It was a straightforward question and Kitty knew she would have to deal with it. The path had been laid out for her and I was time to settle this question once and for all. She could not deny the truth in what Lucinda had said. Her only argument was there was a danger that she could lose Bruno. She loved him with all her heart, but was that enough to lose the things that would last forever? It was a tough decision and too much was riding on this to make a wrong choice.

"You know I will be taking a big chance if I do this, but I think you are right. What do I do?"

"Just follow me in this prayer, and if you mean it you will be a Christian. Dear Father, I know I am a sinner and need Your forgiveness. I believe Jesus died for me and I am willing to turn from my sin. I invite Jesus to come into my heart and life and be my personal Savior. I am willing to follow Christ as the Lord of my life. Amen."

Reverently Kitty followed her in the prayer and when she raised her head there were tears in her eyes. A great weight had been lifted from her shoulders and for the first time in her life she felt free. Words had failed her and all she could do was smile.

Lucinda understood. "Welcome to the family of God. I really envy you because you are in for quite a ride."

The smile changed to a look of concern. "Lucinda, I don't know what comes next. I have no idea how to be a Christian. What do I do?"

"Do you have a Bible?"

"No. My father had given me one, but I left it at the ranch when I went to Denver. "

"That is the first thing you will need. We have them at the store and I will get you one. It is very important that you read it every day. You are going to have lots of questions and I will try to help you as much as I can, but you need to get into God's word to find the answers on your own. You should start with the book of John."

"I can ride back with you today and pick one up," she said, "I have another problem, what am I going to tell Bruno?"

"Just tell him the truth. Tell him what you did."

She looked doubtful. "That might not go over too well."

Lucinda's face showed the concern she felt. "If he loves you, he will stay with you. If he doesn't, you will find out things about him that you need to know before you marry him. There's one more thing. You need to be in church and there is a new one in town. I have heard good things about it. Parson Tom is the pastor and they meet in a log cabin behind the Grand Hotel."

The thought of church brought back more memories of the ranch. Not being able to go to church was a disappointment for her father. It was a price he paid for living so far from people. His solution had been to build a small chapel behind the house. Often she had seen him slip away to spend an hour in that place. It had seemed foolish to her when he had built it and it represented a part of his life that she could not share. Now she understood. Fortunately for her, church was only a few miles away. She was anxious to meet other Christians and to share what she had found.

"One more thing. You need to spend some time talking to the Lord every day. You can expect some trouble from the devil, now that you are not in his camp anymore. The Lord will help you with those things."

The ride back to town was a pleasant one for the women. Kitty was full of questions and Lucinda did her best to answer them. At the store the first items on Kitty's shopping list were a Bible and a notebook to write down things to pray about. The women had decided the best way to break the news to Bruno was to soften him up with a fine meal. Starting in the dry goods store, Kitty covered the town and by the time she started for home she had assembled the makings for a grand feast.

Before he reached the clearing in the trees Bruno could already smell the aroma of home-cooked food. It had been a long time since he had anything but restaurant fare and his anticipation was ignited. When he stepped through the door, he was amazed at the changes that had been made. His eyes swept the room. Was this the right place? Kitty ran up to him and threw her arms around his neck and greeted him with a kiss.

For a moment he stood there trying to absorb all the changes. Somehow, he sensed that it was not only the room that was different but there was something in the woman's attitude that he did not recognize. While he tried to puzzle that out Kitty led him to a chair at the head of the table and seated him with all the fanfare of the finest restaurant in Denver.

On the simple table before him Kitty had carefully laid

165

out the silverware and dishes. Various pots and pans were assembled by the fireplace and the aroma of fresh-baked bread filled the room.

Bruno looked at her with a crooked smile on his face. "What did I do to deserve all of this?"

Kitty took the pot from the fire and poured a steaming cup of coffee. "You didn't have to do anything. I just wanted to show you how much I appreciate you. Now if you will give me a moment, I will get your supper."

Bruno watched the woman as she went about setting the food on the table. She was a rare beauty and he knew he was fortunate to have a woman like her. He knew he had found a rare prize and she was the definition of what a woman should be. Without consciously making the decision, his direction had been changed. He would spend the rest of his life making her life as happy as a man could make it.

When the meal was finished, he leaned back in the chair and built himself a smoke. Seating herself next to him, Kitty scratched a match on the table and lit the cigarette. Taking a puff he blew a smoke ring and watched it drift away. "That was a fine meal, Kitty but I suspect you are trying to set me up for something. I'm not a very patient man, so why don't you just tell me what it is you want."

A modest smile crossed her face and she took a moment before she spoke. "I'm not exactly sure how to tell you this, but something happened this afternoon. I made the most important decision I have made in my life and it's going to affect you too. I became a Christian."

There was silence in the room. Then he grinned. "So you became a Christian. So what does that have to do with us?"

"I don't think you understand. You are going to see a lot

of changes in me and I just hope you love me enough to accept them."

"What do you mean changes? You mean you are going to start going to church and reading the Bible now? I guess that is all right, as long as you don't expect me to change my ways. I'm not a religious man and don't ever plan to be. As long as you keep those things to yourself, we will be all right. Does this have something to do with your dad?"

"Not really. It is a decision that I made on my own."

"I thought you left home because of your dad's religion. Why would you want to take that on after all the problems it has caused for you?"

Kitty poked at her cup as she tried to think. "This is so new, I really don't know how to explain it. Lucinda showed me what Christianity was about in a way I could understand. To be honest, I don't want to go to Hell and she explained to me how I could miss that. What she told me made a lot of sense. We are going to live forever and I want to do that with the Lord in Heaven. Bruno, it's something that you need to do too. Every day you take your life in your hands. What would happen if you were killed? Do you ever think about that?"

Bruno shook his head. "I never thought much about it. I never expect to lose a gunfight. If you start thinking that way you start to doubt your ability and then you will lose. That is a dangerous way to think."

"You need to think about it. As much as I hate the thought of losing you, I hate more to think of you going to Hell. This is too important to just pass off as a woman's silly idea. You, of all people, need to deal with it. I'm ready to die now, but you aren't. I could help you to…"

Bruno leaped to his feet, turning his chair over. "Wait a

minute now. I said if you wanted to be a Christian it would be all right, as long as you keep it to yourself. That is your business, so don't start setting traps for me. I've gotten along just fine without religion this far and I don't intend to start playing those games now. You go ahead and do what you have to do, but leave me out of it. I think I had better go now before one of us says something that we will be sorry for."

He went to the door, but Kitty ran ahead of him and stood in his way. A tear ran down her cheek as she looked up into his face." Bruno, I'm not trying to shove religion down your throat. It's just that I love you and I don't want anything bad to happen to you. I don't know if I could live without you!"

Bruno's face relaxed and he gently wiped the tear away. Tenderly, he gathered her into his arms and for a moment neither spoke. Finally he tipped her face up to his and kissed her lightly. "I'm sorry that I got upset, but this is something that I didn't expect. You will have to give me a little time to get used to it. I haven't been around Christians much in my life and I don't even know what they are. Can you understand that?"

She studied his face, trying to see something that would give her the hope that she needed, but it was not there. She put a brave smile on and tried to hide what she really felt. "Yes, I can understand. I just love you so much I don't want to lose you. Will you promise me you will think about it?"

Bruno stepped out into the fading light of the day. "I've got to go now. I have a lot of thinking to do."

He mounted Hawk and cantered off into the trees. Sadly, Kitty watched him disappear into the forest. What had she done? Had she lost the only man she had ever loved? Was that the cost of being a Christian? Silently she resolved in her heart that no matter what price she had to pay, she was not going to turn back. This must be what Lucinda meant when she said she would learn new things about Bruno. Whatever it meant she had made her stand and there was no turning back now.

CHAPTER 9

Bruno was a puzzled man. Kitty's new fascination with religion had given him a sleepless night and when the dawn came he had still not found the answer to the new developments. For 30 years he had lived without any woman problems and now this had happened. Just when he had found a woman that he wanted to spend the rest of his life with, she had to go and mess things up. If another man had been involved he could have dealt with that, but what do you do when the other man is God? He would have gladly faced another gun to win her, but God did not carry a gun. He had no desire to get crosswise of Him. A bolt of lightning was something he had no defense against.

Maybe the best thing to do was ignore it. Given enough time, it was sure to blow over and things could get back to normal. He had seen the woman's heart and it was just like his own. They wanted the same things and like him, she was a woman that would go after what she wanted, no matter what the cost. They were kindred spirits, so how could there be an interest in religion in her when there was none in him? She had gotten this wild idea from Lucinda, but she would soon be out of their lives. When they left Leadville, she would only be a bad memory. He would just have to give Kitty a little time and this crazy idea would go away.

While he was thinking on these things the door slammed bringing him back to the present. The man who entered the office was dressed in miner's clothes and on his face was several days' growth of whiskers. In his mouth was a large wad of tobacco. Looking about, he searched for a place to spit but there was none. Shifting the wad to the other cheek, he looked at the marshal.

"Mr. Turnbull, I got a problem. I'm missing a partner and I think he has been murdered."

Bruno leaned back in his chair and put his arms in back of his head. "And who might you be?"

"Lem Dorset and my partner has been missing for a couple of days. Sometimes he goes on a drunk, but he hasn't been seen by anyone lately and that is darn peculiar."

"Where'd you see him last?"

"At the mine. We were running low on powder and a few other things, so Scotty McBain, that's his name, went to town to pick the stuff up. I stayed at the mine while he was gone. We just hit a rich pocket and somebody had to stay and guard it till we cleaned it out. Scotty never came back, so I went to the cabin to see what was going on. I found Billy Sharp and Tray Allison there and they had moved in. I think Clay Coffin is living there too, 'cause they pal together, but I didn't see him. Scotty wouldn't just up and move and let them fellers take the place over and I think they killed him. When I asked what was going on, Billy told me they had claimed the cabin and I needed to find another place to live. I knew Scotty wouldn't have given the cabin to a bunch of coyotes like that for any kind of reason. It was Billy that done all the talking and I think he killed him. I ain't no gun hand and I ain't aimin' to get myself killed over it. Can you do something about it?"

Bruno scowled. "So that's how they did it."

"Did what?"

"Never mind, I was just thinking out loud. You might be right about Billy. I want you to do me a favor. Go on up to the Bon Ton and tell Billy I'm coming for him. We have to get this straightened out."

"How do you know he is in the Bon Ton?"

"Go on now. I'll be along directly."

When the man had gone Bruno got to his feet and checked the loads in his gun. He had dealt with men like Billy all too often and he knew he would not be long on talk. There was only one answer to how Kitty had gotten the cabin and Billy was a killer.

After taking a moment to study the street, he headed toward the saloon. He had seen Billy handle a gun and there would be little chance that he would give it up. There was only one way to handle a man like that and if Billy wanted a showdown, he would be ready. As he walked his confidence began to rise and he could feel the anticipation of trouble growing inside. He fought against those feelings and reminded himself that it was the law he was there to enforce. This was not just a chance to feed on the excitement that always filled him when he anticipated a fight. He tried to ignore those feelings and prepared himself for any possibility that might arise.

When he reached the saloon he spotted Billy and Clay on the boardwalk. The men stood quiet as they watched his approach and it was clear that they were expecting him. With confidence he approached the men and stopped a short distance from the hitching post. When he stopped the men stepped down into the street.

"Billy, I've come to settle the business about your cabin. That cabin belongs to Scotty McBain and he has turned up missing. I think you know what has happened to him and we need to talk about it. I'm going to take you down to the jail for questioning and Tray you stay out of it. This is between Billy and me."

Tray grinned and spit a stream of tobacco juice in the direction of the marshal. "Let me have him Billy."

"Stay out of this, Tray. I don't need you to handle this tin horn."

Billy squared off and dropped his arms to his sides. "Turnbull, I've had a score to settle with you ever since that day you killed Dan. You can drag iron anytime you are ready 'cause your time has come."

Disgusted, Tray glanced at his partner. "This is my play, Billy. I don't need your help."

"Tray, I told you to stay out of this. Unless you want to admit to killing Scotty and taking his cabin. You want to admit to that?"

"I ain't admittin' nothin."

"Then shut up. It's between me and Bruno, so you stay out of it. What's on your mind, Marshal?"

"I want you to tell me what has happened to Scotty. I have it on pretty good authority that you killed him. I want you to come down to the jail where we can talk about it. Before we go, I want your gun."

Billy's hand edged toward his gun. "You ain't getting my gun and I ain't goin' nowhere. What are you going to do about it?"

By this time the street had cleared and the crowd had taken safe positions on the boardwalks where they could see what was going to happen next. Bruno dropped his hand beside his gun. "Billy, you got a choice. Either hand me that gun or make your play."

"Marshal, I've never liked you and I don't think you're fast enough to take me."

As he spoke he went for his gun. Billy was fast, but this time he was too fast for his own good. His shot went high and before he could fire again a bullet slammed into his chest, spinning him around and knocking him into Tray. Tray had also pulled his gun, but the jolt sent his bullet into a post on the boardwalk. Before he could fire again Bruno put a bullet in his arm, spilling his gun into the dirt. When he looked to Billy his gun was rising again, but before it came level he put two bullets through the spreading red stain on the front of his shirt. He dropped to the ground and lay still.

Desperately Tray reached for his gun, but Bruno fired a shot that ricocheted off the dirt in front of it. "Hold it right there, Tray. Unless you want some more you had better leave it lay."

Desperation filled the man's eyes and he glanced around in hopes of finding a friend, but there was no one to back him. Reluctantly he did as he was told. Turning to Bruno his eyes turned ugly. "This ain't over with, Marshal. I still got a score to settle with you and I'll wait my time." Slowly he picked up his gun and slid it into his holster. "You remember what I said." Turning he pushed his way though the crowd and disappeared.

For a couple of days things were quiet in town and Bruno enjoyed the break. He allowed himself a little time at the card tables and life began to look bright again. There was a temptation to visit Kitty, but he was not ready to deal with the religion problem yet, so he decided to let it ride.

Then one afternoon a stranger came calling. He was a tall, slim man with a wide black hat that covered his long blond hair. He wore a black broadcloth suit that was set off with a string tie held together with a silver clasp. His pants were tucked into well-polished black boots.

"Mr. Turnbull?" he asked, as he extended his hand. "My name is Edward Bush and I would like a few minutes of your time."

Bruno took the hand and shook it. "If you're not selling something, you can have a seat. What can I do for you?"

"Mr. Turnbull…"

"Bruno."

"He nodded. "Bruno. I represent Mr. Tabor and I think we need to have a talk about your job. It seems you have made quite an impression on the town in a short period of time and I'd like to say that we have also been impressed with what you have done."

Bruno shot an amused look in the man's direction. "Let me guess. You don't like the way I get things done and you would like to suggest using a little restraint. Am I right?"

The man shifted nervously in his chair. "Something like that. The truth is, it would be better if you let the courts decide how a criminal should be dealt with and the district judge can make the choice on what needs to be done."

Bruno threw him a hard look. "Mr., this is a hard country and it makes hard men. I'm a man that knows how to deal with hard cases and you best leave the law enforcement to me. Before I came here, you didn't have anyone that could hold this job for more than a few weeks and now that I'm here you want to complain about how I do my job. I'm dealing with men that don't understand any other kind of law but the law of the gun. I suggest that you tend to your business and let me take care of this office."

The man gave Bruno a cool appraising glance. "We will take that into consideration, but you must remember that this job was not given to you by Mr. Tabor. Until the town council takes this up you are operating on your own authority."

"That's right and I intend to continue doing that until a better man comes along. So far I haven't seen one. Are you that man, Mr. Bush?"

Anxious to change the subject, the man ignored the challenge. "There's one other thing that I need to talk to you about. The judge you put off the stand has gone to Denver and I am sure he will get the ear of some important people. We are a state now and you can't just go around making up your own rules. That judge you appointed is no more a judge than I am. Mr. Tabor is in Denver on business, but when he gets back you can be sure he will be very upset with what you have done. Getting rid of that judge is not only illegal in the state of Colorado, it is illegal in…"

Bruno slammed his fist down on the desk and leaned forward in his chair. "You better get this straight, Partner, the government of Colorado does not keep the law in this town and neither does Horace Tabor. Otto Lynch tried it and got himself shot. So did Tex Bloodson. Do you want to try taking over this chair, Mr. Bush? I can tell you right now you wouldn't last a week before those miners would run over you. As for that judge, I'm not going to risk my life bringing felons into that court just to have some spineless judge turn them loose. I don't know if you have noticed, but this town has been pretty quiet the last few days and I intend to keep it that way. We have a pretty good system going now and I don't need you or Mr. Tabor to interfere with what works. Now, unless you have some other business with me, you'd better get on your way."

The man scowled as he searched his brain for an answer. Finally in a skeptical voice he spoke. "There is one more thing. I went up to talk to Mervin Flynn the other day and he filled me in on what is going on at the mine. Joe Growler is still mining the vein that ran into the Poker Chip property. Word has it that Joe is paying a kickback to Clay Coffin for that decision they got in your court. Is that what you call justice?"

"That claim was all settled legal and proper and whatever agreement Joe might have with Clay is none of my business."

The man stood to his feet and leaned over the desk. "Mr. Turnbull, you know very well what is going on and it is as illegal as a three dollar bill. I promise you there is going to be an investigation and we will get to the bottom of this. We are not…"

Bruno leaped to his feet. "You are not going to do anything. That case has been settled by the courts and that is the end of it. I'm going to tell you one more time, Mr. Bush. We will take care of any violation of the law in this town and we don't need any help from you. Now you take that back to Mr. Tabor and I don't expect to see you in this office again!"

Edward Bush was not a man who was used to being spoken to in that way and he raised himself to his full six-foot-two height. "Let me give you some free advice, Marshal. This little empire that you are trying to set up is not going to last. Leadville is becoming an honest, upstanding city and we will not put up with this kind of corruption. Cheap hustlers like you come and go and your time is up. My advice to you is pack your bags and get out of town. If you stay here, you are in for some real trouble." Casting a look of contempt at the marshal, he marched out the door.

Bruno stared at the empty door for a long moment. He could feel the heavy pounding of his heart and his mouth was dry. He was mad at himself for letting that arrogant "gentleman" get under his skin. He needed a drink. Maybes a few hands of poker would help him feel better, so he headed for the Bon Ton. When he passed the dry goods store he noticed Buck tied to the hitching rail. For a moment he entertained the thought of paying a visit, but he was not sure he wanted to deal with that situation yet. Maybe he could take a ride out to Kitty's place this evening when he was in a better mood. Maybe by now she was ready to listen to some common sense. For now he would let it ride.

Pushing the bat-wing door open, Bruno stood there for a moment allowing his eyes to adjust to the dim light. The saloon was full of boisterous miners and he made his way through the crowd to the poker tables. Spotting an empty chair, he was about to sit down when Tray stepped in front of him. Bruno was not in the mood for a confrontation so he tried to step past him, but Tray blocked the way. It was obvious that the man was stupid with drink and was now spoiling for a fight.

Drawing heavily on his patience Bruno tried to rein in

his short temper. "I'm not in the mood for this today, Tray, so why don't you go on home and sleep it off before you overload yourself."

Tray's face twisted into a snarl. "We got some unfinished business, you and me and we are going to settle it right now."

"I've already settled my business with you, so get out of my way."

Tray stood his ground and his chin lifted in defiance. "Not in my books. You killed my partner and I'm going to settle the score."

"If you're talking about Billy, that business is over. Now if you are a smart man you'll let it ride. Why don't you let me buy you a drink and we'll forget all about it."

Tray's eyes grew ugly. "I ain't drinkin' with no back-shootin' polecat like you. I want you outside where we can settle this like men."

"Tray, I'm trying to give you a break. I could have jailed you for what you did, but I'm willing to let it go. Now let me buy you a drink and we'll forget about it."

"I want you on the street," Tray demanded roughly. "I ain't takin…"

Reaching over, Bruno grabbed the man by the shirt collar and the seat of his paints. Dragging him across the room, he hurtled him through the doors and into the dust of the street. Spinning around, he reached for his gun, but Bruno's gun was trained on his chest.

"You pull that gun and you are a dead man. I've taken all I'm going to take from you and I want you out of town. Now git."

With disgust Tray watched the marshal as he walked back into the saloon. He had never been humiliated like that before and he shook with hatred. Bruno must pay for what he had done and his mind searched for a way to get even. He had just been made to look foolish in front of the whole town and now he would prove that Bruno had prodded the wrong man.

Then he spotted Kitty's horse. It was standing in front of the new dry goods store. Slowly a plan began to take shape in his drunken mind. What better way to get to the Marshal than through his woman? Dusting himself off, he gathered his horse and led him to the store. A look around assured him that no one was watching and the street was back to normal. Entering the store, he sighted his prey. She was examining bolts of cloth and she was by herself. Walking up to her, he took one more look around. No one was paying any attention.

"Excuse me, Miss. Is that your buckskin outside?"

"Yes. Is there something wrong?"

"I don't know. He is acting kind of strange like he is getting sick. Maybe you had better come and take a look."

When they reached the horses, Kitty stroked the animal's nose and with reassuring words looked for signs of trouble. After a closer examination she could find nothing wrong. With a puzzled look she turned to Tray. "What was he doing? I can't see anything wrong with him."

Pulling his gun, he shoved it into her ribs. "There's nothing wrong with the horse. I just needed to get you out of the store. Now we are going to take a little ride and you are going to act like nothing is wrong. I promise you I will shoot you right here in the street if you don't do what I tell you to. I'm going to holster my gun, but if you scream I will shoot you down on the spot. Get on that horse and follow my lead."

Kitty's mouth went dry and she felt sick inside. She realized the seriousness of the situation and she was all alone. She knew about Tray and knew the threat was not just idle words.

Mounting the horse, Kitty glanced over at the man. "Tray, you're crazy. I'm the marshal's girl and you know what he will do when he catches you. Your life won't be worth two cents."

Tray stepped into the saddle, drew rein and turned the horse into the street. "You let me worry about the marshal. You just concentrate on making me happy. I'm not a very patient man."

Kitty moved up beside him. "I know who you are. You're one of Clays outlaws and I have heard about you. He's a friend of Bruno and he isn't going to back you up on this one. You are going to have two men ready to kill you if you don't get smart. If you will let me go back to the store right now, I am willing to forget about this, but this is your last chance."

Ignoring the woman Tray turned his horse west. Together they rode down the street until it entered the forest at the edge of town. A crude trail led off into the trees and much traffic had established a clear path. After riding a short distance, it turned to the north. When they came to a stream Tray pointed his horse into the tall timber that climbed the mountain to the west.

By now Kitty had regained control and anger was replacing fear. This was not the same as being accosted by some drunk at the Palace. This time she was truly on her own with no experiences to draw on for support. Lucinda had told her about Tray and of the outlaw gang that he was a part of. She knew that they would stop at nothing to get what they wanted, but what was it they wanted with her? They had to be trying to get to Bruno. Were they counting on him to come to her rescue so they could ambush him? That was unlikely. This time she was on her own and she would have to handle it. Silently she asked the Lord for help.

As she prayed she began to realize that she was not alone. The Lord had promised her that He would never leave her alone and He would not leave her now. This was just one of those dangerous times that Lucinda had warned her about. That very morning she had read: 'Casting all your cares upon Him; for He careth for you.'[14] This had to be a test to see if she really believed it. It was time to prove to the Lord that she really did believe what He had said. Silently she made the Lord a promise that no matter what happened she would trust Him.

"Tell me Tray, do you know how much danger you are in?"

"What?"

"I think you should know this because it could seriously change your life. I am a new Christian and that means I am under the protection of God. If you try to hurt me you are setting yourself up for the wrath of God. Are you really sure you want to take a chance on that?"

Tray shot a glance at her and laughed. "So you're one of those Bible thumpers. Well, you can save your breath because I don't believe any of that hogwash."

"You'd better believe it because you are playing with fire. I might not be a widow, but the Bible says if you exploit widows and orphans and they ask for the Lord's help He would give it to them. That means me too. He might even kill you.[15] Now I don't know if He is going to do that, but I don't think I would take a chance if I were you."

Tray ignored the woman as he searched for a way through the thick forest. Scattered through the trees were many large boulders. When they had fallen from the slopes above they had taken large trees down with them and their decaying trunks had formed a barricade all the way to the stream beside them. Turning toward it he led the woman into the rushing water.

"Tray, I'm serious. You are not only in trouble with Bruno; you are in trouble with the Lord."

"I can take care of myself and I don't want to hear any more of this God talk."

"Can't you see that I am trying to help you? You are the one that is in danger here, not me."

He turned toward her and his eyes were cold and measuring. "I told you to shut up and I meant it. We have more important things to take care of right now."

Angrily he turned his eyes back to the tumbling waters and cautiously they moved forward. The brush that lined the stream was thick and impenetrable and offered no opportunity to regain the bank. Finally after several tries to penetrate the barrier they found a place where they could get the horses through. The clatter of the horses' hooves rose above the sound of the stream as they scrabbled up over the rocks that lined the bank.

After clearing the brush they were faced with a new problem. Scattered down the slope of the mountain were more boulders. They were part of a giant rock slide that had redefined the side of the canyon. Over the course of years the constant cycles of freezing and thawing had torn them loose from the slope, leaving a trail of rocky debris. The jumbled snarl of rocks and broken trees offered no easy trails through to the upper part of the canyon.

Tray drew rein and considered the scene before him. Kitty

pulled up beside him and shook her head. "This looks pretty bad. Maybe we should head back now."

He shot her a disgusted look. "You just follow me and we will get through this. It ain't nothin."

As they moved forward the trail narrowed into a channel of rock that was barely wide enough to admit a horse. For a moment the horses hesitated, unsure of the perilous path that lay before them. With a gentle nudge from Tray they began to move cautiously forward until they rounded a point of rocks that led out on a short ledge. Fifty feet below, the stream roared over a cataract of jagged boulders that threw white water high in the air. Tray spoke to the horse and touched it on the shoulder. Reassured, it moved forward with great care. Slowly they picked their way along the jagged slope of coble and broken boulders until the path widened out and the ground became passable again. A short ride through the thick forest brought them to a small clearing. Pulling up Tray dismounted.

"This is the end of the line for you. Get down."

Looking around Kitty was bewildered. "What do you mean this is the end of the line. There's nothing here."

Gathering her reins in his hand he looked up. "You're staying here and you are going to give the marshal a message for me. You tell him that bringing you here is only a warning. I could have killed you right here, but I am going to give him one last chance. If he doesn't leave Leadville in one week I am going to shoot him down like a dog. There will be no warning. You tell him that, you hear?"

Kitty swung down beside him. "You can't tell him that. He's the marshal. He can't leave town, He's got a job to do and the town needs him."

Taking her by the arm, he led her over to a tangled pile of dead trees. With a practiced hand he tied her hands and fastened the other end of the rope around a large trunk. Stepping back he inspected his work. Satisfied that the ropes would hold he mounted his horse.

"You tell him. One week." Turning the horse he crossed the stream and disappeared into the trees.

Bruno had just drawn his first hand when Lucinda burst through the door of the saloon. She quickly located him and she ran to his side. "Bruno, you've got to come right now. Tray just took Kitty from the store and they headed out of town."

"Which way did they go?"

"They went into the woods west of town. Tray had a gun on her and he's crazy enough to use it. You better hurry."

Bruno dropped his cards on the table. "You boys are going to have to excuse me. I've got business to take care of."

Once they were outside, Lucinda pointed down the street. "They went that way. You better hurry before something happens."

"I'll take care of this." He said as he turned toward the stable. "You go on back to the store and don't worry about Kitty. I'll get her back."

"I'll be praying for you," she called after him. "And be careful."

Bruno wasted no time in getting to the edge of the forest; he reined in his horse to study the ground. Many tracks converged on this point and it appeared to be a well-traveled trail. Hawk was anxious to go and it took little urging to move him forward. Bruno's eyes were alert for anything that might offer a clue to where they had gone. Seeing no sign where a horse could have left the trail he followed it for nearly a half mile to the stream. Barely visible in the rocky ground were the tracks of two horses that had turned and entered the water. Following the trail upstream he searched the rocky ground for more sign. Finally the brush opened on the bank and there were tracks that led up out of the water. The track led into a field of boulders and broken trees and with great care Hawk moved forward. Many of the rocks were as big as houses and scattered among them were tall aspens.

Stopping for a moment he searched the rocks ahead. This would be an ideal place for an ambush but there were no other paths to travel and he would just have to take a chance. With a watchful eye he moved forward until the rocks thinned out into an area where he picked up the tracks of the horses again. Branches slapped his face as he continued along the slope. The trail angled down to the stream where the waters had not yet entered the cataracts below.

Breaking free of the trees he followed the stream until the rocks that lined it forced him higher into the forest. Here the ground was rocky again and there were no more tracks to follow. Running up from the stream was a thick grove of aspen with many large trees scattered among the young growth. Above the aspens he could see a large stand of spruce that covered the mountain until they tapered out thousands of feet above. Surely Tray would not be stupid enough to try to take her over that pass into the country beyond without making provision for the trip. What did he have in mind?

Moving through the trees Bruno's senses were alert for anything that might look out of place. Once past the aspen grove the forest thickened again. Scattered through the trees were the bones of long dead lightning-scarred trunks that had fallen under the weight of the heavy winter snows. On his left the trees were spread among the large granite boulders that marked the edge of the giant rock slide. There were no paths through the boulders that would allow a horse to pass. They could not have gone that way. Turning his horse into the stream he allowed him to find his own way through the rocky bottom until a break in the brush appeared where they could leave the stream.

When he had cleared the bank he picked up the trail and followed it along the stream. After a short distance the trees thinned out and the tracks of the horses appeared again. The ground was wet here and the horses had sunk deeply into the soft soil of the forest floor. Suddenly Hawk's ears went up and his muscles stiffened. Pulling up Bruno peered through the trees before him, searching for anything that appeared out of place. In the distance there was a small clearing that had been cleared by large boulders that had tumbled down the mountain and leveled the trees in their path.

With his senses on alert he urged the horse forward. At the edge of the trees he stopped. Tied to a large deadfall and all alone was Kitty.

Leaping from his horse he ran forward and cut the ropes from her wrist. Freed from her bonds she threw her arms around his neck and clung to him. For a long time they savored the moment, enjoying the rich comfort of the silent communication that comes from the joining of kindred spirits. She had known he would come and had not considered any other possibility. The strength of his encompassing arms took away any fears that might remain.

Finally she looked up and smiled. "I knew you would come. I prayed for you to come. And my prayers were answered."

Bruno returned the smile. "What kind of a prayer could you say that I would be the answer to? God didn't say anything to me about it."

"You will just have to take my word for it," she said. "I just hope I don't have to get myself kidnapped again to get your attention. You have been a little scarce lately. What did I do to deserve that?"

Embarrassment flooded Bruno's cheeks. He knew he could find no answer that would satisfactorily answer her question. He could only look into her eyes and he could see the hurt he had caused and he knew he would never make that mistake again. When he thought about what he had done, he knew he had been a fool. He had found the ultimate woman and he had risked losing her over something as petty as religion.

He looked at her with an understanding grin. "You didn't do anything wrong, it was just my stupidity. I got a little nervous about all this religious talk and I was being selfish. Will you forgive me?"

Reaching up, she kissed him tenderly. "You know I will."

"Kitty, I am going to make you a solemn promise. With God as my witness I am going to get you out of this dangerous place and make a proper home away from all of this. You deserve the best and I promise you I will never fail you in making your dreams come true. I give you my word on it. That is the best commitment I know how to make."

"You said that before. When are you going to do it?"

"Very soon. I am going to take you to a place where there will be no more danger like you faced today.

"Is that a proposal?"

"I don't believe in proposals. It is a statement of fact and when the time is right I am going to marry you."

"Don't I have anything to say about it?"

"No. Women are too given to changes in their minds and are given to whatever mood strikes them, so I will save you all the stress that comes with that kind of that trouble."

"What makes you think that I will agree to this?"

"Because you love me. There is only one logical thing to do in a situation like that. When you find that kind of love, you don't go looking for it somewhere else. We have found what everyone is looking for and we would be foolish to throw that away. I could never love anyone like I love you and I know you feel the same way. Admit it."

Kitty turned away in an effort to hide her feelings. For a long moment she stared at the rushing water of the creek. When she looked back, her face shown with a yearning that only this man could satisfy. "Bruno, I have wanted to be your woman from the day I met you and I do love you with all my heart. I give you my commitment that I will never let you down. I will love you until the day I die. Now let's get back to town before we do something we will be sorry for."

CHAPTER 10

With Kitty safely home, Bruno returned to town with one thing on his mind. Tray had become a threat to Kitty's safety and the problem had to be resolved. Over the years he had come to know the workings of the outlaw mind and Tray was worse than most. He was not a man to forget a fight, especially one that made him look foolish. Like a child he would have to have satisfaction and like a child he would probably handle it badly. He had thrown down the gauntlet for all to see and if it wasn't dealt with now someone was going to die. Tying his horse in front of the Bon Ton, he went inside. Spotting Clay at the bar he joined him.

"Ben, give me a whiskey and I want the good stuff."

Ben looked to see who was giving the orders and switched from the bottle he had grabbed to another one under the bar. "You're right, Bruno, we serve only the best to you."

When he had gone Bruno turned his attention to Clay. "I got to have a word with you."

Clay stepped away from the bar. "That's a funny thing, because I was about to say the same thing. What's on your mind?"

"Not here. Follow me."

Downing his drink, he led the way to an empty table in the corner. When they were seated his face grew serious. "You are going to have to get rid of Tray. I've taken all the trouble I'm going to from him and if he crosses me again I'm going to kill him. Either you send him back to the hideout or I'm going to plant him right here. It's your choice."

Clay tasted his beer and set it on the table. He wiped the foam from his mouth as he looked up. "Bruno, you got to take it easy on Tray. I need him here for when we have trouble with the mine owners. He's my muscle and without him to back me up these mine owners might not come through with the money. I can try to keep him away from you, but let's not get hasty about sending him away."

Bruno looked at him critically. "Apparently, you don't know what he just did. When I threw him out of the saloon he kidnapped Kitty and I had to run them down to get her back. He crossed the line and as far as I'm concerned he's finished here. Either you get rid of him or I will."

Clay nodded grimly. "I understand your feelings, but things aren't that simple. You're doing a great job, but in the process you have just about wrecked the gang. I lost Stew because of you and you have killed Dan and Billy. I have no idea where Tray has gone."

"What difference does it make? We don't need him."

"Yes, we do. I keep an ear to the ground on what's going

on at the hideout and Gil is pretty mad. He isn't a man that has much patience. I sent word to him that we need more help up here and he's going to start asking questions."

"Let him. We're getting the job done and the two of us can handle anything that comes up."

"I told you I need him, so don't mess this up because of a few personal problems. We've got a great thing going here if we can keep peace in the family. You can put up with Tray for a little while longer. You've already made a lot of money and there is more to be had if you will just be patient. These hills are full of mines that we can squeeze. This is not the time to argue with each other."

"I told you what I want. You get him out of here or I will handle it myself."

Clay's jaw tightened and he took another sip of beer. He was in a difficult position that could destroy everything that he had worked for. He had to find a way to buy a little more time.

"Listen Bruno, when this is over you can do whatever you want with Tray. Gil is sending up a few men, but they won't be here for a few days. In the meantime I'm going to be short handed. I know Tray pretty well and he will head for the hills to cool off. He's pretty independent and he's got a lot of Injun in him. He does show up when I need him, but I don't know where he is right now. We got some more business coming up with the Black Cloud. They have mined into a vein on the Larkspur property. We know how to play that and we need to get this into court as quick as possible. I'm going to need both of you. Don't make things any worse than they are."

Bruno's expression did not change. "I told you to get rid of him. I can take care of the mine owners until your help gets here. You better listen to what I say because the clock is running out on this operation and I can't protect you forever."

"What are you talking about? You said yourself we were going to run this town by mining camp law. That should buy us a little more time."

"And you believed me? That was for the judge's benefit and you can take my word for it we better grab the money while it is there. I don't know how much time we got, but it's not as much as you think. We can get it done without Tray's help."

Clay shook his head. "Maybe so, but you got a bigger problem than that partner. I didn't want to tell you this, but I talked to Tray about an hour ago. He's planning to bushwhack you the first chance he gets. I think I can talk him out of it, but I might not see him before he gets to you. You better watch your back until he cools down. You really got under his skin."

Bruno stood to his feet. "He might try, but I'm pretty hard to kill. When you see him you tell him if he ever goes near Kitty again he is a dead man. You can take that to the bank."

Just then the sound of loud voices rose from the back of the room and Bruno glanced around. A quarrel had broken out at one of the card tables and two men were facing off. He recognized one of them as Jonas Thorpe and he was spoiling for trouble.

"You are not going to get away with it, Sam," Jonas roared with fire in his eyes, "I had an ace in the hole and you switched the cards on me. You been stackin' the deck all day and I'm callin' you a cheat and a thief! That means you forfeit the pot and I'm going to take it all."

He reached down to pull it in but before he could Sam

shoved him against the wall. "You keep your hands off that money. It ain't yours! You go on home and sleep it off."

When he reached for the money again, Jonas struck and struck hard. Sam looked up just in time to see the blow coming, but it was too late to avoid it. It caught him on the side of the head and knocked him over a chair onto the floor. Severely shaken the man took a moment to regain his wits. Then he came off the floor with a lunge. He came in low and was met with a knee in the face. The blow smashed his nose and knocked him to the floor. When he tried to get up Jonas grabbed him by the shirt and jerked him to his feet. Before he could regain his senses he struck him three times in the face knocking him back against the wall. Dazed the man reached for his gun, but before he could draw Jonas grabbed his arm and pinned him against the wall. As he struggled to raise the gun Jonas pulled a knife and thrust it into his stomach. With a stunned look he slid to the floor.

By this time Bruno had reached the men and grabbed Jonas by the arm. When he reached for the knife he pulled it back in an effort to stab him, but before he could Bruno hit him on the head with his gun. He dropped to the floor and lay still.

In the meantime a crowd had gathered around and Bruno lifted his hand. "OK, folks, the excitement is over. Just go on back to what you were doing. Ben, you go and get the doc and see what you can do for Sam."

Picking up the unconscious form he threw him over his shoulder and headed for the door. Clay caught up with him on the street. "That was pretty impressive what you did back there, but I think you made a mistake."

Bruno shot him a glance. "What are you talking about?"

"Jonas is a good friend of Horace Tabor. Are you sure you want to lock him up?"

"What do you mean? He stabbed a man and that's against the law."

Those were not the words Clay wanted to hear and it reflected in his face. "You don't understand. Tabor is going to be pretty upset and we don't want to make an enemy out of him. We need to keep him pacified and this is not going to help."

"I don't care what Tabor thinks. I'm going to do my job and if he doesn't like it, too bad."

"He has a lot of power in this town."

Bruno ignored the remark and they walked along in silence. When they reached the jail he opened one of the cells and rolled the man onto the cot. When he turned to his friend his eyes were cool and defiant. "Clay, I'm the marshal in this town and it's my job to keep the law. This has nothing to do with our deal and I am going to do my job. I didn't just take this job to feather your nest; I took it because I wanted to get the job done. There's no reason I can't do both."

Clay looked at him as if he were a stranger. He had not planned on this change of direction. Things were going well so far, but this new attitude did not fit the plan. He had wanted Bruno to do this job because he was a man who got results and now he was starting to make sounds like a real citizen. He was already in enough trouble with Gil and he sure didn't need this. Billy's death had changed the situation and for the first time he began to wonder if their plans were going to work out.

Inside the office the men were just settling themselves in their chairs when Edward Bush came through the door. Not expecting to see Clay, he looked at him as if he were an insect that needed to be squashed. Choosing to ignore him he turned to Bruno. His face was grim and he wasted no time in getting to the point. When he spoke his voice was low and hollow and sounded like it came from the bottom of a grave.

"Mr. Coffin, I will thank you to leave. I have some business with the marshal."

"Clay, you stay where you are," Bruno demanded. "I'm the one that gives the orders in this office, Mr. Bush, and you would do well to remember that."

He looked at Bruno and his face twisted with fury. "That may be for the moment, but that can change if you don't start using a little judgment when you lock someone up in that jail. I want you to go back there and turn Jonas loose before Mr. Tabor hears what has happened. I came here to give you a chance to set things straight before I see him."

Bruno's expression did not change. He did not like this man and he was certainly not going to be intimidated by him. The arrest had been a legitimate one and he was not going to entertain any challenges to his authority.

"Mr. Bush, I don't need your advice on how to run this office and you don't have any say about who I lock up. I'll make a deal with you though. I promise I won't come up and help you run your hotel if you will not come down here to tell me how to run this office. That includes Mr. Tabor. Now you go on up there and tell him whatever you want, but you remember this. Jonas broke the law and there may even be a charge of murder against him. You people are not going to tell me what the law is and I intend to enforce it the way I see it. This matter will be decided in court. Now there's the door. You'd better use it before I lock you up for interfering with justice."

"You mean Clay is going to decide what happens to Jonas?"

"That's right. He's the judge and I will enforce whatever he decides."

The full significance of the remarks registered on his face and he threw a contemptuous look in Clay's direction. Then he spun around and stomped out the door. When he had gone Clay turned to the Bruno. "He may be trouble. You sure you don't want to change your mind?"

"I'm sure."

Clay shook his head. "You're setting yourself up for a pack of trouble. You don't want to get crosswise of Tabor."

"I can handle him. You just worry about making the right decisions when these cases come up. I will take care of the rest. "

Clay leaned back in his chair and began building himself a smoke. "That ain't the only problem you got, Partner. There's something you probably didn't know about Billy Sharp. I suppose I should have told you this before, but I doubt it would have made any difference. He was always on the prod and it was inevitable that someone would punch his ticket. I should have told you that he was Gil's son. I'm afraid that is going to complicate things for you. Gil set a lot of store by him."

Bruno shot him a look. "I thought you said Gil's last name was Davis."

"It is. He talked Billy into changing his name. He figured when they finally made their fortune he could walk away and start a new life somewhere else with a clean slate. When he finds out what you did, your life won't be worth two cents."

Both men sat in silence. Finally Bruno looked up. "I

suppose we can look forward to a visit from him. How long do you think it will take him to do something about it?"

Clay scratched a match on his pants and touched it to his cigarette. "It's hard to say. We keep a pretty good line of communication going, but I imagine it will be the better part of a week before we need to do any serious worrying. He won't come up here anyway. He'll send someone and he won't be lookin' for a fair fight. "

"And what have you done on the Black Cloud case?"

"We're in good shape on that one," Clay said as he drew on the cigarette. "They knew what we did with the Emperor deal and they've already paid up. All we have to do now is run it through the court."

Bruno's eyes narrowed. "I have an idea. We could move the date ahead and try the case in two days. Then when it's on the books we could split the money and I could leave. You could tell Gil I stole the money and left town. That would get us both off the hook."

Clay shook his head. "I don't think you understand Gil. He'd come after me for losing that much money and he'd find a way to track you down. We'd better come up with a better idea than that."

For several minutes neither man spoke, each busy with his own thoughts. Finally Clay spoke. "What would you think of this. You make yourself scarce for a few days and when Gil's boys get here I'll just give the whole operation to them. Then you and me can go on down to the hideout and join up down there. You can change your name and I can give Gil some story on who you are and let him handle this operation."

Bruno looked skeptical. "That sounds pretty shaky. Why would he want to take us in?"

"Because he trusts me. By the time I give him a new story on you and how handy you are with those guns he'll put you to work. If you got a better idea I'm willing to listen."

"That sounds pretty risky. Somebody's bound to figure out who I am."

Clay dusted the ashes from his cigarette. "Not really. Gil will keep us pretty busy and we will hardly ever be at the hideout. We can make a ton of money in a short time and get out. No one will ever figure it out."

Bruno looked skeptical. "We got a couple of days to think about it. To tell the truth, I'm not too happy about the whole idea. In the meantime we'd better get this Black Cloud case taken care of before this whole thing blows up. Now you go on and get yourself a drink while I think this over."

Ed Bush was not a happy man as he trudged down the hill from the Tabor store. He had been in a bad mood since he had left the marshal's office and the visit with Horace Tabor had not helped. It went against his grain to be an errand boy for Tabor, but he was a rising star in the state and it would be wise to cultivate a friendship with a man like that. There was a good chance that the state would give him the job of senator and that would put him in a good position to further his own career. That was worth putting up with a little humiliation now.

Today's mission was to call on a local minister. Yancy Riddle[16] was a newcomer to Leadville, but was already making a name for himself. With a large donation from Wilber Mudd, a local mine owner, he was starting a new church and had already attracted a sizable congregation. Horace had told him of Yancy's offer to help with the problems the marshal had caused and he had decided to see if he meant it.

When he reached the hotel, he was directed to one of the rooms upstairs. His did not expect his knock to be answered by a beautiful woman. Women this attractive were rare in boom towns and he was caught off guard. She had lovely, long, black hair which was set off by hazel eyes that penetrated the man to his soul. She was middle-aged and had managed to maintain the beauty that would normally be expected of a much younger woman. When she spoke her voice carried the authority of a woman who was used to being listened to.

"May I help you?"

Sweeping his hat from his head he bowed. "I'm Edward Bush and I represent Mr. Tabor. I have some business with Yancy."

Swinging the door wide the woman smiled. "Please come in, Mr. Bush. My husband will be right with you."

The room was quite small, but a door had been cut through the wall to the adjoining room. It had transformed the two hotel rooms into a very attractive suite and it was evident that the couple had set up housekeeping for a long stay. At a desk sat a dignified man with coal black hair and long sideburns that were neatly trimmed. He wore a black broadcloth suit, with black trousers tucked into hand-tooled boots that were covered with the dust of the street. He had the face of a man who had seen much of life, but had managed to retain a touch of youth. He rose from his chair to greet the visitor.

"My name is Yancy Riddle," he said, extending his hand. "Who do I have the honor of addressing?"

Taking the hand, he shook it vigorously. "Edward Bush. I

represent Horace Tabor and I have come to talk to you about a problem with the marshal."

"And what problem is that?"

Glancing at the woman he cleared his throat. "Can we step into the other room where we can talk in private?"

Yancy followed his gaze and grinned. "I'm sorry. I forgot to introduce my wife. This is Frenchy and we can trust her with anything that needs to be said. Now tell me about the marshal."

The man glanced at the woman and she returned a smile. Raising an eyebrow he turned back to Yancy. "As you wish. I am sure you are aware of the liberties that the marshal has been taking in enforcing the law. Today he did something that we can no longer ignore. He locked up Jonas Thorp and he is a good friend of Mr. Tabor."

"And who is Jonas Thorp?"

"He is a close friend of Mr. Tabor and a business associate. Jonas was one of the men who found a silver vein that turned out to be one of the richest finds in Leadville. Mr. Tabor had grubstaked him and he is not going to be very happy if something happens to him."

"Go on."

"We have been trying to ignore the liberties he has been taking. I'm afraid the situation has come to the place that we can no longer allow him to get away with what he is doing. He does not legally hold that job and has appointed a judge to try his cases. He did not have any authority to do that. The truth is he is setting up a scheme to bilk the mine owners and anyone else that he can take advantage of. We need your help to fire him. The town counsel is afraid to throw him out and we were hoping you might have some ideas on what we can do."

Yancy was quiet for a moment as he considered what he had heard. "What makes you think that I have some special power that will get the job done?"

"We thought because you are a preacher he might respect you and listen to you. At least long enough to tell him how much trouble he is in. We are calling in some officials from the capitol in Denver and they will be here in a few days. They are bringing a warrant for Bruno's arrest and also Clay Coffin. He is the man he appointed judge. The charges are serious enough that they could go to prison. They are also bringing with them an attorney who will represent the state and two Federal marshals to enforce the law. If he's here when they arrive, we will hold a trial with a real judge that the city council will appoint."

Yancy nodded. "It sounds to me like you have the situation under control. Why don't you just let the marshal's do their job?"

"Because Bruno is a very dangerous man and someone might get hurt. Besides, he has done some good for the town so we want to give him a chance to avoid that kind of trouble. You need to convince him that the smart thing to do is get out of town while there is still time."

Yancy's face was grave. "That all sounds very convincing, but I'm still not sure they would listen to me. Being a minister does not give me any special powers."

"Maybe not, but you are the kind of a man who can appeal to his common sense if he has any. Personally, I think we are giving him a bigger break than he deserves. It was Mr. Tabor who wanted to give him that one last chance. To be truthful, Mr. Riddle, I don't give a hoot if he goes to jail or dies right here. You are the only break he is going to get. Can we count on you to help us?"

Yancy considered what he had heard. "I have been aware of Bruno's history since before he came to this town and in the past he had understood nothing but force. It would be hard to believe that he would just saddle his horse and ride out of town. I'm going to take Mort Steel along to help enforce my words. That old mountain man knows more tricks than a carload of monkeys and he can be very persuasive if it comes to that. I will give this matter some prayer, Mr. Bush, and we will do the best we can. I believe with the Lord's help we can get the job done."

The next morning Yancy arrived at the marshal's office with Mort at his side. When he stepped inside he was pleased to see that both the marshal and his deputy were there. There was a disapproving look in the deputy's eyes, but he ignored it and extended his hand. "I don't believe I have met you. My name is Yancy Riddle."

Ignoring the hand, Brace scowled. "I know who you are, Riddle. You are the preacher that stirred up all that trouble in the saloon a while back, trying to start that church of yours. If you're trying to drum up some new business here, you're out of luck."

Yancy withdrew the hand and smiled. "That's not why I'm here, but I am sorry that you feel that way. From what I have heard lately, we could be of some help to you."

"Don't mind my deputy, Preacher," said Bruno and he pointed at a chair. "He hasn't had his coffee yet and he gets a little cranky without it. Have a seat."

Yancy's face was grim. "No thanks, I don't expect to be

here that long. I'm on a mission of mercy. The town has asked me to talk to you about the way you have been running this office. I'm afraid what you have been doing is not legal and they are calling in some officials from Denver to arrest you. They will be here in a couple of days and that will be just enough time for you to leave. I'm afraid if you stay, you will be going to prison."

For a moment silence filled the room. Somewhere in the distance could be heard the squeak of a pump handle and from outside the office came the sounds of boots tromping along the boardwalk. Bruno looked up into the preachers face. "Is this your idea of answered prayer?"

"What do you mean?"

"A while back when you were asking me to help you get your wife back from those two coyotes that kidnapped her you said you would pray for me. Is this what you were praying for?"

"You know better than that," Yancy said gently. "I prayed for you to become a Christian and I am still doing that. If you would do that your future would look brighter than it does now."

Bruno snorted. "I suppose you think I should just repent and turn myself over to those men from Denver. No thanks. My woman just did that and it has caused much trouble for me. I'm afraid it is going to take a good bit of time to get her straightened out again. What you are selling just doesn't make sense."

Suddenly Brace stepped forward and gave Yancy a shove, knocking him into the stove. "You better shut up about this religious talk. We got bigger problems to deal with than…"

Stepping out of the shadows, Mort grabbed him by the

shirt front and picked him up. With a shove he pinned him against the wall. "You better back off, Partner. We came here peaceable like and if you got any brains in that thick head of yours, you'll listen to what this man has to say."

With a quick toss he threw him into the corner. "Yancy, you go on with what you're doin'."

Looking down at his deputy Bruno had to grin. "Mort, I thought you were one of Yancy's new Christians. Is that any way for a Christian to act?"

The big man turned his attention to the Marshal. "That's right. I am a Christian, but I'm kind of new at it. You will have to pray for me until I get it right."

Just then Clay walked through the door and looked at the man on the floor. A grin lit his face. "What's the matter, Brace, couldn't you find a chair?"

"I just tripped," the man snarled as he regained his feet.

Spotting the preacher, Clay's grin widened. "Well, it looks like we are stepping up in the world. What brings you down here, Preacher? Are you looking for new converts?"

Yancy nodded. "I'm always looking for new converts, but today I have something else on my mind and it concerns you."

Clay's eyes swept the room. "Looks to me you got a good congregation right here and they could all use some preachin'. I'm not too sure you will get any satisfactory results though."

"I came down here to let you and Bruno know what's going on. There are some Federal marshals and an attorney coming up from Denver. If they have their way, you will end up behind bars."

Clay's face sobered. "What are you talking about?"

"I'm talking about the high-handed way you men have

been handling law enforcement. What you are doing is against the law and it's time to close up shop and get out of town. If you stay here, you will be going to prison."

"Who told you that?"

"It's not important where I got my information. It is important that you believe what I say. I've already filled Bruno in and it looks to me like you boys have a lot to talk about. It's decision time for both of you and I pray that you will make the right one. Come on, Mort, let's go."

When they had gone, Clay turned to Bruno. "What's going on? Is it true what he said?"

"Probably."

Clay dropped heavily into the chair. Behind him Brace took the opportunity to slip out the door. Clay was not a happy man and his face showed it. "If that's true, we have some bigger problems than some lawyer from Denver. We're going to have to shut this operation down for a while and that isn't going to set too well with Gil. He's got some big plans for Leadville and he's already mad enough to kill you."

Bruno leaned back in his chair and concentrated on a spot on the ceiling. Anger was beginning to rise inside of him and he cursed the bad luck that had caught him again. Just when things were beginning to come together, this had to happen. He was counting heavily on the money from this scheme and now it appeared to be falling apart. What could he tell Kitty? She was depending on him and he could not let her down. Maybe there was a way to salvage something from this mess.

Clay could see the frustration in the man and he shared it. One thing was sure; he was not going to jail over money. Life was too short for that. "Bruno, there's only one thing we can do. I can go back to the hideout but we're going to have to do something about you. I know Gil and he's going to kill you on sight. You got one thing going for you and that is he's never seen you. Why don't you change your name and go with me. We can come up with some story about you and how you are good with a gun. He'll find something for you to do."

Bruno was quiet for a moment. Whatever he did it would have to be quick. He knew that he had already gained a good reputation with the people in town, but that would not help when the marshals got here. Maybe he could take a job on a ranch and get out of sight for a while. At least it would be honest work and it would buy him a little time.

"I'm going to have to give this a little thought. I got Kitty to consider too and I hadn't planned on any of this. One thing is sure; we're going to have to get out of town for a while. We're leaving tomorrow morning so you be ready. I'll have a plan by then."

Bruno urged his horse up the trail that led to Kitty's cabin. Easing back in the saddle, he let the horse set his own pace. He was in no hurry to get to the cabin and it would give him time to sort things out.

There was no sound but the sound of the horse's hooves on the rocky ground and it was nice to get away from the noise and complications of the town. The fresh pine scent reminded him of the camps in California and his heart yearned for the simple life where he did not have to deal with other people's problems. There was still good ranch country west of the San Juan Mountains and this was the time to make the break and build a new life. He had been able to put away a good nest egg and the money from the Emperor Mine case had given him a good start toward what he needed. But it was not enough to get stock to start a ranch. He would have to have one more big payday to pull it off. If Clay's idea was good he could join the gang and get the money he needed. There was much gold being taken out of those mountains and he would find a way to get his share.

When he reached the clearing, Kitty was coming up from the stream with a bucket of water. When she saw him she dropped the bucket and rushed to meet him. He dismounted and greeted her with a smile. Happily she embraced him, but there was an indifference in his response. Something was wrong. Something had changed. Looking up, she studied his face for a clue. It was clear there was more on his mind than just a visit.

"You are a little early today," she said as she led him to the cabin. "I was planning on making you a grand feast for supper. There isn't anything wrong, is there?"

Bruno was silent for a moment. It was hard to bring up anything that would make life difficult for her, but he had exhausted every possibility that he could think of. He would just have to give it to her straight.

"Kitty, something has come up that is going to change the plans we have made. We're not going to be able to stay in Leadville and I know you would like to get a chance to see your dad again. What would you think of going back to the ranch for a while?"

"I think that's a great idea. It will get you off the streets and I have been praying for that."

"I hear they are finding a lot of gold in the San Juans and I am sure I can find something to do down there. There are gold camps popping up all over and I could try my luck in one of them."

Kitty's eyes lit up. "You wouldn't have to. You could go to work on my father's ranch. I am sure he will be thrilled to have you."

"I was thinking of Animas City. It's not too far from the ranch and I could hole up there for a while. Would you mind staying at the ranch until I can get a place for you? I've got a thing working that can get us the money we will need to get started on our own."

Kitty shook her head. "I think it would be better if you went to work on the ranch. That's what you want to do, so why wait. Father always needs good hands and that way we can be together."

Bruno looked uneasy. "I don't know about that. This thing I have working is going to take a lot of my time and I can't make the money we need by working for your dad. I think it would be better if I stayed in Animas City until I get this business taken care of."

Disappointed, Kitty turned away. It was clear he was hiding something again and she was not going to be left in the dark. There was danger on the horizon and he was trying to protect her from something. She felt uncomfortable and disappointed. She had to know what was going on.

"Something has happened and you are holding out on me. What is it?"

"It's nothing you need to worry about, but I am going to give up the marshaling job and there is no reason for us to stay here any longer. How quick can you be ready to go?"

That was not the answer she was looking for and anger began to rise inside of her. "That's not good enough, Bruno. This involves me too and I want to know what is going on. Anything that would make a man give up what you've got going here and go to a place you've never been is serious. I want to know what it is."

Bruno shifted nervously. "There are some things that have happened in town that I don't have any control over. The best thing for us to do is clear out as quick as we can. We need to get out of here tomorrow."

Kitty struggled to contain her emotions. "Bruno, you are hiding something from me and I'm not going to put up with it. We are going to get this secrecy thing cleared up right now. I am your woman and I am not going to be left in the dark. Now you tell me what has happened."

He shot her a puzzled look. It was clear that she was not going to give any ground on this one and he searched for the best way to explain. "I'm afraid some of the things we have been doing in town are illegal and the city is bringing charges against Clay and me. There are supposed to be some Federal marshals coming up from Denver and we need to be gone before they get here. There is no way we can beat this one and the only thing we can do is get out of town before they get here. That doesn't give us much time. Clay even recommended that I change my name because this thing could follow us. He is going to stay another day to see if that story is on the level. Can you be ready to go that quick?"

Kitty smiled. "Are you kidding? If we are going back to the ranch, I could be ready tonight."

"I said you are going to the ranch."

Kitty put her hands on her hips and glared at Bruno. "If you are in trouble I want to be with you. If there is going to be danger involved that is all the more reason that I want to be with you. I appreciate you trying to protect me, but it isn't necessary. I can take care of myself. If I'm going to the ranch you're coming with me."

"Kitty, I told you I have some business to take care of. I'm not sure…"

"Listen to me, Bruno. You're going to come to the ranch and there will be no discussion about it. Father can surely use the help and you can take care of that business from there. That's the end of the discussion. When do we leave?"

Bruno threw up his hands. "You win. We leave at first light."

CHAPTER 11

There was a chill in the air when the couple mounted their horses. It was the beginning of a dream fulfilled for both of them and excitement filled the air. The anticipation of the riders was shared by the horses that were also eager to be on the trail. In the early morning the forest was a sanctuary of peace and tranquility. The only sound that broke the silence was the creak of saddle leather and the clatter of the hooves on the rocky ground. Soon the sun rose above the ridges warming the thin air and bringing freshness to the forest that awakened their senses. At this early hour the scent of pine mingled with fresh clean air brought a freedom of spirit that had been missing in their lives. The giant trees that lined the trail gave a comforting sense of escape from the evils that had taken over the valley and their lives. When they emerged from the forest they got their first glimpse of the valley of the Arkansas River. Lining the banks were scattered groves of cottonwoods that were just now putting out the new, green leaves of spring. To the west rose the high snowy peaks of the Sawatch Range with their timbered slopes that marched down the valley to the distant forests and purple hills on the horizon.

It was good to be on the trail again and Bruno filled his lungs with the fresh air. Towns had always cramped his style and he had to admit that deep down inside he was nothing more than a country boy. All the years of pursuing the dream would soon be over. Now he could create a new world for the woman who had given him more than he had ever expected to get from life. There would be much to do and he anticipated the challenge.

Soon the trail intersected the road that followed the rock-lined river. This was the main road into Leadville and the ruts were deep from the many stage coaches that traveled it every day. In this area there was little evidence of mining because it had been prospected in the early days. When Abe Lee stuck his pan in the gravels of California Gulch and discovered gold, the mining interests had moved up the valley. Most of the prospectors had abandoned the area and followed their urge to discover even richer finds in the Gulch. That was a reprieve for the land, as it had left the valley abandoned and in its natural pristine state, with the exception of the road.

It was new country to Kitty and she was anxious to see what secrets this land held for her to discover. She had never ventured beyond the valley of the ranch and had always yearned to see what lay beyond. She knew it was a wild and lonesome land that would be filled with wonders she could have only imagined. The best part was she had someone to share the experience with. So much was new and it would be a chance to really find out what this man was about. As she rode, she studied her companion.

He had been quiet all morning and her curiosity was aroused. He had gone to town last night on a mission that he had not been willing to talk about. The excuse was there were a few things he had to take care of to make preparations for the trip. She knew that was a lie and it irritated her to be kept in the dark.

"You're awful quiet this morning. Did something happen in town last night that I should know about?"

"Nothing special," Bruno said casually. "I just filled Clay in on how to get to the ranch and told him you might have a job for him. He seems to know that country pretty well and he was familiar with your dad's place. He said a friend used to work there a while back but he was fired."

Kitty was quiet for a moment as she recalled that time. It was a bad memory she had thought was gone forever, but she was not going to let it ruin the peace she had found. It was in the past and she did not take pleasure in the thought of reliving it.

"I remember it very well and it was a bad time. This man tried to get me to tell him the location of a gold mine that was supposed to be on the ranch. There was no gold mine, but he was convinced there was. When I explained that to him he got mad and tried to grab me. I swung my horse around and she rose up and tried to get in the saddle with him. He went backward out of the saddle and hit the ground hard. Before he could get up I grabbed the reins of his horse and headed for the ranch. When he got back father fired him. That was the end of it."

"You didn't tell me about a gold mine."

Kitty frowned. "That's just it. There isn't a gold mine. We had worked hard to build up the ranch and in time that paid off. Over the years the herd grew and money started coming in. Before that we went through some pretty hard times. There were some mines up in the high country that were taking out gold so we thought we would give it a try. We made several trips up there, but we never did find anything. Gil knew about those trips and was convinced we were holding out on him. He thought we had discovered gold and that was why we were doing so well. The truth is our success came from dirt-hard work. He never believed that."

Bruno contemplated what she had said. "Did you say this cowboy's name was Gil?"

"That's right. Do you know him?"

"I knew of a Gil that lived in that country. What ever became of him?"

Kitty shrugged. "I don't know. Father said he rode off and that was the last we ever heard of him. Why?"

"Just curious. He never came back to bother you again?"

"Never saw him again."

Bruno turned his eyes to the road and tried to look uninterested. "By the way I hope you have room for Clay at the ranch. He might be staying there for a day or two."

Kitty's eyes brightened. "Your friends are always welcome at the ranch. As a matter of fact, I wouldn't be surprised if father could use another hand. Maybe we can put him to work."

"I told him that, but he's got some other business to take care of. I doubt if he will be there for long."

They had reached a fork where the main road turned to the east and rose to Nine Mile station. From there it crossed the Mosquito Range and descended into Denver. Below the fork the valley narrowed and small granite dikes rose along the banks of the river. In many places there were tiny paths where deer had walked parallel to the road until they disappeared into the brush that lined the river. As they continued south the trail narrowed and became rougher. The ground that followed the river was strewn with large rocks and there were very few places where the land was level. When the valley widened out again they came to a washout that ran down from the trees to the west. Bruno's eyes searched the gully and the slopes above it. The bottom would make a good place to be drygulched and he took a few minutes to study the land. Finally satisfied that it was safe he led the way across. When they gained the other side the trail had greatly improved.

"Another thing has come up," said Bruno. "I'm going to have to change my name for a while. There are men where we are going that would not hesitate to kill me if they knew who I was. Maybe you can help me with that. I've never thought of changing it and you're probably better at things like that."

"OK, but you are going to have to agree to my choice."

Bruno looked a little skeptical. "As long as it isn't parson something or other there shouldn't be any problem."

"You don't need to worry. I'll figure out something that will fit you."

They rode on in silence. "I don't want to be Methuselah or some other big shot out of the Bible either."

Kitty laughed. "Don't worry; your dignity is safe with me."

"Promise?"

"I promise."

Before them was a small grove of aspens that had sprung

216

up after a fire. The fire had killed many of the large cottonwood trees that had once lined the bank of the river. The giant skeletons of the long dead trees displayed a dignity and beauty that could not be destroyed even in death. Now their large darkened branches offered a graceful sculptured splendor that stood in contrast to the new green shoots of spring. Scattered among the dead trees were tender young pines that had managed to gain purchase in the rocky soil. A slower growing tree, they were tenacious and given the opportunity they would take over the valley. The horses picked their way through the grove until the trail turned to follow the slope of the mountain.

Kitty turned to face him. "You seem to know a lot about the San Juan country. I thought you had never been there before."

"Clay told me a lot of what I know. He wants me to go into the mining business with him. He knows quite a bit about it and I might partner up with him. I told him I would think about it."

Kitty knew she was being lied to again, but did not want to make an issue of it. There was a part of him that he would not share and it was beginning to frustrate her. Anger began to grow and it was time to deal with it.

"Bruno, you are going to have to start trusting me. I told you I will not put up with a man that will lie to me. I'm sharing my life with you and I need to know what is going on. Now tell me the truth!"

"I told you the truth."

"No, you didn't. I read you pretty well and I'm not going to put up with this. If we don't learn to share our hearts with each other we could be headed for trouble. I know you have had a tough past, but things are different now. We're starting a new life and we're both going to have to make some adjustments."

Bruno turned his head to avoid the piercing look that had been aimed in his direction. Finally he pulled up and stopped. "You are right; I have not been giving you the whole story. I was afraid you might not be able to handle it. You are going to have to trust me for a while because I have some things to work out on my own. Can you do that?"

She looked at him quickly. "If I knew what was going on, I could help you. I want to be a part of your life and whatever this deep, dark secret is I want to share it with you. I'm a lot tougher than you think."

Bruno started his horse forward. "This might take a little time. I never dealt with a Christian before and I'm going to have to work out a strategy for that. Now if you want to help me, think up a name for me."

"I've already done that. Trent Lovejoy. How does that sound?"

Bruno flinched. "Trent Lovejoy? Sounds like a Bible salesman. Is that the best you can do?"

"No one will expect you are a gunman with a name like that. You better get use to it because that is what I am going to start calling you."

"Then I'm going to start calling you Lilly White."

"No, you aren't. I'm not the one that needs a new name."

Bruno shrugged. "Suit yourself."

The trail they were following had descended several hundred feet and was following along the edge of a large stand of aspen. Suddenly through a break in the trees Bruno saw a flash of light. It was the kind of a flash that could come from a gun barrel and his guard went up. When he took a closer look, his suspicions were confirmed. Standing in the trees was a riderless horse.

Before he could give warning a shot rang out and bark flew from the tree beside him. He kicked his horse in the flanks and the stallion leaped forward. "Get down in that dead timber," he yelled. "And stay under cover!"

Before she could answer he was gone. The trees on the slope above him were thin and scattered, offering little cover and he raced for the stands of spruce that stood above them. Three more shots rang out as he sped across the ground until finally the boughs of the trees closed around him. Once in the trees he pulled up and leaped to the ground. Pulling his Winchester from the scabbard, he angled up the slope toward the spot where the shots had come from. The gunman had picked a poor place for an ambush. The pines above him ran out into a grove of fire-scarred trees that offered little cover. Behind him was a rock-lined draw with a stream running through it. No horse was going to take on that route. Both men were trapped and they would have to stand and fight.

Bruno had narrowed the distance to a hundred yards when he stopped to take a breather. Up the slope he could see the horse that he recognized as Tray's. Clay had been right about Tray. He had waited until the odds were in his favor. He was a man who was at his best in rough country and with a heart filled with hatred, he would not back down. Only one man would walk away from this fight.

He crouched behind a fallen ponderosa and listened for any kind of movement. As the minutes dragged on he considered his situation. The temptation was great to work his way up the mountain. Not knowing where Tray was, made that a bad idea. There was also a danger in staying here. Tray was an excellent tracker who could move through the forest like a shadow. Given enough time he would expose this position. He could not wait for that to happen. He had to move now.

Just as he readied himself to move a voice rang out. "Your time is up, Turnbull, and the devil has come for you. I have waited a long time for this moment and now you are going to die just like Ben and Billy."

To emphasize his point he fired a shot that ricocheted off a rock at Bruno's feet.

Quickly Bruno looked up to where the shot had come from. He spotted a rifle barrel protruding over a log and he shifted himself to a better position for a shot. "Tray, why don't you come down here and we can talk this over. I don't want to add your name to that list."

The only answer was another shot that tore bark from the side of a tree. Bruno dropped to the ground and rolled coming up behind a log. Pushing his Winchester over the log, he pointed it at the spot where he had seen the rifle barrel, but it was gone. Nothing was moving. Suddenly Tray's horse picked up his ears and turned to watch something moving on the slope above. Tray was on the move and working his way toward this position. Inching his way across the slope, Bruno crossed the distance to where the creek had changed direction to move up the hill. He found a spot behind a jumble of boulders to the left of the last position Tray had occupied and looked for any sign of movement.

Searching the slopes he saw nothing, so he moved up the stream until he was blocked by a large pile of dead branches, logs, and other material left by the last high water.

For a long moment nothing happened. Then for a split second he saw something between the trees. Tray was coming down the slope to where he could get a better shot at his old position and he had momentarily exposed himself. Raising his rifle Bruno fired, clipping a branch above his head. It fell knocking his hat off and he dropped to the ground out of sight.

"That's my last warning, Tray. Give it up now or I shoot to kill."

His answer was a shot that ricocheted off a rock near his head, scattering fragments into the air. Silence followed and for several minutes he could detect no signs of the man. Then he caught a flicker of movement out of the corner of his eye. He spun to fire, but it was too late. Moving around the rocks he inched his way forward. For fifty feet the rocks offered good cover, but ended in a tangle of brush that lined the stream. Crawling along the edge of the brush, he reached a spot where he had a good view of the area above. Protruding from behind a rock was a man's boot. He took careful aim and sent the boot heel flying. The foot was withdrawn, followed by some language that would make profanity sound like a prayer.

For a long time there was no sound and from his position Bruno could cover any attempt to escape, but Tray was not moving. Cautiously he eased himself down to the stream and crossed to the other bank. The side of the stream was lined with a steep cliff that appeared to be impenetrable. Working his way down stream, he came to a place where the rock had fractured leaving a crack that ran up the face thirty feet to a narrow ledge. Picking two fist-size rocks, he jammed one of them in to the crack giving himself a step to lift himself out of the water. From here the crack began to widen and after trying several positions he managed to jam the second rock in the crack five feet higher up. The next section was almost a foot wide, so he wedged his forearm into it and pulled himself up to a new position. The crack was now wide enough to chimney his way up to where the rocks were broken and angled back toward more level ground. Moving quietly, he climbed up to the top and crept silently along the ledge toward Tray's last location.

When he had moved 100 feet he spotted him crouching behind a tree. Silently he stood to his feet and pointed the Winchester at the man. "Drop the rifle, Tray. You don't have a chance."

Spinning around he froze in his tracks. He looked up and it was clear that there was no place he could go for cover. Slowly he set the rifle against the tree. "I should have figured you wouldn't have the guts to face me in a fair fight. You knew you couldn't beat me, didn't you?"

"I'm just trying to spare your life. I'm giving you a chance to get out of this with a whole hide if you promise me you will pack your kit and get out of Colorado. There's nothing left for you here."

Tray's eyes turned ugly with hate and he glared at the man. "I'm not taking you up on it so what are you going to do about it. If you will put that rifle down, we will see who is going to give the orders."

For a long moment Bruno was tempted. The simple answer was to pull the trigger and the problem would be solved, but he was not that kind of a man. He lowered the rifle. "If that's the way you want it, it's your call."

He leaned over and set the rifle against a rock and as he did the ledge beneath him crumbled, throwing him off balance. Taking advantage of the opportunity, Tray grabbed for his gun, but very quickly he realized that he was not in the same class as Bruno Turnbull. Bruno drew and fired before his gun had come level and the bullet slammed into his chest, knocking him back against the tree. Suddenly he realized that something was wrong with his arm, for he could not raise the gun. Then his legs began to give way beneath him and before he knew what was happening he crumpled to the ground and lay still.

Kitty was relieved when she saw Hawk break out of the timber. When Bruno dismounted she threw her arms around him. She clung to him until he reached down and kissed her. When she looked into his face she saw a man she didn't recognize. There was a hollow look that she had not expected. She was seeing a side of the man that she had never seen before. Although he tried to hide it, she could see pain that she could not believe a gunfighter could feel. Whatever had happened on that hill had left an impression. This was a man that had been hurt. Somewhere inside him were emotions that had been suppressed too long.

The day was still young and the couple pointed their horses south. The Arkansas followed a wide and grassy meadow that stretched across the bottom of the valley to tree-covered slopes. In many ways it reminded Kitty of the mountains that surrounded their ranch and the anticipation began to grow to see that beautiful land once again. The trail was easy and they made good time, but for Bruno it was a place of danger. Who else knew where they were? Had Gil sent men to find them? Would there ever be a time when he could ride through this beautiful country without the presence of danger?

The rest of the day passed without incident and it was late when they came to the Fork of the river. Turning their horse to the west they began the climb toward the Continental Divide. As they rose into the thick pine forests apprehension began to trouble Bruno. Most of the trail followed the river and when the trees enclosed them it made a perfect place for an ambush. Every tree and rock offered a danger that could not be avoided. Who else would know that they were here? He was being foolish. He knew there was no one that would bother to go to this much trouble to find him, so he dismissed the idea. He was acting like an old woman and he was disgusted with himself. Leadville was far behind them and so, he hoped, were their problems.

The hour was late when Bruno found a good stopping point. A notch in the rocks led to a patch of grass with a small trickle of water running through it. It was situated in an aspen grove that provided excellent cover, well away from the trail. The tall white trunks would help to hide the smoke from the campfire and there were many dried branches scattered about that would make an excellent supply of smokeless wood. After staking the horses in the grass, he made camp. Kitty took over the cooking duties and together they enjoyed a fine meal of beef and beans, with some baking-powder biscuits.

When daylight came they were on the trail. The going was slow at first, as the way was filled with many deadfalls and scattered rocks. Except for hunting bands of Utes there were few that traveled this part of the mountains and that suited Bruno just fine. In spite of the difficulty of the trail he was enjoying the wild country. As the elevation rose his mind began to absorb the peace that the mountains can bring to a man.

When they reached the pass they gave the horses a breather while they took in the view. It was a lonely place, but before them lay a rugged, beautiful country. Below the rocky ground of the pass were magnificent stands of lodge-pole pines that covered the slopes like the waves of an ocean in unbroken symmetry. In the distance thunder rolled across the ridges and in places sheets of rain fell into the valley. They were standing on top of the world. For a little while all the land they could see was theirs. It was a place of wonder that brought a comfort and security that could not be found in the towns below.

"The mountains shall bring peace to the people," Kitty breathed.

"What?"

"It's a verse I read in the Bible. The mountains shall bring peace to the people and the little hills, by righteousness."[17]

"It sounds like you have been reading that Bible quite a bit."

"What do you think I was doing while you were making the streets of Leadville safe?"

Bruno snorted. "Well, just don't let it corrupt you too much. I have heard people can go crazy from reading that book."

Kitty shot an amused look in his direction. "Don't be too quick to judge. It's got me praying for you and God answers prayers. Your time is coming."

Bruno shook his head and smiled. "Well, don't get your hopes up. I wouldn't want you to be disappointed."

He urged his horse forward and they began their descent. The trail lead down through a barren section of loose shale and the horses began to stumble, forcing them to dismount. For several hundred yards they led them until the ground offered better footing.

With the high country of the divide behind them, the country dropped quickly into valleys filled with vast open plains of fresh, new grass. Streams of clear rushing water danced along rocky streambeds that wound through the grassy meadows. The beautiful country they were traveling through made the miles melt away and they made good time as they crossed the open country. After several days of steady riding they came into Animas City and took rooms at the San Juan Hotel.

Not wanting to compromise Kitty's name, Bruno took a separate room. It was not a practice that he had followed in the past, but this was a special woman and he would never put her in a compromising situation. She was right after all, this was a new day and changes would have to be made.

For Kitty, it was good to be back into civilization. The days in the saddle had worn her down and she needed a break. It had been a long time since she had spent this many hours riding, but it was worth it to be back in her own country again.

It was an easy day's ride to the ranch from here. Anticipation began to grow inside of her as she looked forward to the reunion with her father. How things had changed since she had seen him last! Finally she could understand his heart, for she knew he would be overjoyed when she told him of her conversion. But how could she explain Bruno? Would he be able to accept a man whose life had been marked by killing and violence? Surely there was a way. The Lord had not failed her so far, so why would He start now? What was it she had read in her quiet time? 'You will keep on guiding me all my life with your wisdom and council; and afterwards receive me into the glories of heaven'[18] She would just have to trust the Lord to handle the situation. It would be another chance to trust Him and strengthen her faith.

When daylight came they were on the way. The path to the west followed high above the creek and it was one she had ridden with her father many times. In those days it was an Indian trail, but it was no longer the narrow path she remembered. Wagon traffic from the mines had widened it and it was now beginning to form a recognizable road. It was an easy ride and by mid day they reached the Mancos River. From here the river ran north to the ranch.

The country before them was unlike any Bruno had seen before. It was the kind of country he had longed for all his life. It was a man's country and he knew he was man enough to match it. It was a wide beautiful land that carried a sense of adventure. He was drawn to it as if he were coming home to a place he had never been. To the west were hills of scattered ponderosa pines and scrub oak. To the east the ridges gradually rose in elevation as they crossed the broad land. In the distance, ravines ran up to the slopes of the mountain until they separated the high divide into a series of small summits. In the low country the Mancos River followed a series of bluffs. In many places small caves ran back into the sandstone, offering refuge from the brilliant sun. Many dry streambeds ran down through breaks in the bluffs to join the river. A well-established trail followed the river through the forests and meadows.

As they traveled up the river the gambel oak gave way to a series of groves of Ponderosa and meadows of the best grazing land Bruno had seen since they had left the Arkansas. Scattered among the trees were juniper and pinion to add variety to the forest. The scent of pinion filled the air to bring freshness to this beautiful land.

The ranch house was set in a small cove on the edge of a clearing. The river had gouged out a long shallow cave in the base of an escarpment, leaving a large open area for the buildings that made up the ranch headquarters. A few ponderosas grew by the gate and several of the trees close to the road had been cut down, giving a good view of anyone approaching the house. The range to the east was covered with more groves of trees separated by lush green meadows of grass. Cattle could be seen grazing on the land as far as the eye could see.

Close to the river were several pole corrals with a small stable and a bunk house. The ranch house was large and constructed of adobe with a veranda circling three sides of it. Behind the house was a cook shack that was joined to the house with a long shaded arbor. Next to it was another small adobe building with a steeple and a cross. On the east end of the yard was another, larger stable with a hay loft above it. Adjoining the stable were more corrals.

When they reined their horses in they were met by a man holding a shotgun and it was pointed in their direction. One glance would tell you that Zeb Duncan was a man of rawhide and iron from the top of his battered hat to his dusty boots. He looked to be a man of 50 years with well-muscled arms and shoulders, a result of years of wrestling broncos and steers. His face radiated strength of character that had not given in to the hardships of building a ranch in an empty land. Yet there was a twinkle in the eyes that lent an air of mystery. The stern face softened when he recognized Kitty and he lowered the gun.

Leaping from her horse, Kitty ran to him and threw her arms around his neck. Caught by surprise the gun clattered to the ground and the man staggered back a step. Recovering himself, he returned the hug. "Kitty! You are the last person I expected to see. I thought you were in Denver."

"I left there several weeks ago. I have been in Leadville for a while and I got a chance to come home, so I took it."

"Who's your friend?"

"This is Trent Lovejoy. We met in Leadville and I invited him to come home with me."

Bruno grinned as he stepped down from his horse and extended his hand. "Mr. Duncan, I'm glad to meet you."

Taking the hand, Zeb pumped it vigorously. "It's a pleasure. Any friend of Kitty's is a friend of mine. Come on in the house and we'll have a cup of coffee."

The room they entered was spotlessly clean. On the windows were curtains with a Navajo design and the room was filled with finely crafted furniture right down to the cushions on the chairs. In the center of the room stood a large, well-rounded black woman. She was neatly dressed in a full black skirt and a red and white checkered blouse. When she recognized Kitty her face lit up and she rushed to her, enclosing her in a giant bear hug.

"Lody, lody, Miss Kitty! It's so good to see you. Have you come home to stay?"

"We will have to talk about that. I want you to meet a friend of mine. Trent, this is Hattie Sanford. She has been taking care of my father since before my memory."

Bruno touched his hat. "Ma'am, it's a pleasure."

"Hattie, could you get us a pot of coffee?" Zeb asked. "We got a lot to talk about."

"Yes sir, right away."

The woman disappeared and Zeb pointed them to the table. "She's a good woman. Been with me since my little girl was born. Now tell me what has happened to bring you home."

Kitty shot a glance in Bruno's direction. "The biggest news is that I became a Christian. I'm still pretty new at it and I'm

229

going to depend on you for some sage advice on how to make that work."

Zeb smiled. "I knew that was going to happen. Tell me all about it."

Kitty's face beamed. "I met a lady on the stage to Leadville and to make a long story short, I prayed the prayer and my life is changed. Now I understand things a little better and I can't wait to see what happens next."

Zeb's smile broadened. "Well, praise the Lord! That is an answer to years of praying. And where did you meet Trent?"

Kitty's cheeks flushed red. "That was before I became a Christian. He was the marshal in Leadville and he arrested me for a mix-up I got involved in and helped me get clear of it. We fell in love and we are going to be married."

There was a silence in the room. Bruno shifted uncomfortably. Finally Zeb turned to him. "Kind of quick, wasn't it?"

It was a situation that Bruno had never found himself in before. He searched for the right words. "Mr. Duncan, I love your daughter and I intend to take care of her for the rest of her life. You, too, if you let me."

Another silence. Just then Hattie came through the door balancing a tray and she placed it on the table. "I'll just let you serve yourself. If there is anything you need, just give me a call." Sensing the apprehension in the air, she turned and disappeared.

Zeb glanced around casually, one brow lifting. "Tell me Trent, how long have you been a Christian?"

"Father!"

Bruno held up his hand. "It's all right, Kitty. I can handle it." He turned to Zeb, "Mr. Duncan…"

"Zeb."

"OK, Zeb. I didn't just fall off the turnip wagon yesterday and Kitty is not the first woman I have ever known. I've been around long enough to know that your daughter is very special and I intend to marry her. We want your approval, but win, lose or draw I intend to marry her. We have some differences of opinion on religion, but I am sure we can work that out. I also want to be your friend, but our minds are made up. I'd like to ask for your blessing."

"You didn't answer my question."

"That depends on what you call a Christian. I believe in God and I believe He has been there for me many times when I needed His help. I would never cross Him up and I am happy with things the way they are. I believe in 'live and let live' and I can handle Kitty's new ideas. Not everyone thinks the same way and we have to make allowances for that."

Zeb turned to the woman. "Kitty, why don't you get Hattie and she will help you get settled in. Bruno, I'd like to take a ride with you in the morning and kind of show you around. Now, you will have to excuse me, I have some praying to do."

CHAPTER 12

The men were up at first light. It was cold and gray in the early dawn light, but the stars were already gone and the air was fresh and crisp. Zeb moved out on his Morgan stallion and Bruno matched his pace. Above the ranch a stream ran into the river and they crossed where the land began a gentle rise onto a grassy plain. The stream was already running cold and swift with the winter snow and the horses carefully made their way through the rushing water. In the distance a ripple of rock lifted from the valley floor and ran for several miles until it joined the heights of the distant mountains.

"That's the Hogback over there," said Zeb as he pointed to the tree-covered ridge. "It runs up to where it joins Indian Ridge. Part of my range is behind it and runs as far as Burro Mountain north of here. Part of the Mancos runs behind the Hogback through Hells Hole and that's the only way to get to the high range. There's a lot of good grass and water up there and that's where most of the cattle spend the summer. Hells Hole is the canyon you saw running north of the ranch. South of here there's a long canyon that runs up to the La Plata Mountains and that's where the East Mancos River runs. That is the south end of the ranch. I've got thousands of acres here of good grazing land and we have been blessed by the Lord to have it. This year we had little snow, but it was cold. Good for the grass and it cures on the stem. It's mighty fine country for grass up in those northern mountains too. Its high country, but most years the cattle winter right here on this range."

Bruno lifted his hat and scratched his head. "You were mighty lucky to find this country when you did. I hope I will be able to do that before the land runs out."

"Is that your plan, to set up a ranch and marry Kitty?"

Bruno nodded his head. "That's what I had in mind. I've got some business going right now that should give me what I need to get started. Do you know of any land around here where we can make a start?"

The ground before them had become rocky and Zeb turned his horse from the stream and he scrambled up a bank to an opening in the pines. Before them was a magnificent sweep of open range that ran for miles across the mesa. In places there were stands of ponderosa pine and gambel oak with lush grass filling the spaces between.

It was a beautiful land and for Bruno the manifestation of his dreams. The only problem was it was not his. In his heart he envied Zeb for the luck that had put him here at the right time. Could that happen again or had the times changed and opportunity disappeared forever? Time would tell.

Following Zeb's lead, they walked the horses south across a series of small hills toward a small dome that rose above the land. It was the culmination of a long ridge that defined the rim of a deep canyon that ran up to the peaks of the mountains. Below the dome was a small lake. Turning his horse toward the lake, Zeb cantered up to a place where several dead trees lay on the ground. There was a well-used fire ring there with a large stack of firewood beside it. When the horses were tied, Zeb built a fire and fixed a hot meal. Bruno took the horses to the lake to drink and picketed them again. When he returned to the fire the coffee was ready. After they had eaten, Zeb poured the last of the coffee and banked the fire. Settling himself on a log, he studied his companion for a few moments before he spoke.

"Trent, in the last few years many ranchers have come in here and set up cattle operations. All of the good range has been taken and it would be hard to find a ranch like this one. The D bar D is a very successful ranch because of all the hard work we put into it. Other than a few problems with rustlers, we have a good operation going and I'd like to keep it that way. I'm getting older now and I need to think about Kitty's future and the future of the ranch. You say you want to start a ranch and I can understand your feelings on that. If you had been here 20 years ago you might have been able to do it. Times have changed and you'd be buckin' a stacked deck if you tried to do that now."

"I'm not asking for an easy ride."

"That's good because you won't be getting it. Like I said, I'm getting older and I would welcome you to join us in running this ranch. You could look all through this country and not find a better place. I could save you a lot of hard work if you would join us. Would you be interested in working with me?"

For a few moments Bruno was silent as he watched buzzards circling above the ridge. He turned his eyes to the snow-capped mountains to the east and his soul was filled with wonder. This was a big country and a man could ask for nothing more. Yet it was not his land and that was not the way he had planned it.

"That's a mighty generous offer, but I want to do this myself. I want a place where a man can spread his shoulders and answer to no man. I hadn't thought about working for someone else."

Zeb smiled. "I understand those feelings and they were the same ones I had when I came into this country, but there is a difference between that time and now. When I came here this was open country and the only people were the Utes. It was a tough place to start a ranch, but my mind was made up. I was going to make a home here or die tryin'. It took a lot of years, but we did it. It still takes a man to hold the land. You would have more to fight than just the elements. In a few more years, there will be law to help out, but until then it is up to us. We can be a lot of help to each other. I can give you a hand up that wasn't there for me. It would be a place for you to start."

Bruno watched a duck playing in the rushes beside the lake. "I will admit that is a tempting offer. I will have to give it some thought."

Zeb poked at the fire with a stick. "There's one other thing that I have to get cleared up. Yesterday I asked if you were a Christian and I didn't get a satisfactory answer. You're not, are you?"

Bruno looked up and their eyes met. He smiled "Not the way you see it."

"That is a real concern for me when you tell me you plan to

marry my daughter. The Bible says 'Be ye not unequally yoked together with unbelievers'[19] and that is what you are planning to do. I'm not going to tell Kitty that she can't marry you if that is her choice, but I can't put my blessing on a marriage like that. It goes against what the Lord planned for his children. I can't stand with anything that goes against His will."

Bruno's face darkened. "We love each other. Doesn't that count for anything?"

Zeb nodded his head. "Yes, love is important and in the beginning it would carry you through some of the tough times. Eventually your differences would cause real problems and your marriage would suffer. It might not even survive. There is only one answer that I know to solve the problem."

"You mean for me to become a Christian?"

"That's right. You need to accept God's love and He will teach you what love is all about."

Bruno smirked and looked into the fire. "I know what love is about."

Zeb shook his head. "You might think so, but God's love is different than the love you know. Let me explain it in a way you might understand. You made a living with that gun. A gun, like any other source of power, is a force for either good or evil. People know you and respect you because of your gun. The good people are comforted by it. The evil ones fear it. If they know it or not people's lives are changed by the way they react to that gun and the authority behind it. Love is like that. God's love protects those who receive Him and His protection. It gives them a safe future. The ones that reject it have much to fear. Like the authority of your gun, their future is determined by how they respond to that love. It is much more powerful than a gun. Like the men you faced, you will have to choose how it will affect your future. With that gun you are a defender of the right. God is a better defender because of His love than you are with that gun."

"You mean God has a gun?"

"A gun of the heart. His love changes lives and it will change yours if you let Him. It's up to you to make the right choice."

"The only love I am interested in is the love that Kitty and I share."

Zeb nodded his head. "God knew you thought that way. It just might be that He put Kitty in your path so He could show you His love. It might have been the only way he could get your attention. The most important thing is not if you love each other. It is if you accept God's love and let Him change your life with it. The choice you make will determine where you spend eternity."

Bruno was anxious for the conversation to be over and searched for a way to change the subject. "Looks like you're having a good year for calves. When do you do the branding?"

"That will be coming soon. I've got a good bunch of boys and they know how to handle it. Why don't you throw in with us and give us a hand?"

Bruno threw his stick into the fire. "You've got a deal. I have a friend coming down from Leadville and he could use a job for a while. Could you use two hands?"

Zeb stood up and emptied his cup into the fire. "If he's not afraid of work. Now let's get going, we got a lot of ground to cover before the sun sets."

Gil stood in the window of the ancient cliff dwelling

and studied the canyon below. Beyond the edge of the cave the canyon stretched out in a long, meandering expanse of sand and sagebrush. For miles the canyon lay flat and was surrounded with high cliffs that rose to the canyon rim. In many places the walls of the canyon were shear with a drop of several hundred feet to the talus slopes below. The trail that lead to the hideout was barely visible in the stream bed that followed the narrow canyon floor.

He studied the lone rider as he approached. Even from a distance he recognized the pinto that Clay rode. It had been a long time since he had talked to the man. Some of the reports he had gotten from Leadville had not been good and he was anxious to clear the air. The whole setup was in danger of collapse and if he was going to lose it, he was going to find out why. Clay would have the answers he needed. He was a good man and one of the few men he trusted.

Urging his horse up a small draw, Clay pushed his way through the scrub oak that blocked the entrance to the draw until he stood before an elaborate corral. It had been built in this small ravine in such a way that it was completely concealed from the main canyon. The stable had been built in a small hollow and not even the roof rose above the brush to reveal the presence of the structure. In the corral were several horses. Stripping the gear from the pinto, he slapped it on the rump and turned toward the stone pueblo that filled the hollow in the side of the cliff.

Gil had found this place years ago and had set it up as his headquarters for the many enterprises he was involved in. The spot had been chosen well. It offered many comforts that could not be expected in this remote location. There were many cliff dwellings in the area, but this one stood out from the rest.

Situated several miles from the Mancos River, the ruin had never been visited since ancient times. It was one of the few ruins that had a spring. It was a good source of fresh water and it flowed year round. There was enough water to take care of the many horses that came and went.

There were many rooms in the ruin that had been worked over to make living quarters for a dozen men. Most of the time the rooms were empty and that was the way Gil liked it. It was a place of deployment and not a pleasure resort. Only the outlaws knew of the existence of this place and if anyone strayed into the canyon they would never be allowed to leave. As the operation had grown Gil had found he needed to concentrate his time on running the show, so it had become a home that he seldom left.

Mounting the stone steps that led to the main room, Clay reviewed his facts. There would be questions to answer and he had better have the right answers. Gil was not a man who cut much slack on the basis of friendship. If the money from the Leadville operation was drying up, there had better be a good reason for it. Clay had given it much thought and he was ready.

When he stepped into the room Gil looked up from behind a makeshift desk and motioned toward a crude bench. "Have a seat, Clay. Been a while since I have seen you."

Clay dropped the saddle bag by the door. "That's all right. I been riding for days and it feels good to be standing."

Gil pulled a cigar from his pocket and offered it to Clay, but he refused. "I thought you were a cigar man. You giving up all your vices?"

"Na. I just ain't in the mood. This isn't a pleasure trip. I wanted to find out what you plan to do about the situation in Leadville."

Gil scratched a match on his britches and lit the cigar. "I was hopin' you could fill me in on that. The things I been hearin' aren't making me very happy. It sounds like your new man is taking that marshaling job pretty serious. Did you explain to him whose side he is on?"

"I expect you get your information from Stew and his friends. There is more to it than what he told you. Bruno didn't have much choice with Dan. You know he was a hothead and all he did was defend himself. Stew should consider himself lucky that he is alive. If Bruno hadn't cut him some slack, he would have been dead too."

Gil took the cigar from his teeth and scowled. "I ain't worried about that, Dan was bound to catch one sooner or later anyway. It's Billy I want to know about."

"He didn't have much choice on that one either. Billy killed a miner to get his cabin and when Bruno went to talk to him, Billy called him out. He was just a little too slow, that's all."

Gil leaped to his feet, his eyes ugly with hate. "That's no excuse for what he did. Billy was my son and I want his hide! He's going to pay for what he did and I got just the man to take care of it."

Clay put up his hands. "Take it easy Gil. It's all over now and if you push it, more people are going to die. My advice is just let it ride. You can't bring Billy back by killing someone else and right now there is a lot of money to be made up there. Opportunity won't last forever.

Regaining control, Gil sat back down and stuck his cigar

back into his teeth. "I don't need any advice from you, so shut up about it. Bruno has got to pay and the sooner the better."

Just then a scar-faced man stepped into the room, his bulky body blocked out much of the light and he stopped. Spotting Clay, he frowned. With difficulty he suppressed the bitter hatred inside and turned to Gil. "I'm ready to go. I'm taking Henry and Bernie with me." He shot a glance at Clay. "Is there anything you need done before we leave?"

Gil dusted the ashes from his cigar. "Not at the moment. Just get up there and do what I told you to do. If you can't take care of the marshal, don't bother to come back."

Stews lips tightened "You don't need to worry about that. This is one job that will be a pleasure." He shot a glance at Clay and stalked out of the room.

When the men had left Clay turned to Gil. "There's one other thing. I got a new man that can replace Bruno. He's just as fast with a gun and he knows how to think. I can bring him here if you want to take a look at him."

"If he's anything like the last one you brought I'm not interested."

"You'll like this guy. He's ten times the man Stew is and there's not a man here that he can't lick. He's got sand and he can take orders. Why don't you give him something to do and let him show you what he's made of? "

Gil gazed out the window. "If he's as good as you say he is, I'll give him a try. I've got a job that needs checked out at the Smuggler Mine up above Columbia.[20] Word has it that they are taking ore out of there that runs $1,200 to the ton. We need to get a piece of that action. They are packing it out over the range to Ouray on burros and on to Alamosa from there. I heard they're taking mule trains out that are packing $10,000 at a time. I need somebody to go up there and see what kind of security they are using. That would be a chance to try out your new man."

"We'll take care of it."

Gil smiled. "Be sure and take a coat. That mine's at 12,000 feet and you're going to need it."

"I said we would take care of it. I want to know what you're going to do about Leadville."

"Stew is going to see if it can be salvaged. If it can be, he will be running the show up there. I've got some other things for you to do."

"Like what."

Gil rolled his cigar in his teeth and glanced up at Clay. You take care of that Smuggler business first and when that's done we'll talk about it."

"Fair enough. I'll see you in a couple of days. Then I will introduce you to my new friend."

For Clay the land through which he rode was new. In the past he had always come to the hideout from the east through the Red Mesa country. It was a country that no one traveled and there was enough cover to stay out of sight. This canyon was confining and he preferred country where he could control the situation around him. This was a place of steep draws and escarpments of standing rock that offered few exits. Years of riding the owl hoot trail had taught him to leave himself a way of escape whenever he could. A man that was careless in this line of work did not last long.

When he reached the Mancos River the land opened up and he followed the river north. Bruno's instructions had been good and he enjoyed riding in this beautiful country. The trail followed the river through the open range and onto the ranch. When he rode into the yard, Bruno was there to meet him.

A quick look around brought a smile to Clay's face. "Looks like you found yourself a home." He said as he stepped down from his horse. "Before you get too comfortable I have some business for you."

Bruno grinned. "That wouldn't be a note of jealousy I hear, would it?"

Clay chuckled. "I just don't want you to go soft on me. We still have some unfinished business to take care of."

A glance toward the house assured Bruno that they were alone. He motioned for Clay to follow. "Let's get that horse taken care of before we get into that. Not everyone around here knows what we do for a living and it might be easier to talk in the stable."

When they were inside, Clay stripped the saddle from his horse and hung it on the side of the stall. "Had a little talk with Gil this morning. He said he was willing to give you a try."

Bruno hesitated. He hadn't thought about the gang since he had gotten to the ranch and the idea of going back into that life was not as appealing as it had been. This new arrangement was already taking a hold of his soul and it was hard to think of leaving it, even for a little while. Yet the old problem still remained. To build a herd cost money and that was something he did not have enough of. There were still some hard trails to ride before he reached that dream.

He frowned. "Tell me what you got."

"Does that mean you are in?"

"That depends on what you tell me. I'm not making any long-range plans right now. I been thinking it over and this is a pretty good deal I have here."

"It's not going to get you that ranch."

"I could do a lot worse. Even if I do go along, don't make any long range plans. When I get the money I need I'm leaving and I don't care what Gil thinks."

Clay nodded. "Suit yourself. Right now I got a little piece of business to take care of and I'd like you to ride along. Another thing. From now on you are going to have to use another name."

"I've already done that. You can call me Trent Lovejoy."

"That sounds like a Bible salesman."

"Kitty came up with it so you are going to have to live with it. That is the only name Zeb knows me by, so don't be calling me Bruno. I have enough problems with him already. "

He nodded. "Suit yourself."

"Now what's this business we have to take care of?"

I want you to take a little ride with me. We're going up to Columbia to check out the security on the gold coming out of the Smuggler mine."

"Were breaking into mines now?"

"Not exactly. We're interested in how they ship the gold. They're taking a lot of gold out of there by mule train. We have to find out what kind of security they are using. "

The sound of approaching footsteps caught their attention and they turned to see Kitty coming into the stable. Clay grabbed a handful of grass and began rubbing the horse down. Bruno began searching for an explanation.

"It's good to see you again, Clay," she said as she sized up the situation. "I hope you will join us for supper."

He tipped his hat politely and grinned. "Yes, ma'am. It would be a real pleasure to have home cookin' again. It's been a while."

While it was still dark the men were on the trail. By sunup they had crossed Haycamp Mesa and dropped down to the Dolores River. As they followed the river, the land rose out of the juniper and pinion country into forests of Douglas fir and aspen. It was a lonely and desolate land of rock, trees and water. Gradually the ragged canyons gave way to mountain slopes that followed the river for many miles, giving way to lush valleys of green grass and groves of aspen and spruce. When the canyon forked the men followed the river to the east. Many times the riders crossed the icy waters, weaving a crooked trail through the valley until the land widened out. It was wild and beautiful country and Bruno's heart was filled with delight as they moved through the pristine wilderness. This was country that Bruno understood and it was refreshing to be traveling it again. It was late in the day when they saw smoke rising from the chimneys of a town. Neither man had seen Rico, but the stories of the new finds there had been told far and wide.

Rico reminded Bruno of Leadville, only on a much smaller scale. Silver had been discovered the year before and the streets were full of miners, boomers, and other fortune seekers. Small businesses and saloons had already appeared and the scene was all too familiar. There would be miners here from Leadville that would recognize the men, so to avoid that they pushed on up the canyon.

Night was closing in when they made camp. The spot they found was almost perfect. Situated in a jumble of large boulders, there was just room enough for a fire and their bedrolls. There was good grass for the horses and an abundance of dry wood for the fire and with the thick grove of trees between the camp and the trail their small fire could not be seen from below. Clay was elected cook, so while he fixed supper Bruno gathered spruce boughs and made some comfortable beds. After a meal of beef and frying-pan bread they settled back with a cup of stiff, black cowboy coffee.

For a long time Bruno lay awake. The long ride had given him time to think about the changes in his circumstances. He knew the plans he had made were coming apart at the seams with little chance to salvage them. How long would it be before Gil figured out who he really was? Sooner or later someone would finger him and his life wouldn't be worth the price of an old boot. The smart thing would be to move on, but Kitty had made that impossible. Could he buy enough time to put together the money he needed? The chances were not good. On the other hand, if he took Zeb up on his offer he could get out of it now and no one would be the wiser. Could he work for another man again? Was his pride worth the price that it could demand? The path before him was getting narrow and time was running out. It was only a matter of time before they found him out. One thing was sure; Kitty was worth any price he had to pay. He was committed to building a good life for her no matter what the price. It was time to come up with a new plan.

Early in the morning they rode into Columbia and it didn't take long to learn the location of the Smuggler mine. It was the largest operation in the area with half the town working there. The trail to the mine began at the foot of the mountain, just a few hundred yards from town. The trail was little more than a narrow ledge that clung to the mountain where the winds swept down from the heights with a chilling gale. Pulling their coats tightly around them, the men followed the winding trail along the rocky cut. As the trail ascended the horses labored bravely, their nostrils flared as they fought to fill their lungs with air.

With the elevation rise deep banks of snow began to appear. They had been sculptured into beautiful shapes by the bitter winds that frequented the higher elevations. In places the trail had been covered by snow slides that had broken loose from the snow pack that clung to the peaks above. In some places the trail dropped off for a thousand feet and any movement of snow would have brought instant disaster. Hawk was a sure-footed mountain horse and Bruno had learned to trust his judgment even on an icy trail.

Finally the buildings of the Smuggler came into view. Situated on several large benches they clung precariously to the mountain. Narrow flats had been enlarged to accommodate the large mining operation and no space had been wasted. Scattered across the mountain were large buildings that housed the mill, dry house, offices, and mining equipment. The snow fields that covered the side of the mountain were broken occasionally with fir trees and stumps were beginning to show through where the snow had begun to melt. At the end of the trail stood a log building that appeared to be an office.

At the desk sat an old man intensely studying a large ledger that lay open before him. His face was deeply lined and tanned from many years of exposure to the elements, but his clothes were neat and clean. When he glanced up his eyes took in every detail and he laid down his pen. "If you boys are looking for work you will have to go to the main office. That's where they do the hiring."

Clay pulled his hat off and ran his fingers through his hair. Making an effort to smile, he put out his hand. "My name is Clay Coffin. This here is Bruno Turnbull. "We heard you was lookin' for guards for the gold shipments. We'd like to hire on."

The man looked puzzled. "Somebody sure did steer you wrong, mister. We ain't looking for guards but we can always use two good strong men in the mine. They can put you on right away."

Clay frowned. "We ain't interested in that. We heard you were shipping a mule train out of here every week and sending it down to Ouray. That's some tough country and you need two good men like us."

"We're shipping a lot more than that, but we don't hire just anybody that walks in the door for that kind of work. We got people we brought up from Texas that can handle any security we need. Used to be Texas rangers and you can't get any better men than that. Now if you boys don't want jobs underground, you had better head back to where you came from. We don't allow strangers on the property."

Clay grinned. "Suit yourself." Then his eyes brightened. "It was a long ride up here. Do you suppose you could make an exception and show us around the place? We heard a lot about the Smuggler and we shore would like to see some of it."

A frown appeared on the man's face and he stood to his feet. "Mr., we don't make any exceptions to that rule. Why are you so interested in knowing about what is going on here anyway?"

"Just curious that's all. We never seen an operation this big before."

"No, I'm not buying that," the man growled. "I know what you're doing. You came up here to check out our operation. That's it isn't it! I had a bad feeling about you the minute you walked in the door. You're nothing but a couple of thieves.

You better get on your horses and head back to town before something bad happens to you. If I ever see you on this property again, I'll sic the dogs on you, now get and don't ever come back."

"Wait a minute, you don't understand…"

"I understand very well. I know everything I need to know about your kind. Now get out of here!"

When they were outside Bruno laughed. "Clay, I got a good piece of advice for you. Next time we have to sweet-talk someone you better let me do it. I was afraid you were going to get us shot."

Turning toward his friend Clay's face turned ugly. Then thinking better of it he grinned. "You may be right. I might not have won any friends, but I did find out that the stories were true. Gil will be glad to know that. It will be up to him to decide what he wants to do about it. Our work is done and it's time to head for home."

The day was already warming when they reached the fork in the canyon. It had been a long ride from the mine and the country had transformed itself from the deep snows of winter to the baking heat of the canyons. The men had talked little on the way back, each busy with his own thoughts. It had been a time of reflection for Bruno. The offer Zeb had made was looking better all the time. The times had changed the country and things were different than what he had expected. What the times had not changed, Kitty had. She was a woman any man would give his soul to have and he had allowed himself to be manipulated. Somehow it didn't matter though, because he knew if he looked all of his life he could not find another like her. She was the ultimate woman. Now he had put her in

249

a place of danger. She was a woman with spunk, but was that enough? And what about this new religious kick? At first he had not taken it seriously, as he had thought it was a passing fancy. He was no longer sure that was true. What would he do if it didn't go away? He shook his head. There would be enough time to deal with that later. The world was closing in on him and it was time to regain control. The first step was an obvious one. He had to get out of this gang as quickly as he could, but how. Gil was no fool. He would have to play along for a while. His chance would come.

Clay turned his horse to the east and pulled up." The hideout is up that canyon and from here on you need to be on your guard. Gil keeps a sentinel hidden in the rocks up in there and there is no telling where he might be. They won't know you and I can't promise they wouldn't take a shot at you. "

"But I'm with you."

"Doesn't matter. They might figure I am a prisoner. Gil doesn't take any chances on having this place found out."

Bruno took in the scene before him. The canyon was a lonely place of desolate and barren ground. Scattered through the sagebrush were a few pinions and Junipers that had managed to cling to life in a place dominated by red rock and sand. The walls of the canyon formed a trap and there were few places where a man on a horse could escape. It would be a bad place to die, but what place was good for that? It didn't matter though; he was not going to back up. He was not in the habit of running and whatever he was getting into he would handle. There was always a way.

"I just hope they aren't too trigger-happy. I don't have many friends in this country."

"Don't worry, you're probably safe. My horse is the only

pinto that comes in here and they will recognize it. If I'm wrong you better find a rock to get behind."

"Is this the only way in?"

Clay kneed his horse forward. "From this end. The hideout is in a notch in the side of the canyon and just before you get there it splits and runs out on Red Mesa. There is a spring up behind the ruins and that is where we get our water. The ravines are short and steep, but on the plateau there is better grass for the horses."

The men rode on in silence. As the distance dropped behind them the canyon wound around and narrowed as they gained elevation. Here and there in the walls there were ravines that cut through the slopes that ran up to the top of the mesa on each side. When they reached another split in the canyon they turned to follow a barely discernable trail that led off to the right. Suddenly a man stepped out from behind a large rock with a rifle in his hands.

"Hold it right there, Boys." He turned the rifle toward Bruno and for a long moment looked him over. "Who is this hombre, Clay? I don't recollect seeing him before."

"It's OK, Jed. This is Trent Lovejoy. He's the new man I told Gil about. He's expecting him."

"Lovejoy, aye. Sounds like a Bible salesman."

Clay grinned. "You wouldn't know a Bible salesman if I hit you over the head with one. Now put up that rifle and let us go."

"I got orders not to let anyone in that I don't know. Nobody told me about a new man coming in."

"Well, I'm telling you now. I'll take the responsibility."

Reluctantly the man lowered the gun and nodded. "If I

got your word, I guess it's OK. You mind your manners when you get up there. Gil's in a bad mood."

Clay tipped his hat with a grin and urged his horse forward. When they were out of earshot he nodded his head toward the man. "Jed's a good man and you don't have to worry about him. Gil's the one you better watch out for. He's got no sense of humor at all."

Bruno scowled. "Neither have I. Lets go see if this big man is all he is cracked up to be."

It was only a short distance past the fork to the hideout. From the canyon floor a narrow trail led up to where the cliff dwelling had been built. When they put up their horses Bruno got his first chance to look around.

"Gil found this place several years ago," said Clay. "There's no way to get into the ruin from the mesa except the ravine behind the stable. Gil figured it would make a great hideout and has been using it ever since he organized the gang."

Tucked into the cliff wall was a high arch that enclosed a bench of considerable length. On the bench were several small stone buildings and one house that was larger than the rest. All of the structures were built well back from the edge and were partially concealed from the bottom of the canyon. A man with a rifle across his lap was sitting outside of the house where he had an excellent view of the whole canyon. When they approached, Clay gave him a nod and stepped into the building. Sitting behind the desk was Gil Davis.

CHAPTER 13

Gil stood to his feet and extended his hand. "Come on in Mr. and make yourself at home. My name is Gil.?"

Bruno took the hand and shook it. "Trent Lovejoy. I've been hearing a lot about you. This is quite an operation you have here."

"We make out. Clay has been telling me some good things about you. He says you are good with that gun. Are you, or is it just talk?"

Bruno's face sobered, but he caught himself before he spoke. "I've sent my share up the flume when they needed killing. Is that the kind of man you are looking for?"

The jab had hit a nerve and he smiled. "What I mean is, I hear you are a man that nobody tackles head on without giving it some serious thought. Is that true?"

"You're wearing a gun. You want a demonstration?"

Gil's face went sober. He had never seen eyes that cold and

he had faced down many a man that had made a living with a gun. "Are you trying to pick a fight with me? I wouldn't advise it. You don't have many friends here and I don't want to ruin your day. Now why don't we back up and start again. What makes you think I can use you?"

For a long moment Bruno looked into the man's eyes. This was a man that could help him if he played his cards right. There was nothing to gain by confronting him and a great deal to lose. He relaxed and tried to look pleasant. "I've been around and had my share of trouble. I've faced some of the worst men that hell ever spit out and I punched their tickets to send them back. I'm not afraid of man or beast and I'll take on anybody you can stand up in front of me. I came here because I heard there was money to be made and that is my only interest. If you are as good at running this show as I am at getting the job done, we'll get along just fine."

Gil smiled. "That's the kind of man I'm looking for. How'd you meet Clay?"

"Had a few drinks with him in Central City a while back. He said you could use a good man. I had to give it some thought before I decided to join up."

"Well, if you are as good as you say you are, we'll get along just fine." He turned toward Clay. "Tell me what you found out at the Smuggler."

"Only that the stories you heard were true. They're puttin' out so much gold up there it will break your back to carry it all away. They are running burros down to Ouray every few days, but they have hired on some Texas Rangers to guard it. Whoever you send up there had better be ready for trouble. Those Rangers are a salty lot."

"Trent, do you think you are up to that?

"We can take care of it."

"I'm going to send you and Clay and a few of the boys up there to take care of it. That will be a good chance to get your feet wet."

While they were was speaking two men stepped into the room. One of them was a big man with a scar on his face and when he saw Bruno he froze in his tracks. His hand dropped for his gun, but before he could bring it level Bruno pulled his and chopped it down on his wrist, knocking the gun from his hand. When he tilted his gun a little it was pointed at the man's heart.

"You might want to think twice before you pick that gun up. I won't cut you any slack the next time."

Stew's face went red with fury. It had been a long time since that day in Central City, but the memory of it had not dimmed. Angrily he turned to Gil. "Is this the new man you said was coming? This is Bruno Turnbull. He's killed off half the men you sent to Leadville."

For a moment the room was silent and then Gil sat down and smiled. "So this is the famous Bruno Turnbull that I've heard so much about. I admire your courage, but not your good sense."

"You can't believe everything you hear. If you're listening to this tin horn you've not heard the whole story. He's wanted to kill me ever since that run in at Central City. He's a lying coward and he's going to get you in trouble if you keep him around."

While he was talking the other man had slipped into the shadows of the back of the room. Moving up behind Bruno, he jabbed his gun in his back. "You better drop it Turnbull, 'cuz I can put a hole in you anytime I please. What me to kill him, Gil?"

There was a reckless light in Gil's eyes when he leaped to his feet. "Henry, you just back off. I've been waiting for this moment for a long time. No one is going to deprive me of the pleasure of killing this sidewinder myself."

"Hold on a minute," Clay burst out. "You forget he made you a lot of money on the Emperor deal and if the boys had behaved themselves, there wouldn't have been any trouble. He's a better gun hand than any one of you and he's worth ten times the man Stew is. He can make you a lot of money."

Turning slowly toward Henry, Bruno kept his gun pointed at Stew. The gun was still pointed at his heart when he looked him in the eye, he smiled a little. "Why don't we all put our guns down and talk this out before some one gets hurt. Gil, I can fill you in on what happened in Leadville and I'll tell you the parts that Stew left out."

"The only part I'm interested in is the part where you killed my son. You shot him down in cold blood and you're going to pay for that."

Bruno spoke quietly. "Lem Dorset came to my office one day and explained to me how Billy had killed his partner to get their cabin. I went to the saloon to find out what Billy had to say about it. When I asked him to come to the office, he refused and pulled his gun. I had no choice but to kill him."

"That's a lie!" Stew barked. "You shot him down in cold blood on the street without even giving him a call. You murdered him!"

"Stew, you weren't even there and some one has givin you a bum steer. The only…"

Before he could finish Stew jerked a knife from inside his

shirt and lunged at Bruno. When he sidestepped, Stew fell into Henry, knocking him off balance. Grabbing for Henry's gun, he ripped it from his hand and swung it around toward Bruno. Before he could fire, Clay's gun roared and the bullet caught Stew in the chest spinning him around. Swaying unsteadily on his feet, he tried to raise the gun, but his strength was gone. He tried to open his mouth to speak, but it was too late for words. The gun slid from his fingers and he fell to the floor. With one last effort he tried to rise, but to no avail. His fight for consciousness was lost and death closed his eyes forever.

"OK, everybody just stay where you are," Clay ordered. "We're getting' out of here and I'll kill the first man that comes through that door. Bruno, are you all right?"

"So far. Let's go"

When they burst into the sunlight the guard met them. Before he could aim his gun Bruno caught him in the jaw with a punch that drove him over the side of the bench and into the rocks below.

Other outlaws began to appear and guns roared. Sprinting down the stairs, the men reached the corral while confusion reigned above. A whistle brought Hawk running and Bruno leaped into the saddle. Reining him around he headed for the back of the corral. Hawk was eager to run and he cleared the four rail fence at a dead run. Encouraged by what he had seen, Clay's horse followed suit and they headed up the ravine and into the trees before any of the outlaws could reach their horses.

The ravine was filled with scrub oak and Pinyon, but there was a faint path that led up through the brush. Bruno pulled up to consider what his next move would be. When he turned to look back Clay flew past him through a narrow space in the brush and up into the trees above.

"Come on, I know the way," he yelled over his shoulder. "We got to keep moving."

The loose rocks of the path offered poor footing for the horses, but their determined feet carried them forward. When they reached the mesa top they had gained a substantial lead. The outlaws were just getting organized and some of them had started up the ravine.

The mesa top offered more open space. Once they had gained a little distance they slowed the pace to give the horses a break. After they had covered several miles Clay pulled up on a little knoll to allow Bruno to catch up. Hunching over in the saddle, it was clear he had been hit.

Clay urged his horse alongside and stopped. "How bad is it?"

"Bad enough. I can handle it, though."

"We're going to have to keep moving, Partner. Are you going to be able to keep up?"

Bruno forced a smile. "You just lead the way. I'll keep up."

"We got to get off this mesa before they catch us. I know some safe places where ... are you sure you are going to be all right?"

Sitting up in the saddle, Bruno pulled open his shirt and inspected the wound. "Maybe we'd better split up; I'm afraid I'm going to slow you down. I'll meet you back at the ranch."

"Don't talk foolishness. How bad is it?"

Bruno made an effort to hide the pain. "Looks like it went on through and I don't think it hit anything important. I can patch this up and meet you later. You better get moving."

Clay leaned over and inspected the wound. "You're losing a good bit of blood there. We're going to have to get you to a doctor."

Tearing a piece off of his shirt, Bruno plugged the holes. Then he looked at Clay and tried to look indifferent. "That's going to have to do for now. You lead out and show me this safe place you had in mind. I may need a place to go to ground."

Clay looked skeptical. "I don't think your doctorin' is going to hold up very long. Are you sure you can ride?"

"Partner, I don't have any choice. Right now, we had better make some distance or those boys are going to add some more holes to my collection. I'm going to have to get back to the ranch before Gil decides to go there and cause some trouble. We'd better split up."

Clay scratched his head and frowned. "I don't want to leave you like this. If they…"

"Partner, this is only a scratch. We'd better get moving. You know this country, and what to do so show me the way."

Clay shrugged. "Suit yourself. If we ride east we will come to the La Plata River. There is a place where Cherry Creek runs into it. I could lead them south from there and join you later. We got some miles to make before we get there. Are you really sure you can do it?"

Bruno raised his head. "If we don't get moving, it won't matter. Let's go."

"You're sure?"

"Let's go."

Clay looked back and scanned the mesa. In the distance he could see a small cloud of dust. "They've made the rim and they're headed this way. We better get off this hill before they spot us."

Turning their horses toward the east, they moved out at a ground-eating lope. The country was relatively flat and there were no tracks, which suggested the area was rarely traveled. A light wind stirred the juniper and kicked up clouds of dust from the horse's hooves.

"With any luck at all those men will head to the south," said Clay. "There are some trails that way and I'm guessing they will figure that's where we went."

"Where's this going to take us?"

"To a place close to where the waters join. If they are still behind us I can leave enough trail to lead them south. That will buy you enough time to get to the ranch. Red Mesa is south of here. I'll head for that."

Both men knew that the lead they now had would not last and they pushed the horses as hard as they dared. The soft sandy soil of the mesa top was hard on the animals and it left a trail that a blind man could follow. With Bruno's wounds, it was only a matter of time before they would be overtaken.

Finally the hills gave way to a green valley with wide expanses of grass and sagebrush. "I think we lost them," said Clay as he looked over his shoulder. It's only a couple of miles to The La Plata. Looks like we're going to make it, Partner."

Bruno looked skeptical. "Don't count your chickens before they're hatched. It doesn't take much of a tracker to figure out where we went."

Clay pulled his hat off and dusted it on his leg. "Well, we'll know shortly. Once we make the La Plata, we should be clear."

It was a short ride to the shallow canyon where the river ran. At the rim of the canyon Bruno pulled up and looked back. In one of the gulches that ran out of the mesa he spotted a dust cloud that was growing larger and several riders leading it. "Clay, look over there. Looks like we will have to stand a fight."

A look to the west confirmed to Clay that the riders were gaining ground. "I don't think it would be smart to take that bunch on. I'll leave some tracks and hopefully they will follow me."

"That's a bad idea. If those guys catch you they'll kill you sure. If we stick together we can lick them."

"I don't think so," Clay said as he watched the distant riders. "This is where we part ways, Partner. Those boys know this country too and they will figure us to go south to Red Mesa."

"It wouldn't be smart for you to go there would it?"

"It's the safest place I can go. There are people down there that know me and it will be the best chance I'm going to get."

"Well, when you get clear of this you come to the ranch."

"I will. You shouldn't have any trouble getting' back. Just follow The La Plata to Cherry Creek and that will take you to the ridge behind the ranch. You follow that until you see the hog back. You can drop on down to the ranch from there. Zeb will help you and you'll have a chance. Just remember these boys will be out for blood and they won't be taking any prisoners."

"You take care of yourself."

"Don't worry about me. You just get back there and take care of that little girl of yours. She's worth fightin' for."

Bruno touched his hat and reined his horse around. "I'll see you there."

Dropping down to the river Bruno urged Hawk into the icy water. He spoke softly to the horse and he began to move up the river. The big Morgan seemed to know that his master was in trouble and he was eager to do his part. They had developed a bond over the years they had been together and it took little guidance from Bruno to make his wishes known. He spoke softly to the horse as if he were talking to a lover. He knew he loved the sound of his voice and he pricked up his ears to listen.

It was an effort to stay in the saddle and every step brought a stab of pain, but Bruno was a man who had experienced his share of pain. Sagging in the saddle the temptation was great to stop and rest but that was not an option. There were many miles ahead, but he could not think about that. Gil was not a stupid man and he would put things together. Kitty's life was in danger and Zeb could not stand against a gang of outlaws. If he failed now they could both die.

As they moved up the river it became cluttered with large rocks. Hawk stumbled over the unseen obstacles, but bravely continued forward. Finding a good spot he urged the horse up onto the bank. Finally they came to the dividing of the wasters where the LaPlata turned to the east. The trail ran north along the creek and they turned to follow it. A small forest of Ponderosa covered the flat between the creek and the slope beyond. Many game trails ran through the brush as the land began to rise. Finally it broke out of the trees onto a large grassy park. At the edge of the trees he drew up to listen. A large bull elk was grazing in the meadow and it raised its head to consider the stranger that had entered his domain. Irritated at the intrusion he moved off to graze where he would not be disturbed.

Across the meadow stood the mountain he would have to cross. A feeling of hopelessness began to rise in his spirit as he gazed at the high peaks before him. He would have to cross that rocky barrier before the outlaws reached the ranch and time was running out. Shaking off the feeling, he urged Hawk on. It was not in him to fail and he would just have to find a way. To the west a lower ridge rose to where it joined the high mountain. There would be a place on that ridge where he could cross to the land beyond and he would have to find it. Soon they were moving up the pine-covered slope of the mountain.

A small stream flowed down and he followed it up toward the divide. Soon the trail narrowed to a ledge that divided the stream from the forest. The deer with many years of use had defined a path through the narrow space. The trail hugged the trees for a short distance until they thinned out again. The rapid elevation gain was sapping Hawk's strength and Bruno dismounted to give him a break.

Barely discernable through the trees was a small peak which was the first of a chain of rocky cairns that followed the high ridge. As they gained elevation fir trees began to appear. Bruno studied the slope looking for a good place to climb out of the gully that was beginning to close them in. The ridge above was the one that Clay had mentioned and if he could cross it the country beyond might look familiar. The slope they had been traveling was giving way to rougher country and the gully was becoming a trap that would keep them from reaching the ridge at this lower elevation. They would have to cross now if he wanted to avoid the high ridges.

With the exertion of walking, the wound had begin to bleed again. Giving Hawk a well-deserved break, he plugged the wound with a piece of his shirt tail. Fighting off the temptation to lie down for a little rest he pushed on. Pushing their way through the brush and downed timber they gained elevation until he finally came out onto the ridge.

The land before him was magnificent and despite the pain he took a moment to enjoy the scene before him. In the north the sky was overcast and lightning danced along the ridges. Below was the Mancos River Canyon and on the far side he recognized the knoll he had ridden to with Zeb and the lake where they had eaten dinner. In the distance was the Hogback and from these heights he could see the buildings of the ranch. If he could cross the canyon it would be an easy ride and no power on earth was going to keep him from making that ride.

When Bruno was gone, Clay turned his horse to the south. The river was already running strong with the spring runoff and as they crossed the river the horse fought to keep his footing in the swift water. Searching the bank he found a place where the rocks were flat and smooth. Urging the horse out of the river he stopped to survey the situation. It was not far to Red Mesa and it would no longer matter if the outlaws found his trail. The town would offer a safe haven and plenty of witnesses to discourage any plans they might have to kill him. A look to the west assured him that he had opened up enough lead to make it.

He patted his horse on the neck and smiled. "Looks like it is up to you, pal. If you keep me ahead of that pack I'll see that you get a good bate of grain when we make town."

The big horse bobbed its head and snorted. Sometimes he was sure the horse spoke English, and he was sure he had a bigger heart than most of his friends. When they reached the top of the bank Clay stopped to search for a trail. He had only been in this country a few times and there were no well established routes of travel. To the east he saw a lazy column of smoke rising from the flats and he turned toward it. An easy ride brought him to the town.

When he drew up at the end of the deserted street he breathed a sigh of relief. The town appeared empty except for a stray dog that wandered along the board walk in search of a free meal. He tied up at the Red Dog Saloon and stepped inside. He was just finishing his second beer when the door burst open and the outlaws strode into the room.

When the leader of the pack walked up to the bar Clay recognized him. Tex Hartsel was a man that needed no excuse to start trouble and this was his chance. Before Clay could speak, the big man slapped him across the mouth, knocking him against the bar.

"Where is he, you little weasel?"

Taking a moment to compose himself, Clay looked up into the cruel eyes. "Tex, you better relax before you mess this up. When I tell you what I learned at the ranch you won't care about Bruno anymore. It's about the gold and I will only tell it to Gil."

A confused look appeared on the big man's face. "I don't believe a word of that. All he wants from you is to see your face when he puts a rope around your neck. He doesn't take kindly to people that double-cross him."

"He'll look at me a little differently when I tell him I know where Zeb's gold mine is. If you get me back to him you will be a hero."

Tex studied the situation, while his dull mind tried to

sort out the new information. "You're just giving me a story to save your worthless neck. Where would you get that kind of information?"

"From Bruno, where do you think? I've been setting him up ever since we left Leadville. He got it from Kitty and she wouldn't hide anything from him. I even know where he's got the gold stashed that has already been taken out. Now if I was you I'd be real careful to see that nothing happens to me until I see Gil."

"My orders are to get you and Bruno."

"Forget about him, he's not important. When I tell Gil what I know, we will all be rich. Even you ought to be able to figure that out."

The man pushed his hat back and scratched his head. "Are you sure about this?"

"Sure enough to know it will make you a rich man. Now what do you say?"

He glanced at the others for guidance, but all he got were blank stares. No help there. He turned back to Clay. "Get on your horse. We got some ground to cover."

Bruno urged his horse forward, but before he had gone a step a rifle shot rang out and clipped a branch by his head. The motion of the horse had saved his life, but he had no time to think about that now. A quick glance down the slope revealed a large cairn of rock protruded out of a scree slope. Below it a flat ridge ran down the mountain into the trees. Scattered around it was a jumble of boulders that would offer good cover. The trees on that side of the ridge were few and too far away to reach in time. The cairn was his best bet so finding a bare spot in the rubble he slid his horse down the slope into the rocks.

"Just you hold it right there, Turnbull." A voice boomed out. "We've come to take you back and if you come peaceable you won't get hurt."

Carefully Bruno searched the ridge. How many were up there? His cover could only protect him from fire from above. What if they worked their way down the gullies that paralleled his fortress? He would be exposed and he could not wait for that to happen. He would have to take the fight to them.

Suddenly a rider burst from the ridge and he was moving fast. Caught by surprise Bruno threw a quick shot in his direction, but it was a clear miss. Dropping down onto the slope, he slid his way into the gully and out of sight. When Bruno heard the horse stop, he knew it would be only a matter of seconds before the rider reached the top of the gully where he would have a clear shot.

Protruding from the other side of his rocky fortress was a dead tree. It had been torn out by the roots in a winter storm and the top had broken off when it fell. The trunk ran from the cairn to the gully offering cover from the ridge above. There was no time to think, so Bruno hit the dirt crawling as fast as he could along the tree and into the gully. The man on the ridge had not seen him move, but it would be only a few minutes before they realized what he had done.

The movement had opened his wound again, causing the blood to ooze down his side. Taking a moment, he adjusted the makeshift bandage until the bleeding stopped. Then silently he scrambled up the gully until he spotted the man crouching behind a rock with a rifle in his hand. So intent was he in searching the rocks for a target, he failed to see anything else. There was a small stand of dwarf firs and thick brush just over the ridge, so Bruno slipped in behind them. Silently he crossed the distance until he stood behind the man.

"Drop the rifle and don't make any sudden moves."

The man's body stiffened and he did as he was told. Bruno stepped up to him and kicked the rifle aside. "Now with two fingers lift that gun out of the holster and drop it on the ground."

The man's eyes turned ugly with hate and he snarled. "You ain't takin' my gun. If you want it come and get it."

"Suit yourself," said Bruno and he stepped forward and reached for the weapon. Before he could reach it, the man grabbed the gun and started to draw. Bruno caught the hand and jerked it up over their heads, causing the gun to fire.

"He's up here, Bernie," the man yelled as they fought for the gun. "Shoot him."

Bruno glanced down the slope and saw the rifle coming around toward him. As the gun fired he spun the man into the line of fire. With the impact of the bullet, the man's body jerked and went slack in his arms. Dropping him to the ground, he dove for the rifle. With a quick roll he came up firing just as Bernie dove for the rocks. There was no return fire and for a few minutes he lay there and studied the situation.

There was no sign of movement below. "Mr., your friend is dead and if you don't want to join him come on out with your hands in the air."

Silence. Bruno fired a shot that ricochet through the rocks, but there was still no response. "This is your last chance to come out. You don't want me to come down there."

More silence. He fired three more shots but there was no reply. Standing to his feet he fired one more time with the same results. Cautiously he worked his way down over the scree until he reached the cairn. Peering over a boulder he saw the man lying in a pool of blood and he was not moving.

The mountain was silent and the danger was past. He moved down the slope stumbling and crawling toward the trees below. His body hurt, but he ignored the pain and pushed on. Below him he spotted Hawk grazing on some of the brush at the edge of the trees. He was a welcome sight and he leaned against the saddle for a moment to rest. All the exertion had left him weak and his body ached. Across the river he recognized the dome that he and Zeb had eaten dinner under and his spirit was lifted. The ranch was only a short ride from there. With great effort he pulled himself into the saddle and pointed the horse toward the river. The day was well spent when he made camp in the trees on the bank.

When he rolled in his blanket he passed out and slept the night through. He awakened to a cold gray morning with a raging thirst. Stepping over to the river, he drank his fill of the cool, refreshing water. When he inspected his wounds he was relieved to see that they were closing and the bleeding had stopped.

After he crossed the river he followed the canyon a ways until he found a place in the cliffs where a horse could make the climb. The talus slopes were very steep, making it difficult for both horse and rider. The plateau was still hundreds of feet above him so he dismounted to give Hawk a break. When they began to move again, he was overtaken by a sudden weakness which made it difficult to stay on his feet. By holding onto his mane and taking many stops they were able to make the climb. At the top they paused for a minute while Bruno searched the country for anything familiar. A few miles to the west he could see the notch in the mesa where Hells Hole opened a way to the upper range. He remembered it from the ride he had taken with Zeb. The ranch would be near that cut.

With his spirit lifted, he mounted Hawk and pushed on. It was a short ride to the ranch and when he stepped down in front of the house, Kitty burst from the door and rushed to his side. When he had dismounted she threw her arms around his neck causing a spasm of pain.

She pulled away, dropping her eyes to his side and her smile disappeared. "You're hurt!"

Bruno grinned sheepishly. "It's just a scratch."

His face sobered. "There's no time to deal with that right now. You're in danger and there will be men coming here that will be looking for blood. We need to get ready. Where's your dad?"

"Right here," said Zeb as he stepped off the porch. "What are you talking about, men coming here?"

"I had a run-in with some outlaws and I am sure they will be coming to find me. I want you and Kitty to get somewhere out of sight where you will be safe. I'll handle them."

"From what I see you are the one that better find a safe place and let me handle it."

"What are you talking about?"

Zeb's face grew serious. "If what you say is true there will be men dying here and until you are ready to do that you had better let me handle it. I've taken care of this kind of business before and I can take care of it now. You go on in the house and let Kitty doctor that wound. I'll see if I can round up some of the boys."

Dumbfounded, Bruno watched the man walk away. "Is he crazy? This is what I do for a living."

Kitty took his hands and looked up into his face. "He's

right. Bruno, if something happens to us we are ready. You aren't and I'm not going to let you be gunned down. I know what you have been doing.

I know about your business with the outlaws. They are evil men and they aren't going to take any chances with you. They know your reputation and I am not going to let you commit suicide."

"This is about religion isn't it? This is not the time for that. These men are not kidding and when they get here they will kill you and your dad just as quick as they will me. Now let's go to the house and get ready."

When he tried to move Kitty held tight to his hands and forced him to turn and face her. "I mean it, Bruno. There is only one way I will let you do it and that is if you will pray with me right now and give your heart to the Lord."

"We've been through this before and I don't need to do any praying. Most of my life I've been a good man and I am sure God will let me into heaven on that. If He won't, I will just be dead and that will be that. Now get inside. This is no time to be talking religion."

Kitty shook her head. "That's not true. The Bible says salvation is not a reward for the good we have done, so none of us can take any credit for it.[21] There is a hell[22] and if you don't give your life to the Lord you will go there. I can't make that decision for you. Please Bruno, quit being stubborn and pray with me. You've just got to believe me before its too late."

Before he could respond the sound of galloping horses came to their ears. When they turned to look, three horsemen rode into the yard and reined in in front of them. Bruno recognized Henry from the hideout but the other men were strangers to him.

Henry's dark eyes showed contempt as he glared down at Bruno. "Where's Zeb?"

"Zeb's out of it. This is between you and me."

Bruno gave Kitty a push toward the house. "You boys are on a fool's mission. I know what you are here for and you will take no one from this ranch. Unless you turn around and ride out of here someone is going to die and I am going to start with you, Henry. Now what's it going to be?"

Just then the two riders came around the side of the house, dragging Zeb between them. He had been severely beaten and when they dropped him on the ground he made a futile attempt to get up but failed. With a groan he slumped to the ground. The rider grinned satanically. "We had a difference of opinion and we had to help him see things our way. You want us to kill him?"

Bruno's face flashed with anger as he spun toward the rider. "You stinking coward, I'll show you what I think of a snake that beats up old men." Grabbing him by the front of his shirt he jerked him from the horse and threw him to the ground. When he hit he rolled over and came up with a gun in his hand. His shot went wild, but Bruno's didn't and the force of the bullet drove him back under his dancing horse. Spinning back toward the riders he saw Henry's gun coming level and he fired again, putting a bullet through the man's neck. As he fell from his horse one of the riders fired, striking Bruno in the head and in an instant his world disappeared.

CHAPTER 14

Suddenly Bruno found himself falling through a great darkness. When he came to his senses he was in a tunnel and it was spinning around him, drawing him deeper and deeper into a darkness that was more intense than any he had known in his life.[23] He knew the darkness of the mines, but this was darkness that penetrated into his spirit and engulfed him in a feeling of terror like none he had ever known before.

He landed with a bone-shattering thud in a small room that appeared to be a prison cell. The room was dark and the tormenting heat was beyond anything that he had ever experienced. No one could live in heat that intense, but he was alive. He could sense, more than see, living forms moving about in the darkness. The foul odor coming from them was overwhelming; their shrieks of torment and pain gave evidence of the bedeviled minds of lost spirits.[24] In the distance, he could hear multitudes of people crying out in anguish and pain. In desperation he strained his eyes, searching for some means of escape, but there was none. The choking sulfurous air was thin and he fought to fill his lungs, but the attempt was futile. When he tried to rise to his feet he found that his strength had been drained from his body and he sank back to the floor.[25] For a moment he sat there in the overpowering heat and darkness trying to put together what had happened to him. A terrible sense of hopelessness and despair settled onto his spirit and he knew he had entered Hell and there was no escape.[26]

While he tried to regain control of his emotions, he heard a grumbling roar from someplace behind him. The deep rumbling sound carried a resonance that could only be made by a giant being. When he turned to see, a massive claw reached down and grabbed him, yanking him to his feet as the long razor-sharp talons sank into his side, tearing away large pieces of flesh. He cried out in pain, but there was no one to hear or come to his aid. The creature hurled him against the wall, breaking bones and shredding the flesh.[27] A powerful kick sent him hurtling across the hot rocks of the floor into a larger space where he came to rest on the edge of a large precipice. With great effort he raised himself up to look over the edge. Suddenly a strange sensation went through his body and he looked down at the opening in his side. Crawling through the open wound were giant worms that had begun to eat his flesh.[28]

Before he could react, a great wall of flame rolled across his body and he screamed in pain. He knew it should have killed him, but he was still alive. For the first time he longed for death, but it was not to be found. This was the second death that he had heard about and he knew it would never end. In horror, he realized that there was no hope and he would be in this place forever.[29]

From behind him came a cruel, cackling laugh that struck terror into his soul and he knew he was in the presence of a demon or some kind of a wicked spirit. A mind-shattering shriek burst from its throat and Bruno drew back against the rocks. "You fool." It snarled. "You would have been wise to listen to your new friends. They could have saved you from this place. Now you can abandon all hope because we have you and you will be here forever." Throwing back his head he burst out with a wicked, tormenting laugh that sent shivers of fear into Bruno's soul. "Take a look around. This is your new home and most of your friends are here. You sent many of them to us. Remember Billy? Look into the pit."

Peering over the precipice, he could see dimly the form of a man twisting in torment as flames washed over his body. When he looked closer he recognized the man he had shot. "And over there is Tray and we have his brother too. We have many more people that you knew. You were a great help and I want to show you how much we appreciate what you have done."

Drawing back, the demon hurled a ball of fire that engulfed Bruno and he twisted in pain as he tried to avoid the hungry flames. Desperately he tried to compose himself, but all that was left inside was hopelessness. When he turned back to speak the creature was gone. In agony he realized that what the demon had said was true. If he had only listened to Kitty he would not be in this horrible place. If he had only taken her seriously, this would not have happened. Could he pray now?[30] It was his only chance. He had never prayed before and he was not sure he knew how. Hopelessness would be his teacher and he would have to try.

"God!" He screamed. "Please help me! I have been an evil man and I know I deserve this place, but I am asking You for mercy! I swear I will give you the rest of my life, if you will get me out of this place! I am at your mercy!"

Suddenly his body began to rise and as he gathered speed the terrible heat began to fall away. As he rose from the depth of the earth he was engulfed in a great burst of light. The next thing he knew he was lying on the ground in front of the ranch house with Zeb leaning over him.

When he opened his eyes he screamed and fought, but Zeb's vise-like grip held him firm. "Easy son, just take it easy. You are all right now."

"What happened? What's going on?"

"You're at the ranch and you've been shot.

Dazed and disoriented, he fought for control. When he sat up he could feel the blood running down the side of his head and he reached up and touched the wound. The blood had matted his hair where the bullet had cut a furrow above his ear. His eyes searched Zeb's face trying to find an explanation for what he had just experienced. "Something has happened to me because I wasn't at the ranch. I was in Hell and after I prayed I ended up here. What does it mean?"

Zeb's face grew serious. "You couldn't have been in Hell, Son. No one who goes there ever comes back. What you had was a vision. God has given you another chance that few people get. Now is the day of salvation for you and there is no time to waste."

"What do I do?"

"You need to invite Jesus into your life. I'll lead you in

a prayer and you just follow me. If you agree with the words that's all you have to do."

Together the men bowed their heads and called out to God. When they finished Bruno looked up. "You mean that is all there is to it?"

Zeb smiled. "That's right. It isn't hard to give your life to the Lord. The important thing is that you mean it. If you do, your life will change. That will be the proof."

Bruno shook his head. "You don't need to worry about that. I prayed something like that when I was in Hell and I meant it. When I give my word, I don't back up. Whatever the Lord wants from me, He's got it."

Zeb pushed his hat back and scratched his head. "You know what our first job is going to be. The outlaws have taken Kitty and we are going to have to get her back. Do you think you are up to that?"

Bruno picked up his hat and gingerly set it on his head. "I'll get her back. You need to stay here and let me handle the outlaws. I know these men and they play for keeps. You just stay here and I'll get her back."

Zeb's face flushed angrily. "Before you start putting me out to pasture you better realize she is my daughter too and I have a share in this. I'm going with you."

Bruno frowned and for a moment he hesitated. Then he nodded his head. "OK, if you are determined to go I'm not going to stop you, but you are going to have to play it my way. I can't take a chance on you getting us killed. Their hideout is in a place called Johnson Canyon and it is about 25 or 30 miles south of here off the Mancos River. There is an old rock tower that was built by the Indians on the mesa top just south of the entrance. That's Johnson canyon and somewhere in that canyon you will run into a sentry. You are going to have to find a way to get past him. The canyon will fork, so go to the right. You will see a ruin on the left. They have a guard on the balcony, so wait in the trees out of sight. When the shooting starts, you will know I have opened the ball. You'll know what to do."

Zeb was not happy and his displeasure showed on his face. Yet he knew he was right and he would have to go along with the plan. "You take care of business up there and don't get my little girl hurt. I will do the praying.

"I'll leave that up to you, but don't forget a gun. You're going to need it."

"I'm bringing a wagon too. People are going to get hurt and we are going to have to be able to get them back here."

"You better pray that Kitty isn't one of them."

"Or you."

The clatter of hooves echoed against the walls of the buildings and Clay Coffin stepped to the window. From down the canyon riders were approaching and he recognized them. Riding in the center of the group was Kitty. Her presence could only mean one thing. They had raided the ranch and he may be the only man left that could help her. It could also mean that the tales that he had been telling would no longer keep him alive. His life could be hanging by a thread, but it didn't matter. By now Bruno would have found that Kitty was missing and he would be coming if he was still alive. That could take more time than they had. He had to find a way to get Kitty out of here.

While he was thinking on these things a man came to the door. "Come on, Coffin. Gil wants you right away."

"What's going on?"

"You'll find out soon enough."

Together the men walked the narrow balcony until they came to Gil's quarters. When they stepped into the room Kitty looked up and her face brightened. She tried to cross the room, but her guard blocked the way.

"Clay, I'm so glad to see you!" she said. "Don't tell Gil anything about the mine. They killed Bruno and beat up my father. They will kill you next if you say anything."

Gil shot a venomous glance at the girl. "Kitty, you are going to put bad ideas into poor Clay's head and he could get himself into trouble. You wouldn't want something bad to happen to him, would you?"

Her eyes blazed with fury. "It doesn't matter what he says. You're planning to kill both of us anyway, so why should we tell you anything."

A mock sadness covered the man's face. "I'm disappointed in you, Kitty. All you have to do to go home safe is to tell us the location of the mine. That's all I want. If you tell me that I'll send you home to your dad."

"I'm not going to tell you anything, you two-bit floor flusher. I told you there isn't any mine. That's a story you made up to explain why the ranch was doing so well. The only gold mine was hard work. We toughed it out when things were hard and in the end it paid off. That's something you wouldn't understand."

"And those trips up into the hills? I suppose they were picnics." He looked around at the men and grinned. "These people are the only ones I have ever seen that take a pick and a shovel on a picnic."

She threw an angry look at him that took the grin off his

face. "I'm surprised a worthless piece of warm meat like you would even know what a pick and shovel is for. I will admit we did look for gold when times were hard, but the only treasure we got out of that was a few pleasant days together. We never found any gold."

"I don't believe that fairy tale for a minute. Nobody builds a ranch up the way Zeb did by selling beef. I want the location of that mine and if you don't give it to me in one minute I am going to kill Clay. If that doesn't do it, Zeb will be next. Now talk!"

Distracted by the rattle of a wagon in the canyon one of the men stepped to the window. "You better take a look at this, Gil. There's a buckboard coming."

Bruno pulled his horse up and studied the canyon. When they had ridden to the hideout he had noticed it and it was the last canyon before they left the river. Would it go all the way to the mesa top? In the distance he could see a point of rocks that seemed to split the canyon, but it could also be a notch in the wall. Even if it opened into another canyon it could be a box canyon. The south wall offered no paths of exit that he could see. He would have to take a chance as there were no other ways to approach the hideout from the west. Riding up Johnson Canyon was no longer an option. The sentry knew about him and he would be shot on sight. This canyon would just have to go through.

Turning into the canyon he studied the land before him. It was a wild and broken land that lifted abruptly from the river with a narrow wash cutting a jagged path down the middle. The canyon was dry with juniper and pinion scattered in the dense brush. Walls rose a thousand feet on either side and were joined to the canyon floor by rocky slopes. He urged Hawk forward. The sandy wash had carved out a narrow path that was just wide enough for horse and rider to pass. It was the only trail through the tangle of brush and the canyon had been deserted since the days the Anistazi had occupied this land. He rode watching for any route that could give him access to the mesas to the south.

Finally a smaller canyon forked off. As the land rose smaller trees and sagebrush appeared and filled the air with a pungent scent. In a short distance the canyon split into several smaller gullies that ran out on the mesa top.

Not sure of where the hideout could be, he headed off to the southeast. Judging by the distance he had covered and the length of Johnson canyon, his best bet was in that direction. Soon the cedars began to thin out and a large canyon appeared in the distance. It had to be Johnson canyon, so he turned Hawk to the south. After a short ride, he crossed a trail that had been made recently by many horses. It was the trail the outlaws had made when they had pursued them across the mesas. That meant it would lead right to the draw that led down to the ruin! A short ride confirmed his speculation.

He sat for a moment and studied the canyon. There were no signs of movement below. Many horses were milling around in the corral and he counted eleven. That was more men than he had expected to deal with, but it didn't matter. Kitty's life was at stake, so losing was not an option. When this fight was over he would be the last man standing.

Quietly he made his way down the draw and tied Hawk to the corral fence. Leaving his rifle in the scabbard, he spun the cylinder of his Colt and checked it for loads. Reaching into his saddle bag, he pulled out a second gun and after checking it, he stuck it in his belt. Whatever was coming, he was ready.

He pulled off his boots and traded them for moccasins. Boots could give him away as they clicked on the stones, but moccasins would allow him to move fast and quiet. Circling the corral he moved silently through brush toward the office. The air was still and he moved cautiously, being careful not to dislodge any stones or raise any dust. With the heat of the day the men would be inside. It was unlikely that anyone would be checking the horses.

His mouth was dry and he had a strange feeling in his stomach. Was it fear? That enemy had been conquered long ago and replaced with indifference. He had been down this road too many times to have to deal with that. But this was different. The cold indifference he had felt in the past was not there. This time the odds were against him, but there was more at stake than just his life. Death was no longer his enemy. This time it was not about him. He had to win for reasons he had never dealt with before. There was one other thing that was different. God was on his side and that changed the odds. Should he pray? It couldn't hurt.

Silently he whispered a few words that seemed appropriate. If prayer worked, this would be the test. There would not be a chance to try it again

When he reached the gate, he stopped to listen for anything that seemed out of place. All was quiet. Nothing was moving but the horse's tails as they brushed the flies away. Then in the distance he heard the clatter of a buckboard. It was Zeb and he was not supposed to be here yet. The time to move was now.

Recognizing Buck, he caught him and tied him to the fence, being careful not to excite the other horses. Quietly he pulled the logs back and slapped the nearest horse on the flank. Startled, the horse jumped and ran for the opening. After a few more well-placed slaps, the whole herd thundered through the gate and down the canyon to freedom.

Rushing to the balcony, Gil watched the horses disappear down the canyon. With a curse on his lips, he spun around. "Tex, you get down there and see what's going on. Dirk, you take some of the boys and get those horses."

The men scrambled to carry out the commands. Anger flashed in his eyes as he reached inside the office and picked up a rifle. *Now whoever is in that buckboard is going to die.*

Kitty had been watching the whole thing from inside, recognized the man in the buckboard and ran to the door. "Don't shoot, that's my father!"

When she grabbed for the rifle, Gil pushed her away. "I don't care who it is, I'm going to kill him."

When he raised the rifle, Kitty gave him a shove and the shot went wild. Zeb dove for the rocks as Gil turned on the woman. "Why you little…"

He drew his hand to strike her, but before he could Bruno stepped into the doorway and shoved a gun in his back. "You touch her and I will kill you! Now drop the rifle."

Gil recognized his captor and his hand dropped toward his gun. Before he could draw Bruno grabbed his shirt front and pinned him in the doorway. "You touch that gun and you are a dead man. Now call back your dogs."

Some of the outlaws began to appear on the balcony and when Gil saw them he yelled. "Turnbull has got me. A hundred dollars to the man that kills him."

The nearest man raised a rifle, but before he could fire he heard the roar of Bruno's gun. It was the last thing he ever heard. The bullet caught him in the chest, driving him backwards onto the ground. The other men froze. "All right, I hope the rest of you have better sense than he did. Now, I want you to pull your boots off and throw them over the wall."

Before they could move, Clay who had been in a room between them, stepped out onto the balcony. Taking advantage of the opportunity, the men drew their guns and dropped behind a broken wall.

Throwing an arm around Gil's neck, Bruno pulled him close. "Clay, you get Kitty back in that office. I'll be with you in a minute."

Just as Clay ran up to Kitty, Gil jabbed an elbow into Bruno's stomach and spun around drawing his gun as he turned. Before he could fire, Bruno grabbed his wrist and punched him in the face, knocking him to the ground. He rolled and came up with the gun in his hand and Bruno shot him. One of the outlaws fired, striking Clay in the shoulder and knocked him against the wall. At the same time a rifle boomed from below and the man leaped to his feet and pitched forward over a short wall. Before the men could put together what was happening, the rifle boomed again and another man fell to the ground. In desperation the last man leaped over the wall and disappeared into the brush below.

When the outlaws that were after the horses heard the shooting, they turned back toward the ruin. Spotting Clay, one of them fired and the bullet caught him in the chest. The impact of the slug knocked him against the wall and he slid to the ground. In shock, Kitty ran to his side to see if there was anything she could do. Bruno joined them, but it was clear that Clay was running out of time. More shots rang out and Bruno dragged him into the office.

The other outlaws had reached the brush below the corral and Bruno threw a couple of shots in their direction. They dove for cover in the rocks.

Silence settled over the canyon and Bruno's eyes scanned the brush. Reloading, he turned to Kitty and she leaped into his arms sobbing hysterically. For a moment he held her close and then he lifted her chin to look into his eyes.

"Bruno, I'm so sorry I got you into this mess. Will you ever forgive me?"

"I'm the one who should be apologizing. If I had listened to you in Leadville this would never have happened."

From behind them they heard a groan and they turned to see Clay trying to raise himself from the floor. Dropping down, Bruno propped him up against his chest. The front of his shirt was covered with a big red stain and foamy blood trickled from the corner of his mouth.

Bravely he tried to smile. "I don't know if I'm going to be able to help you, Partner. They hit me pretty hard."

"You just rest easy now. You are in no condition to talk."

He struggled to put words together. "I'll talk all I want to. I took one in the box and I'm finished."

Tenderly Kitty took his hand. "You're right. You haven't got much time and you've got some business to take care of before you leave."

"What are you talking about?"

"Listen to me, Clay. You are about ready to leave this clay coffin you are living in and you need to make plans for where you are going."

He stared blankly at the woman.

"I'll give it to you straight. You are headed for Hell, but we can help you. You need to give your life to the Lord and we haven't got time to convince you how important that is. You need to do that right now while you still have time."

"She's right, Clay. There is a Hell and you don't want to go there. You need to get right with the Lord."

Clay struggled for a breath of air and his face contorted with pain. "I've never believed in Hell."

"Clay, I've been there and the place is real. I'm your friend and you know I wouldn't lie to you. Just pray with us and you won't have to go there."

Silence followed and Kitty gave Bruno a puzzled look. For a moment they thought he had died and then his eyes fluttered open. He looked up into Kitty's face and tried to smile. "What do I do?"

"All you have to do is ask the Lord to come into your heart and be your Savior. That's all there is to it."

He nodded and with great effort he formed the words of the simple prayer. When he had finished he coughed and blood spilled from the corner of his mouth. He struggled to speak, but the effort was too great. He closed his eyes and his body relaxed.

For a moment they looked at the still form. For Bruno it was not a new thing to see death, but this time it was different. He had never thought about where a man went when he died, nor had he really cared. This man had been a friend and it was generating emotions inside that he did not understand. In a way he envied the man. In his mind he knew he was in a better place, but in his heart there was confusion.

Kitty sensed what was going on and took his hand. "It's OK, Bruno. You know where he is now and it's time to move on. We still have a problem out there."

There was a long moment of silence before he turned to

her. "You're right. I'm going to have to deal with this later and right now I am going to leave you here alone. Can you handle that?"

"Go on and do what you have to do. I will be praying for you.

Dashing outside he leaped over the wall as shots echoed from below. Hitting the ground rolling, he regaining his footing and scrambled behind a large slab rock. Silence settled in and no one moved.

Minutes dragged by. Then from below, a rifle barked and behind him an outlaw crumpled to the ground. It was the last man that had jumped from the balcony and he had been in his sights. Good old Zeb. He had saved his life. Now he could concentrate on the men below.

Suddenly he caught a glimpse of a man moving through the rocks and he was headed for the office. He fired a quick shot that blew chips from a rock close to the man's head and he dove for cover. The shot would draw attention to his position and he scrambled for cover just in time. Fire from below sent lead ricocheting through the rocks behind him.

Quickly Bruno crept through the junipers until he found a good spot below the men. From this position no one could move without being seen. "You boys had better throw out your guns. Gil is dead and this show is folded. You've got nothing to fight for anymore."

A rifle fired and a spout of sand leaped in front of him. "That's a lie! You're the ones that's in trouble. Dirk is in the ruin right now and he is going to take that little girl of yours. You throw down your gun and we'll let both of you ride out of here."

Just then a rifle barked and Bruno looked up toward the

office. A man staggered from the door and turned as if to go to the horses. His lips were moving with an effort to say something but he could not form the words. He took one staggering step and fell.

"Looks like you played your last ace, Boys," Bruno said, his voice dripping with sarcasm. "Now come on out or I will send that little girl to get you. I don't think you got the spunk to take her."

"I'll show you some spunk!" the man yelled and he opened fire on Bruno's position. Then he was moving through the brush to a jumble of boulders. Leaping to his feet Bruno fired a quick shot, but missed.

He waited. The air was heavy with apprehension and he knew it was up to him to start this dance. There was a series of low slab rocks between him and the outlaw's position that were just tall enough to cover a man. If he was careful, he could cover that ground without being seen from either of the outlaw's positions. Carefully he moved forward. The ground was slanted toward the valley floor and many of the rocks shifted under his feet as he worked his way up the slope. When he had covered half the distance he paused. From above he heard a rock click against another. He turned just in time to see the outlaw taking aim. Rolling, he pulled his gun and fired at the same time as the outlaw. He felt a jerk on his sleeve but there was no time to deal with that. The man above made a half turn to the right and tried to bring his gun to bear, but it was too late. The gun spilled from his hand and he fell into the brush below.

From where he was he had a clear view of the rock where the last man was hiding. He sent a bullet in that direction. "Mr., you better give it up. Your friend is dead and you are all alone. It's not too late for you to ride out of here, so what do you say?"

A long silence followed. Finally a small voice called out. "Hold your fire. I'm coming out."

Slowly the man stepped out onto the path and dropped his gun. As Bruno joined him he could see the fight had drained out of him and he holstered his gun. "Mr., I'm going to give you a break. Your horse is down the canyon. You go round him up. When you find the sentry tell him what happened. I am sure he will be glad to join you. I don't expect to see either one of you in this part of the country again. Now beat it."

The man gave Bruno a long look as if he was trying to think of something appropriate to say but he came up empty. He turned and walked away.

When Bruno reached the office Zeb was waiting. When Kitty saw him she rushed to his side. "You're bleeding again."

He grinned. "That's a small price to pay for getting my girl back. Why don't you look at it as an Amen to my old life? Zeb, are you all right?"

"Not a scratch. Looks like we did all right. Too bad about Clay."

"Ya, but we know where he is, don't we? He made it just in time."

Zeb pulled his hat off his head. "Too bad. He had the makin's of a good man. Just what happened here?"

"A miracle," said Kitty. "Bruno, you have a lot to thank this man for. He took a bullet that was intended for me and if it wasn't for him and my father we could have both been dead.

Bruno was quiet for a monument as the truth of what she said sank in. "It's true, then. God does answer prayer. When I

289

was down by the corral I asked God to help me. It looks like He saved my bacon."

"God had this whole thing worked out from the beginning," said Zeb. "If He hadn't gotten me past the sentry this whole thing might not have turned out so good. That man didn't know it, but he was set up."

"I thought you were going to wait down there in the canyon until the shooting started. What happened?"

Zeb grinned. "Not much. I just rode right up to the sentry and asked him if this was where they had taken Kitty. He was about to turn me around when he spotted the basket of doughnuts on the seat. I told him they were for Kitty, but there were plenty if he wanted some. I knew there wasn't a cowboy in the world was going to turn down bear sign, so I handed him the basket. While he was pulling one out I bent the rifle barrel over his head. He didn't give me any trouble after that."

Bruno laughed. "Well, I'm glad you didn't listen to me. I don't think we are going to need that buckboard, though. Why don't you take Kitty back to the ranch while I finish up here. I got graves to dig."

Tilting his head toward Kitty, Zeb grinned. "Aren't you going to tell Kitty what happened to you?"

He glanced at her awkwardly. "I think you know. I took your advice and prayed with Zeb. Now I know why you were so stubborn when you became a Christian. You were right after all."

"I thought something had changed. I can't wait to hear about it."

Together they started up the steps toward the corral. When they reached it Zeb paused for a moment. "Bruno, you remember when I asked you to work for me. You didn't give me an answer and I'm still waiting."

"I have done a lot of thinking on that since we talked. Times have changed since you started this ranch. If I took the rest of my life I could never build what you have done. I had dreamed of a spread like that my whole life and never was able to get one. All I have done is learn how to handle a gun. I've built up quite a reputation and sooner or later it is going to catch up with me. I don't have tumbleweed fever like I used to and I am ready to settle down. There is one thing I want settled though, before I answer that question. I want to marry your daughter and I'm just old fashioned enough to want your blessing. You wouldn't give it to me before, but things are different now. Will you give us your blessing?"

Zeb looked at his daughter and she blushed. Of all that he had worked for in his life and all that he had acquired she was the most valuable. He had prayed over the years for her protection and for a good life for her. He knew that the Lord had answered his prayers. He had sent the man who could turn those prayers into reality. There was a peace in his heart about it. There was only one answer to the question.

"From the day this little girl was born, there has only been one thing that I wanted in life and that was that she would have a good life. I have done the best I could to provide that. Now that job falls to you. I need your promise that you will devote the rest of your life to making her happy. Will you give me that promise?"

"You know I will."

"Then you have my blessing."

Reaching over, Bruno took Kitty's hand in his. "Then I

can answer your question. I'll take that job and I'll be the best hand you ever had."

"And what about that gun of yours?"

The only guns I am interested in now are the guns of the heart. With the Lord's help, we will take those guns and build a life. Zeb, God made your daughter for me and me for her. We're going to do you proud."

"Don't I have any say in this?" Kitty asked.

"Yah. I made up my mind a long time ago that I was going to marry you and now it's the time for you to agree. What do you say?"

"Is that a proposal?"

"Will you let me make you happy?"

Kitty looked into his eyes and smiled. "For the rest of your life."

End Notes

1. II Corinthians 5:17
2. History would know her as Baby Doe Tabor.
3. Later to be known as Idaho Springs.
4. John 3:16
5. Romans 6:23
6. Romans 3:23
7. Philippians 4:13
8. Palms 55:22
9. Matthew 10:28
10. II Corinthians 6:2
11. Psalms 28:7
12. Hebrews 13:5
13. II Timothy 2:13
14. I Peter 5:7
15. Exodus 22:22
16. The complete story of Yancy Riddle is told in "The Legend of the Golden Cross," and "The Miracle in the Snow."
17. Psalms 72:3
18. Psalms 73:24
19. II Corinthians 6:14
20. In 1881 the name of Columbia was changed to Telluride
21. Ephesians 2:9.
22. Matthew 5:29.

23. I Samuel 2:9. II Peter 2:17.
24. Revelation 14:11
25. Lamentations 3:18
26. Isaiah 38:18
27. Amos 5:18,19
28. Job 24:20
29. II Thessalonians 1:9
30. What Bruno was experiencing was a vision. Once a person enters Hell there is no return. None of the prayers that are uttered in hell will ever be heard. Hell was prepared for the devil and his angels and it is a place of separation from God. (I Thessalonians 1:9)